Spaghetti Bolognaise
by
Martin Henson

To Tommie and Jamie

"So, to Lake Como, Signore? Have you visited before?"

"Actually no, I…" Cut short as we thump over a speed hump, I intensify the search for the other half of my fraying seat belt. "…haven't. How long is the taxi journey?"

"From the airport? Just over an hour, Signore. It's a beautiful drive. Even in this car! Business or holiday for you?"

"To be honest, I don't really know. I've been invited to an event there. Overnight stay. Grand house by the lake. All a bit of a mystery."

"Mystery? It means like a puzzle, no? Maybe a surprise?"

"Yes, exactly. A puzzle, a surprise."

"Maybe it's a good surprise for you, Signore."

"Well I'm hoping so. I could certainly do with one after everything I've just been through."

"Hey, listen Signore. If you want to talk, I'm tutto orecchi."

"Sorry, you're what?" I say, finally giving up on my seatbelt.

"All ears, Signore. I'm all ears!"

1

Ten weeks earlier, London

To the best of my knowledge at the time, it all began one rainy afternoon in late June 2018, when I got a call from a firm called City Law Partners. Assuming the worst, I guessed that one of our clients was suing us. It wouldn't have been the first time. Then as they spoke, I thought they were suing *me.*

"It's a private matter that can only be discussed in person. Would you be available for a meeting with Mr Erskine at our Strand offices on Friday at 2pm?"

Partly because the manner in which the girl spoke indicated absolutely nothing sinister, I agreed. She also sounded incredibly sexy. As a single man with a hopeless track record with women, you become alive to any possibilities. Already I had an image of her in mind. I just hoped she would be there on Friday.

"Excellent. Thank you Mr Foster-Fewster. We look forward very much to seeing you on Friday. Take care."

Apart from her beguiling tones, she was also one of a small number of people who didn't stumble over my name on first attempt. I've often wondered what my parents were thinking. Either Foster *or* Fewster would have done, but in an attempt to sound a bit posher than they were, their only practical legacy was to leave me the opportunity of adding "and how are you spelling that?" to my gravestone so that at thirty-eight years old, I was an ordinary chap with a name people tended to remember. A mixed blessing, as I was soon to discover.

Up until this point, my life had been reasonably normal. As for most people, there had been a few twists and turns, but it was an unremarkable life and if success is measured by wealth, then there wasn't much to measure.

I was an only and lonely child. Packed off to a minor public school in Bath until the age of fourteen, when both my parents died within weeks of each other. My father in a freak accident, apparently trying to swipe a migrating puffin from the roof, and my mother... well it turns out she killed herself, although it was covered up for years. All I was told at the time was that she became seriously ill and died very quickly. My aunt Daphne was never willing to go into details, but she proved to be a brilliant guardian when she agreed to look after me in her small but elegant home in Bayswater. A loving, somewhat unconventional lady, she told me that public school was a terrible idea and that if I played my cards right, I may never have to attend, ever again. Music to my ears, though little did I know at the time that she was suffering from early stage dementia and that her advice, although sounding sensible and considered, was in fact akin to that of an excitable ten-year-old.

Looking back, I'm surprised I wasn't more upset about losing my parents, but if public school tried to teach me one thing, it was the apparent necessity to hide emotion. I remember Mr Outridge (obviously renamed Mr Outrage) telling us that we should never reveal our feelings. "If you're told you've won the lottery or that your mother's just died, you must react in exactly the same way. Give nothing away boys, give nothing away." A tight, dry man, Mr Outrage was the epitome of his own words.

So, when I arrived at Aunt Daphne's house on a sunny Saturday afternoon in May, I was keeping my emotions tightly in check, but I was also struck with just how beautiful that part of London was. It helped to keep my mind focused on the present. I'd visited the capital once before, but hadn't seen anything like this. A pretty tree-lined street of Georgian houses, spring sunlight breaking through the leaves and dappling the house fronts. Iron railings painted in various shades giving each house a personality. I knew I was going to be happy here.

But my emotions, despite Mr Outrage's training, gave way that first day. It's one of the few times I let it all out. Standing in the lounge of Aunt Daphne's house, as she cuddled me and said something about how sad I looked, I didn't know what was happening as heat started rising throughout my body. Then as my tears started, Aunt Daphne held me tight, stroking my head which was now lodged firmly on her wonderfully comforting bosom. I remember thinking it wouldn't have been Mr Outrage's way of dealing with emotion, but it was exactly what I needed.

After that, life with Aunt Daphne settled down, and true to her word, I didn't ever go back to school. I was fifteen that first summer in Bayswater and it seemed I was able to slip through the net, thinking that by the time anyone got around to following it up, I'd be school-leaving age.

I ended up staying with Aunt Daphne until I was eighteen. By that time, she would ramble on about the weirdest things, telling me about various grand relatives, war stories and how the Nazis were particularly good at dancing, before adding that Hitler was still alive and lived in the Shetland Isles. She often asked me if the dog was upstairs because she didn't want him on the bed. There was no dog. She would ask after my brothers, too, which always got the same response.

"Aunt Daphne, I think you're a bit confused. It's the neighbours who have three boys – I'm an only child."

"That's right, dear. I think they live in the Shetland Isles, too." Always pleased with her replies, Daphne never seemed bothered by her confusion.

When she passed in her sleep one night, it was a relief to know she'd avoided sinking into full dementia. But it was sad, too. I'd lost a real friend. My years with Daphne had been full of light and kindness, and now she'd gone forever. The raw emotion of the moment slammed into grief from the past and took me to a place I'd never been before, while Mr Outrage's words replayed in my mind again, but I knew that letting the feelings out was the only thing to do. In any case, presumably the end result of bottling everything up is the pale and pathetic image that describes Mr Outrage. It wasn't how I wanted to end up.

At eighteen, losing Aunt Daphne also coincided with the theoretical concept that I was now a man. It was time to move onto the next chapter in my life.

2

Aunt Daphne told me several times that when she died, her entire estate would go to Battersea Dogs Home. But she'd been kind enough to make a small amendment to her will without ever telling me, so when a cheque for £10,000 arrived out of the blue, it was manna from heaven. I'd never had a chunk of money in the bank before. My parents, who on the face of it were wealthy, it turns out were not only shit at creating surnames. They were even worse with money and had ended up owing far more than their assets could cover.

I'd made a few friends during my four years with Aunt Daphne and I was sofa surfing with one of them when I received the money. It enabled me to put a deposit down on a two bedroom flat in Camberwell and begin renting on my own. Twenty years later and I'm still in the same place. It's nothing much to shout about, but I like the buzz of the community and the flat is quite roomy. Every Sunday morning there's a market in East Street across the road, where you can get just about anything you want from the dodgy to the very dodgy. The pubs are good too, down to earth London taverns where someone always knows someone if you're in a fix. Like the Browning Boys, two chunky brothers who could get you anything you wanted as long as it was, "cash only and no questions asked." Others too, loveable rogues, hilarious and strangely reliable when push comes to shove. Even as a small and occasional part of these social circles, there's a sense of safety and belonging.

So that's my patch, where my middle of the road life has played out without any spectacular success or failure, getting on with the same old crap we all face, not complaining or dwelling on things, simply accepting my lot and ticking along, with generally more optimism than pessimism.

But I've always managed to keep in work and over the years have risen to the dizzying heights of account manager at 'Just the Job', a recruitment agency in Covent Garden. It requires no specialist skills, but being personable and organised are considered essential. Despite being a bit of a loner, I think I can tick both boxes most days. I don't have the appetite to get more involved or strive for promotion and ego jostling leaves me cold. I've avoided any temptation to slip into the lingo of corporate bollocks, having never knowingly *reached out, pushed the needle* or *circled back* once. I simply tolerate it all, happy to be Mr 9 to 5, honest and reliable.

Since I don't earn megabucks, I'm careful to make sure ends always meet because there's no safety net in my life. And for the most part I've lived as a single man, although that doesn't stop me fantasising about the perfect woman. There have been girlfriends, but I've long convinced myself that any normal woman considering taking the name Mrs Foster-Fewster would walk in any direction other than down the aisle. Or maybe I haven't met the right woman yet and I'm still waiting to meet someone with a pure, sweet voice that makes my heart melt - like the woman who called from City Law Partners. But when I haven't even met her yet, I'm getting ahead of myself.

3

In the three days before the meeting at City Law Partners, my mind has been focused on the female voice down the phone as much as the meeting. I have no idea what to expect from either. I've checked out the company online and they are clearly an established law firm, but there is no clue as to where I fit in. Maybe they have a need for an internal recruitment specialist, but that idea turns to dust when I think how crap at my job I am.

But the day has come and on a Friday afternoon, I'm on my way to the Strand, trying not to feel nervous as I approach the building. On the face of it I have nothing to be nervous about, but I'm not used to hotshot lawyers and city law firms, or the atmosphere that goes with them.

Making my way up to the third floor via the classic cage lift, I find the door marked, City Law Partners, London. Hesitating only briefly, I ring the bell.

An intercom sounds. "City Law Partners, how can I help?" The voice is unmistakable, the same girl who called me earlier in the week.

"Mr. Peter Foster-Fewster to see Mr Erskine." I try to sound suitable.

"Just push the door open when you hear the buzzer and I'll come to meet you." I do as she says, the door closing firmly behind me as I walk down the wood-panelled corridor. Reaching the door at the other end, it pushes open and there she is, the girl I haven't been able to get out of my mind for the last few days.

"Mr Foster-Fewster. Very pleased to meet you. My name is Jayne Renton. Please follow me and Mr Erskine will be with you shortly. Can I get you a drink of anything? Tea, coffee, water...?" As she leads me through to the waiting area, I'm distracted, thinking how neatly her looks match her voice, trying to remember what she's just said.

"Just... er, water would be nice, I think. Thank you," is the best I can do as I sit on the oxblood leather Chesterfield, trying to imagine how Mr Erskine would tackle my name. She returns with a cut crystal glass of iced water, her hands petite and pale, her slender fingers hypnotic, adorned with blood red nail varnish. I feel embarrassed, as if my thoughts are written on a flag and being waved around in front of me. I've known her for less than two minutes, yet rarely has anyone gone to my head like Jayne Renton. Light but expensive smelling perfume follows her, minimalist make up executed to maximum advantage.

I watch as she sits down at a walnut table in the waiting area and begins typing at her computer, the silence broken only by the sound of her nails gently clicking against the keys. Aware that she must know men stare at her, I try not to be one of them, instead convincing myself that the view out of the window is more enticing. To be fair, London is a wonderful city and when famous landmarks and streets are seen from a different perspective, it's always surprising. Three floors up in the Strand provides some spectacular views; particularly helpful today while I fight the urge to refocus my gaze on Jayne Renton, succeeding for an impressive thirty seconds or so before she stands up.

"Mr Erskine will see you now."

Getting up, like a puppy, I follow her to his door. Then as I go inside, Mr. Erskine stands up to shake my hand above his large leather-topped desk. "Mr Foster-Fewster, thank you so much for taking the time to see me today. Please take a seat and I'll explain everything."

He pronounces my name so richly and perfectly that suddenly my parent's social climbing aspirations seem fully justified. Feeling at ease, I sit and form a quick appraisal of the man. Privately educated, mid to late fifties, tall, slim but not frail, long necked, thick steely grey hair combed back over a boxy cranium, tanned, expensive suit, exotic cologne and, I imagine, a confidence most women would find attractive. He clearly has charm and a skill for relaxing his clients. Possibly too skilful it seems, as his mellifluous tones tempt my mind to drift back to Jayne Renton. But not knowing why I'm here, or what to expect, the next twenty minutes turn my life upside down as Mr Erskine explains the reason for the invitation to his office.

Suddenly, I'm sitting up, fully focused and trying to take in what he's saying.

"So, in addition to being a city law firm, we are also one of the most successful heir hunting agencies. We have entire teams dedicated to it. Don't ask me how they do it, but our specialists find inheritance estates that for one reason or another have gone unclaimed. There are billions of pounds locked up all over the world and very often someone who is entitled to their fair share has no idea! Once we've done all our homework and believe we've identified someone who is the heir to an estate, we offer to manage the whole process for them. And in your case, if you're not already ahead of me… we have discovered you are the sole beneficiary of just such an estate.'

Stunned into silence, my mouth falls open. An inheritance? Me?

He goes on. 'Quite a sizable estate, as it happens. Being a lawyer can be a grind, defending obviously guilty criminals in court, but this is the part of my job I really love. Mr Foster-Fewster, I'm delighted to tell you that you are the sole beneficiary of an unclaimed estate in the region of five million pounds - quite possibly more."

My response is entirely reasonable in the circumstances. "Holy shit!"

"Holy shit, indeed," Mr Erskine agrees. "But there are some details I need to explain. It's not the normal sort of inheritance we deal with, say like a straightforward dollop of money in a forgotten bank account. Your case is far more interesting. But as a result, it will be a slightly longer process than normal before the money is with you. Probably around two months. That's because of the particular circumstances of your case and the way we operate, which I will explain in detail. The whole thing is dependent on whether you choose to go ahead with us as your legal advisors."

I wait with baited breath as he pauses, watching me intently.

"So, the first thing I need to explain is our role, the arrangement and fee structure. If you are happy to proceed after that, we will draw up a contract. Only at that point can I go into the actual particulars relating to your inheritance. Would you like to ask me anything at this point?" Mr Erskine's eyebrows are raised.

I have no idea what to say. My mind feels shot to pieces. Excited and confused, my words tumble out. "Is this normal?" I ask, running my hands through my hair. "Surely if I'm entitled to an inheritance, shouldn't I just get it? I don't really understand why I'd be paying a fee." Deflated after the initial excitement, I'm suddenly suspicious, trying to work out if this is a scam. But after my research, it seems unlikely. City Law Partners are obviously a bone-fide law firm.

"Perfectly reasonable questions." Mr Erskine speaks reassuringly. "Questions I'd expect you to ask and indeed they are all on my list of things to explain. Firstly, the fee comes out of the inheritance money once it's released, so there will be absolutely nothing to pay in advance. Needless to say, you will obviously end up with a much larger percentage than we will." Mr Erskine taps his fingers on his desk. "For the record, you would not be liable for any costs in the event that we *didn't* secure the inheritance. Regarding the point about automatically receiving it, the question to ask yourself is, why you haven't received it?" I try not to look inept. "The answer, in a nutshell is, how would one go about claiming an inheritance one knew nothing about? This case is not only complex, it's international. There's been a lot of investigative work, all done at our own expense and very much at our own risk. If you're not interested, then all that work goes down the drain. But our hope is that when we put a strong enough case to the beneficiary, the outcome will be to the greater good of both parties. We have many clients who have become very wealthy as a result of our work and there is no doubt that in your case, our team has uncovered a legitimate and substantial claim." Mr Erskine looks serious.

I smirk because I know he's got me over a barrel. But not a bad barrel to be over, I have to agree. And they've done all the spade work. Only an idiot would walk away just because they weren't willing to pay for it. It still rankles though, that they have all this information and they're prepared to shred it unless I sign up.

"So, what sort of fee are we talking about?" I ask, still buzzing with conflicted instincts.

"Our fee is 30% of the final figure, and an Italian agency will get a 10% fee. That probably sounds astronomical, but it covers all the work to date, all the work between now and when the inheritance comes through and it'll leave you with at least two and a half million. But this is something you need to sleep on and think about carefully. Take your time to come to a decision."

I stare at Mr Erskine, playing through the scenario he's just outlined. Even though he's knocked me for six, some rational thoughts are returning. I've already decided that I have no real choice, but for now I want to keep him guessing. The fee is high, but what the fuck. This guy can turn me into a millionaire without me lifting a finger.

"I get it, and I'm obviously interested. You mentioned that my case was legitimate. I have no idea how these things normally play out. In your experience how strong would you say it is?" It feels like a sensible question.

Mr. Erskine leans forward on his desk. "Bulletproof."

As I leave the office with my head spinning and still trying to decide whether Mr Erskine is legit or not, I couldn't have known that a week later I'd be sitting in Club Class with Mr Erskine by my side, getting ready to take off for Italy, where my life was about to change forever.

4

It's three days after my first meeting with Mr Erskine and I'm back at City Law Partners, excited but determined to remain cautious. Since my last visit I've done a bit of digging and their website confirms in brief detail about their heir hunting services, which helped settle some doubts I had about being scammed. It seems that Erskine actually runs City Law Partners, which is an offshoot of a larger company and specialises in the legal end of the process. There are no bad press stories about them as far as I can see, and no one seems to have an axe to grind against them. On top of that, I'm excited at the prospect of seeing Jayne Renton again. I'm nearly there, as the vintage cage lift clanks its way up to the third floor.

"Good morning Mr Foster-Fewster," she says quietly as I enter the waiting room. "I do hope you are well. Can I get you a drink of something? Tea, coffee, water?"

"I'm very well thank you. Just a glass of water, please." And she's off, possibly more hypnotic than I'd remembered. As she returns with my drink, I wish I could think of a way to start a conversation, but my brain is suddenly empty, leaving me to sit wait in silence. Thankfully it's not long before Jayne instructs me to go through.

After a few pleasantries, Mr Erskine turns to business. "I know there was a lot of information to process when we last met. I imagine you have some questions you'd like to ask?"

"I'm sure I will have, but right now, I can't see I've got anything to lose by going for it." I could have strung it out, but I've always tended to trust my gut and deep down I know I can't walk away from a few million quid.

"More to the point, Mr Foster-Fewster, you have everything to gain." Mr Erskine is right. There is no downside here. If I thought I had a snowball's chance in hell of finding the inheritance on my own, I might think about giving it a go. But I'm happy to sign on the dotted line, and happy to work with Mr Erskine, who seems to have my best interests at heart. And then there's Jayne Renton. Surely all of that is reason enough to jump into bed with these people.

Two days after the contract is signed, I'm back for another Renton fix and Mr Erskine is now cleared to discuss the details of my case. He reminds me of one of the contract clauses relating to the official appointment of City Law Partners and that should I be a stupid bastard and run off with all this sensitive information to handle it myself, they will chase me down, saw my legs off and sue me for twice the original fee. OK, he may not have used those words, but his demeanour changes enough to leave me in no doubt it would be a very bad idea. With that out of the way, Mr Erskine opens a box file on his desk and takes out a bunch of papers tied with dark blue ribbon.

He unties the ribbon before addressing me. "It relates to your Italian grandmother, on your mother's side. Did you know of her?"

"Not at all," I say dumbfounded. "I hardly knew my mother, to be honest"

"Well, you are the only direct descendant of your grandmother. Her name was Giovanna D'Agostino. She married well you might say, but what must have been a good life in Florence was turned upside down during the war. The family lost everything." Mr Erskine takes a sip of water as Aunt Daphne drifts into my mind, her war stories suddenly not so bonkers. Mr Erskine carries on. "When the Germans occupied northern Italy in 1943, Giovanna was the only family survivor after the Nazis rounded up all the people that didn't fit into their way of thinking and packed them off to concentration camps. Looting by the Nazis was rife, and this is where your inheritance comes in. A Nazi general named Fritz Koenig stole a set of gold and diamond jewels that belonged to Giovanna. There is a paper trail that proves it was hers, there is no question of that. All the receipts, serial numbers, photographs and records are consistent, and there is no dispute from any quarter about the theft or the fact they belonged to Giovanna. All making sense so far? Tell me if I'm going too quickly." Mr Erskine enquires kindly.

"I think so. I'm trying to take it in, but at the same time I'm trying to work out what my mother knew or didn't know. To be honest, it's all a bit of a brainfuck... so sorry, it just slipped out."

"No problem. Entirely understandable." Mr Erskine coughs before carrying on. "The research was done by a division of our parent company in conjunction with my associate agency in Italy. Now that all the detective work and due diligence has been done, the jewels are just one step away from being legally recovered. The last piece of the jigsaw is to complete the identification process, which we'll do at our partner's office in Italy - we'll need your birth certificate, passport and a couple of other bits and bobs. So, we'll be jetting off to lovely Bologna in the next few days to get that done, along with your signature on a couple of official forms allowing the jewels to be recovered from the German authorities. Once the Bologna office has possession of the jewels, the quickest way to realise the cash will be through a specialist auction, which they will organise. There will be an auction reserve of €5 million." Mr Erskine pauses, realising I look worried,

"Sounds a bit elaborate. A bit like a grand heist." There's a nervous laugh in my voice. "Not sure why I feel that. On one hand it seems logical, but on the other it all seems, well, a bit cloak and dagger."

"There is absolutely nothing to be concerned about." Mr Erskine is authoritative. "Every aspect of this procedure is being done through official channels, with transparent legal documentation. Please don't be alarmed if things look complicated at the moment. In reality we just need to dot the i's and cross the t's. There is nothing remotely cloak and dagger about reclaiming your inheritance. It's a legal process."

"What about the auction? Surely that's my decision. What if I don't want to sell the jewels just yet?" I ask, uncomfortable that I don't seem to have much say in what's going on.

Mr Erskine is ready for this one. "And how exactly will you be paying our fee?" There's a moment's silence as I think about what he's said. He carries on. "The contract requires that we organise any necessary conversion of the inheritance assets into cash in the shortest time possible. This is a positive benefit to you, Mr Foster-Fewster, and it guarantees that you get the maximum cash value in your bank account as quickly as possible."

I feel stupid, realising I hadn't understood that part of the contract. Feeling more out of my depth, I'm also uneasy that the contract isn't specific about an auction, a point I put to Mr Erskine.

Nodding, he explains. "Ah, well... that's because in theory there may be another, possibly better, method of expediting the cash nearer the time. It's not impossible, for example, that some mystery character will come out of the woodwork and make a cash offer of €10 million, in which case it would be silly to go to auction for a lower amount. It keeps our options open. And at the moment, the best option is a specialist auction."

It seems to make sense, but then I think of the auction commission, that could wipe out another massive chunk of the inheritance.

As I question Mr Erskine, he slowly taps the side of his head to indicate he's got this one neatly covered, too. "Normally that would be an issue, but the very good news is that the Italian auction house offers the seller - you, in this case - the option of operating what's called a 'buyer's premium'. A facility we would use. This means the jewels will be auctioned to bidders fully aware that the stated commission will be *added* to the hammer price." Mr Erskine's face suggests, 'good, eh?'

This piece of news is a positive surprise, levelling things out a bit in my mind. A few minutes ago, I felt like he'd held stuff back, but he held this back too, something I'd have thought he'd have wanted to mention before. Maybe I've just got to trust him more. Mr Erskine seems to have an answer for everything and maybe that's simply because there is an answer for everything.

But then I think of something else - the cost of going to Italy. The flights, hotels, meals and the general expense of tagging along with Mr Erskine. Then there's also my job. I would love to tell my boss to poke it, but I can't afford to just yet. I put all of my thoughts and concerns to Mr Erskine.

He surprises me again. "Yes, I was going to talk to you about all of those points. I'm going to propose that we financially cover all of that under a separate arrangement. Hopefully this will have two benefits as far as you're concerned. Firstly, it should confirm in your mind how confident we are of a 100% outcome, because essentially you won't be liable for anything if the unexpected happens and the inheritance doesn't materialise. Secondly, it will put you in a much better frame of mind when we travel to Italy and do the paperwork."

Bloody right it will, I'm feeling the benefit right now! I nod my approval as Mr Erskine adds more details.

"The plan is to cover your salary and all expenses associated with the case, flights, hotels and the like until the inheritance comes through, hopefully within the next couple of months. We just need to work out a figure which will come back to us from the inheritance when everything is completed. If that sum needs to be amended up that won't be a problem, after all it's a drop in the ocean compared to what we've spent on this case already!"

His words force a weight to lift from my shoulders as the reality and enormity sink in. This is it. The moment my life changes. I can't decide what I feel most excited about right now, the immediate cash advance in my bank, the impending millions, or having another go at starting a conversation with Jayne Renton before I leave to tell my boss where he can stick his job. All of it's lovely.

5

With my bank account buoyant from the cash advance and no hitches since learning about my good fortune a week ago, I've finally accepted this is all real. It better be, I walked away from my job a couple of days ago. I had planned to tell my bosses exactly what I thought of them, but in the moment, I simply thanked them for everything and told them I had a new job, before creeping out like a mouse. Now however, strapped into seat 1A and minutes away from jetting off to Italy, I feel like a tiger.

Next to me, the lawyer who is about to change my life forever smiles reassuringly as I have a crack at making some casual conversation. "What should I call you? Mr Erskine seems a bit formal."

"Everyone calls me Erskine. No need for mister or anything like that."

"Erskine it is then," I confirm, feeling pleased that I'm part of his circle, even though I'm going to be paying him handsomely for the privilege. He's a man who's worked hard for his success and it's only by outrageous fluke that I can enter his world. But it's already a feeling I like.

As the plane leaves the ground and begins to

climb, I think about Jayne Renton and how nice it would be if she was part of our entourage. Aware I know absolutely nothing about her, I decide to make a few discreet enquiries with my chaperone who is suitably engrossed in his copy of the Financial Times.

The plane levels out and as the engine noise drops, I think of a way to get the conversation started. "The girl in the office... Jayne something... Has she been with you long? She reminds me of someone that one of my colleagues at *Just the Job* was trying to place recently. Would be quite a coincidence!" Feeling about as convincing as a playground liar, I remember that Erskine is a lawyer and can probably smell a motive from outside the aircraft.

"Jayne Renton? Lovely girl. Been with us for about a year. Extremely efficient. Her boyfriend is an interesting chap. A journalist for one of the red top rags. He has a regular column, usually dishing the dirt on someone. Met him a couple of times. Jason Clarke - you might know the name if you read that sort of dross. Most unlikely pairing, you'd never put them together." If he did smell my motive for asking, he was too much of a gentleman to embarrass me. Closing off my line of questioning by telling me about her boyfriend, his expression hints that Jayne's bewitching presence has seeped into his fantasies, too, from time to time.

Erskine carries on. "I know there's no Mrs Foster-Fewster, but is there someone special in your life?" The lawyer is putting on his invisible wig. If I answer no, he'll assume I'm sniffing after

Jayne Renton, if I answer yes, I'll have to lie. But Erskine the diplomat has worked it out, my momentary unease giving me away. He politely diverts. "I'm so sorry, completely personal question, absolutely none of my business. Right. What are you going to have from the drinks trolley? G&T or something?" Erskine rubs his hands together.

"I think a G&T would go down well."

"Excellent, two large gin and tonics it is."

With the benefit of a gin and tonic running through my mind, the view from the window reminds me of gazing into a child's snow globe. The carpet of cloud below like settled snowflakes, the blue parabolic sky encasing everything within it, the whole scene looks ready for its next shake. Feeling wonderfully heady, I take another sip.

"I just need to get some notes from my man-bag," Erskine whispers, unseating himself and rising to the overhead locker. Returning with the same ease, I'm surprised to see his notes are in fact an electronic tablet. I'd thought of him as more of a leather-bound notebook type, but watching him he's clearly adept with modern technology. "OK, I thought I'd just go over a few things. Nothing to worry about, but it's better that you know the form." Erskine scrolls across various photos before stopping at some office images. "This is our partner's office. We'll be visiting tomorrow to sign the papers and to confirm your identity check. I'm au-fait with the process so it'll all be fairly straightforward. I'll just be guiding your hand over the dotted lines." While I get the feeling he's the master of understatement,

Erskine continues scrolling before abruptly stopping at an image of an eye-catching woman. In fact, several images. He scrolls more slowly before settling on one, then turns the tablet full face towards me. "And this is Valentina Russo. She's going to be managing everything at their end. She speaks very good English and I've dealt with her on various international legal matters over the last few years. Very friendly and supremely good at her job." He stops short of saying, "and as sexy as hell", but judging by the look on his face, it doesn't need saying.

Continuing to feed me snippets of information about the process, Erskine shows me a spreadsheet with a pretty accurate assessment of what I'll end up with after expenses and commissions. My cut will be around half the auction sale price, but even if it goes for the reserve, that's two and a half million quid, more than I could ever previously have dreamt about. We've discussed the figures before, but seeing it laid out, I reassure Erskine that I'm more than happy with the arrangement. Despite my earlier worries about the whole thing being an elaborate scam, I feel safe in the knowledge that this thoroughbred Englishman has his hand on the tiller.

Time passes quickly, and it's not long before the captain announces our imminent descent into Bologna. Erskine repacks his overhead locker before returning and securing his seat belt, seeming to float as if in another time dimension, unhurried yet definite in his purpose. His public school drilling obviously went a little deeper than mine when it came to the art of deportment. The thought makes me wonder if he'd had the same pep talk about keeping emotions in check from his equivalent of Mr Outrage. If he did, it hasn't held him back.

6

"I don't often get to say this, but I'm genuinely going to miss you two." The old-school governor of Ford Open Prison spoke in a soft Yorkshire brogue as he sat behind his desk methodically rubber-stamping two sets of release papers. "No matter what the crime, I always say it makes our job so much more rewarding when we have well-spoken residents." With eyes firmly on the task in hand, he made certain he was happy with the running order of the papers, tapping them neatly into shape before stapling each corner. "I hope you don't mind me asking, but how have you coped with the last six months? A bit more bearable finishing your sentences together here I'm guessing, rather than those long stretches apart?" Sincere in his enquiry, the governor stood up and handed both men a set of papers.

"Thank you, sir. I think I speak for both of us when I say that our stay here has, certainly by comparison with our previous accommodation, been a largely agreeable experience." Gerald Bassinott turned to his brother Thomas, who nodded in agreement.

"Well, that's nice to hear." The governor smiled. "But can I ask before you leave, why the temptation to get into fraud? It's always puzzled me, ever since I met you. I mean, you're both smart individuals. I might even go as far as describing you both as tall, dark and handsome. On paper you certainly seem to have it all. So why not the quiet life?"

"I think you've probably answered your own question."

The governor frowned. "And how's that?"

"Well, the truth is that from an early age, people gave us credibility almost no matter what we did or said. Didn't seem to matter who they were or where they came from. We always looked the part. Then, when you add the most delicious ingredient, the world becomes your oyster." Gerald smiled, but his eyes were steely as he looked at the governor.

"Delicious ingredient? Go on, I'm hooked." Sitting on the edge of the table, the governor crossed his arms.

"Twins!" Gerald replied. "As identical twins, we could pull off the most elaborate cons! Even when we were kids. In fact, especially when we were kids. We got a taste for it and it's never gone away."

"Well, one thing's for sure, it doesn't always work, or you wouldn't have ended up in here!" Looking pleased with his quippy response, the governor stood up. "Gentlemen, you are now free to go. But please remember... be good. And if you can't be good, for Christ's sake be careful!"

7

Having landed in Bologna, it's a fifteen minute cab ride into the heart of the city. The journey is largely unremarkable, until the last few minutes when we turn into Via Indipendenza, a wide straight road with porticos either side, leading up to the main square, Piazza Maggiore. I'm hooked immediately by the red ochre buildings, columns and arches, the churches and cathedrals, medieval architecture filling the view from every window in the cab.

I'm just about to share my awe with Erskine when he beats me to it. "Spectacular, isn't it? I think most people miss a trick with Bologna. Florence is only half an hour away by train, but it's just a tourist magnet these days. You can't move without treading on some foreign oik taking a selfie. Venice, which, OK, is obviously something different, is a couple of hours away in the other direction. But again, completely overrun like an ant's nest." Erskine's eyes light up. "While Bologna, by way of comparison, has plenty of culture and a charm of its own, but far fewer people to spoil the view. And talking of views, this is us." Leaning forward, Erskine speaks to the driver in Italian, before the taxi pulls over in front of Grand

Hotel Majestic, a building whose name describes first impressions perfectly.

This is the world of the rich and privileged and as if to underline the point, as we get out and the driver unloads our bags, an old man shuffles in front of us. It's warm, but the old man is wrapped in an oversized greatcoat, wearing a crumpled black homburg. His body bent forwards from the hips, his top half is almost at right-angles to his legs and cruelly twisted, so that he can only make eye contact by straining his head skyward. When he does, I notice both eyes are white with cataracts. Suddenly I feel uncomfortable that I am now part of a privileged world that will separate me from people like him. I make a silent vow to come and find him when my money comes through, and somehow help him, but for now, I give him the fifty euro note in my pocket, at which he wails a harrowing cry of gratitude. Then as Erskine calls my name, a hotel porter, bandbox smart, urges us to follow him up the wide steps into the reception area.

"You'll see quite a few beggars in Bologna, but they know not to walk up the steps to *this* hotel." Erskine's tone echoing the body language of the porter as we climb the steps, clearly thinking I was being bothered by the old man. And I was, but not because he was a pest. Quite the opposite.

Inside, the high-ceilinged reception area has been designed to elevate the senses and I stand there, gaping in amazement at the pristine elegance that hits the eyes, while an assault of aromas rising from huge displays of fresh flowers fills the nose. It's a place created to edit out the riff-raff, in which I don't feel I belong. I've heard it said that to respect serious wealth, money needs to be in a family for a least two generations. It makes sense, standing here in this atmosphere, I can't believe it will ever seem natural to me, despite the fact that very soon, I'll be able to stay here whenever I want to.

Looking at all this, it's easy to understand how sudden wealth could go straight to the head and completely fuck you up. Resolving to keep my head firmly on my shoulders, I'm grateful for those few seconds with the old man outside. There's part of me that feels more connected to him than all these perfect-looking people around me. I guess I'm still in shock about the inheritance, out of the blue. All too easy to worry, too, that the money will never actually materialise. If I had to put in a nutshell how I'm feeling, I'd call it bewildered excitement. Very bewildered.

Turning around slowly, while I'm still taking it all in, Erskine is sorting out the room keys with an immaculate Italian man on reception. "Pleasant chap, that Chief Concierge," he says a few minutes later, handing me a key card. I make a note-to-self. *Chief Concierge, not man on reception.*

Erskine looks at his watch. "It's just after 6pm now, so how does it sound to you if we head up to our rooms, freshen up and meet back down here at say, 7:30? Then we can pop out for a few drinks and a spot of dinner. I know a couple of lovely places just off Piazza Maggiore."

"Sounds wonderful," I reply, thinking Erskine's voice could make the prospect of a burger bar sound equally attractive.

To quote a teenager I overheard recently, my hotel room is "totes amazeballs". Or rooms actually. Bathroom, bedroom and lounge. Each one immaculate, spacious and designed for maximum comfort. Especially the bed which I flop onto, spread-eagled and face down, not noticing three white chocolates subtly placed on the pillow and embedding them into my forehead. After momentary shock, I flip over and eat them. Then, letting a minute or two of luxurious nothingness pass, I get up to open the window and look over Bologna's inspirational views. A huge, flat-fronted cathedral is slap bang opposite, its red brick façade magnificent in the afternoon sun. I'm not a fan of modern churches, but old ones, especially big ones like this, move me to the point that would make Mr Outrage uncomfortable. It's probably something to do with losing both parents as a boy, but I can almost believe there is a spiritual connection inside their restful, echoing spaces.

Making a mental note to look inside tomorrow, I leave the window and wander into a bathroom of shining marble, huge mirrors and gold fittings. Under evenly cascading warm water, the house body wash is luxuriant on my skin, the fragrance classy and exotic. Standing in this rarefied atmosphere, I feel a release of fully matured butterflies flap through my entire body as I take stock of my situation. For all my earlier good intentions to remain grounded, I can sense the magnetic pull of this lifestyle. Even though I'm not ready to fully give into it yet, I feel a thrill just dipping my toes in the water.

Bath-robed and back on my bed, there's time for a little more indulgent nothingness as gentle city sounds drift in through my open window, the butterflies still very much alive and well, usefully preventing me from dropping off to sleep before I get up again and get ready to go out to meet up with Erskine.

8

"Think you'll cope with all this?" Erskine asks with light sarcasm from across the table, his eyes slowly rolling around the splendour of the old Italian restaurant he's chosen.

I assume he means when my money comes through. "Well, it's certainly not the sort of place I've eaten in before. I guess I could put up with it." Then feeling the need to be funnier, "But probably only six nights a week – to start with at least."

Complimenting my good taste, Erskine laughs professionally. Making comfortable small talk while the silky red wine gets to work, eventually I feel brave enough to ask whether anything could go wrong with my inheritance. "I know you've said everything is all systems go for tomorrow and it's just a matter of covering off the formalities... and that my case is bulletproof..." I try not to sound as though I'm worried. "But is there a percentage chance that anything could go wrong?"

"Not one percent chance. Everything's drawn up and the papers have been seen by both sides. It really is a straightforward matter of putting pen to paper. Peter Foster-Fewster on this dotted line here, Peter Foster-Fewster on that dotted line there." Solid as ever, Erskine raises his huge wine glass to meet mine for a gentle touch that chimes not clinks.

My God, this wine is lovely - the perfect accompaniment to the omnipresent butterflies in my stomach, happily fluttering to Erskine's reassuring words and the prospect of two and a half million smackers dropping into my bank account.

After dinner, Erskine is keen to show me around the pretty pedestrian streets of the Quadrilatero. It's charming, a network of tiny streets crammed with bars, restaurants and people standing and sitting outside in the warm of late evening. Remembering his earlier comment, I'm thinking I could very easily cope with all this.

His phone rings. "It's the current Mrs E. Excuse me, I better take it." Erskine says with mock horror.

"Darling, just give me a moment. I'll find a quieter spot to talk." Gesturing to me that he's going down a small alleyway between a couple of restaurants. As he walks away, I loiter, window-shopping, looking into tiny shop after tiny shop, all rammed with local food. Over dinner, Erskine had told me this region is known as the stomach of Italy, and I can see why. Sodding great lumps of parmesan cheese in clumsy stacks, even bigger parma ham joints dangling above them, handmade pasta in all shapes and sizes in open boxes, artistically labelled tins of olive oil and local wine – and that's just what I can see from the street.

Happy wandering while Erskine is taking his call, I walk past the end of the alleyway a couple of times, to check he's still there and passing a third time I stop to watch him. His body language suggests he's frustrated or possibly angry, holding the phone in his left hand, his right hand raised above his head, hand wide open, jarring it back and forth as if emphasising his words. He stops to listen before repeating the same hand actions, this time turning slightly on the spot, a quick knee-bend indicating real frustration. I'm intrigued. This is not the cool Mr Erskine I know. Maybe it is just a barney with Mrs E, but I can't take my eyes off him. About twenty metres away, I'm trying to hold an expression that suggests I've just noticed him, should he look my way. Then things seem to settle down and it's not long before he turns and sees me, waving with a smile and indicating he's finishing the call. I'm fascinated to know if he'll share his news, even if it was just a barney with Mrs E.

"Peter, I'm so sorry. It was just something I needed to deal with back home." Erskine is back to the polished performer, "Charlie, one of my sons, is at uni and there's been a spot of bother with one of his friends. His parents wanted some legal advice - always happy to give some pointers when friends are in a fix. Anyway, I know a nice little bar on the walk back to the hotel. How about a very special Italian grappa nightcap before we call it a day?"

And very nice the grappa was, helping me to relax back at the hotel as I lay on the most comfortable bed I have ever known. But I can't stop thinking about Erskine's phone call. Whatever it was about, I don't actually believe it's what he said it was. Repeatedly replaying his body language as he spoke, it's clear he was not happy at all. I'm not even sure it was Mrs E who called him. If it was, and his account is genuine, then he would have made a call to the parents of his son's friend to give them the "pointers" he referred to, making it even more unlikely he would have been frustrated or angry with them.

Unable to reason it out, as my brain slows down after a day of butterflies, my overriding thought is that Erskine is supremely good at telling people what they want to hear - and that includes me. I shouldn't be surprised, he's a lawyer after all. And he probably was covering up a row with Mrs E, but for no good reason it tickles the occasional worries I have about my money, causing me to dwell on events for a few more minutes, before the heady alchemy of wine and grappa puts me to sleep with blissful ease.

9

I wake up to the sound of my mobile phone.

"Peter, good morning – I'm in the break-fast lounge, just wanted to check you were OK?" Erskine sounds perky. "It's nine o'clock and we ar-ranged to meet down here at eight. Probably my fault leading you astray with the grappa!"

"Shit," I say without thinking. "Sorry, I must have overslept. I blame the beds, they're just too comfortable. I'll be down in twenty minutes."

"Don't worry, it's time that's been useful. I've been catching up on another case. I'll pop out for a stroll. It's a lovely morning and I'll see you here, let's say nine-thirty, if that gives you a bit more time? There's no hurry - they serve breakfast all day." Sounding comfortably reassuring, he con-firms the meeting with Valentina Russo is at 2pm, giving us plenty of time as her office is a just a ten minute taxi ride away.

"Great, see you in the breakfast lounge." Leaping out of bed, suddenly I'm excited. Today is the day I'm signing the paperwork and hopefully the moment I can finally allay my worries that all this will come to nothing.

Entering the near empty breakfast lounge, I immediately see Erskine on the far side. It's a large room full of grandeur and he fits in perfectly. Walking past several empty tables weighed down with the finest tableware, I get another hit of those feelings that this is not a world I could ever feel natural in. My senses heightened, I'm on hyperalert for any flicker of behaviour from Erskine that could indicate all is not well. He's on the phone and hasn't seen me, but when he does, he ends the call immediately, which does nothing to settle my nerves.

But he gives no sign anything is wrong. Smiling and relaxed, he rises to shake my hand. "Peter, a very good morning to you. Big day ahead. How are you feeling?" Erskine's words and manner are welcome. It wouldn't take much to convince me that a last minute hitch was coming.

"I'm scared to bits," I say as we sit down, trying to be light and comedic, but my sporadic worries making me sound far too serious.

Erskine frowns for a moment, before looking more sympathetic. "Frankly, I'm not at all surprised. But I'm here to help you every step of the way today. I'll make sure that you are comfortable with everything before you sign, and any questions at all, no matter what, just ask away." He places a reassuring hand on my shoulder. "This is going to be one of the best days of your life." He pauses to let it sink in. "There's absolutely nothing for you to worry about."

Feeling relieved by the comfort blanket that Erskine has thrown over me, my thoughts turn quickly to breakfast. After making my choice, I savour every mouthful of his recommendation; avocado toast, poached eggs and pepperoncino.

All to be helped on its way with the hotel's own specialty coffee, which he's already pouring from a tall silver jug. Smiling to myself, I can't help thinking about my local pub in London, and how the Browning Boys would tackle a breakfast like this, imagining them eyeing it suspiciously as it was delicately put in front of them, before going nose-to-nose with the waiter. *Are you having a bubble bath mate, where's the bloody chips?*

After breakfast, we head back to our rooms, Erskine to "slave away over a hot laptop" and me to peruse the substantial bedside guide to Bologna. Lying on the bed with the window open and sunshine filling the room, my mind at rest after Erskine's earlier reassurances, at last, I relax.

At the appointed time, I head down to reception, where Erskine is sitting on one of the large sofas under a huge mirror. As arranged, it's 1.30pm and I make my way towards him, edgy with a mixture of excitement and nervous tension. "Peter. How are you?" Erskine shakes my hand. "Apologies. I'll be one minute."

As he finishes methodically reordering the contents of his case, I suddenly realise the magnitude of this afternoon, not just because of the paper signing, but because this is the first time someone else is involved. Not only will I be watching Erskine like a hawk, and ditto Valentina Russo, but also the interaction between the two of them. But the whole atmosphere in the office will be under my hyper-attuned scrutiny, as I try to work out if *anything* isn't going as smoothly as Erskine promised.

"Right… Final check - you've got your passport, birth certificate and proof of address?" Probably sensing my tension, Erskine sounds upbeat.

I reach into my inside jacket pocket. "Passport, yes; birth certificate, yes; and the other thing, yes, it's all here." I match the brightness of his mood.

"Excellent. We're all systems go. The taxi is ordered - I reckon we should wait outside. It's a lovely afternoon."

We walk out into the bright sunshine of early summer, where Via Indipendenza is vibrant with smartly dressed Italians and students ambling in animated clusters. A couple of hundred metres to the right, Piazza Maggiore is alive with people, crisscrossing its magnificent open square with varying levels of urgency. Everywhere I look, I'm surrounded by medieval buildings. Erskine was right. It is a spectacular city.

The beep of a taxi horn stops my daydreaming and we're soon on our way, Erskine by my side, in the back of a cab so quiet it apparently has no engine, the only sound its tyres rippling across the cobbled streets. Leaving the city centre, we head to the business district of Fiera di Bologna. It's 1:45pm when the taxi pulls up outside the offices of Città Legale Italia. A few minutes early, Erskine asks the driver to drop us around the corner and we kill a couple of minutes walking a little way, before turning to head back in the direction of the office.

While Erskine appears cool and relaxed, my

feeling of being out of my depth escalates. I should be ecstatic at the prospect of this meeting, but I can't stop the conflicting thoughts filling my head, convincing myself I've got into something that's too good to be true, something I'm going to regret. But as always, and just in time, Erskine has the power to calm me with just a few words, as we stand in the street facing Valentina Russo's office.

"This should be a lot of fun. Leave the talking to me. Try to relax and just think about that sodding great glass of celebratory wine we'll have later." His confidence and solid smile in the afternoon sun is like a shot of morphine. "Well, if you're all fit, shall we go in?"

Erskine leads the way into the air-conditioned reception area. It's larger than I imagined, modern and uncluttered, with two metal framed seating benches and a low glass table in the centre of the room, half a dozen tall potted plants around the edge completing a minimalist, chic look, each of the four cream walls home to a large abstract painting. As Erskine strides to the receptionist and speaks in fluent Italian, I make out the words Valentina Russo, Erskine and Foster-Fewster, but very little else. The receptionist is attractive, but not a patch on Jayne Renton, I'm thinking, but then who is? Nonetheless, she has a pleasant smile as she indicates to us to take a seat.

While we wait, Erskine and I make small talk about the paintings, neither of us capable of interpreting anything from the jaunty black lines encircling riots of deep citrus colours. As we sit there twisting our heads to see if a different perspective adds anything, our focus is suddenly drawn to the sound of a door opening and closing in the corridor behind reception, followed by the unmistakable sound of stiletto heels on solid flooring. A few seconds later, a woman I recognise as Valentina Russo emerges through an arched opening and walks over to us, her heels tapping confidently, full of purpose.

In the three seconds it takes to reach us, I've already appraised her. Thick, black, shoulder-length hair falling around a wonderfully handsome face, which to my overactive mind portrays intelligence and sexual authority. Eyes highlighted with thin mascara and a hint of pale green eye shadow complement the darker green of her thigh-length dress; her lipstick pale rose, her skin dark olive. A thin gold chain necklace holds an amber teardrop above her cleavage. Nothing abstract here, I'm thinking, guessing she's around my age. I try not to think about Jayne Renton, because even though she's spoken for, in my frustrated mind, it feels like betrayal.

"Erskine. Lovely to see you again," she says softly as they kiss twice on the cheek, while I await my turn.

"And Mr Frosty-Fowster - how lovely it is to meet you."

Mentally forgiving for her crunching my name, as she leans towards me, the world becomes reduced to slow motion as she gently kisses my left cheek, her floral perfume filling my head before she sways to kiss my right cheek. Feeling myself blush, I try to sound composed. "Lovely to meet you. Really, very lovely," I say with far too much enthusiasm, no doubt causing the spirit of Mr. Outrage to despair at my lack of self-control.

As we make our way to Signora Russo's office, there is some Erskine-led small talk during which time I learn that she prefers to be called Tina, not Valentina, while I chip in that Peter will do for me, thinking anything is better that another mangling of my surname.

Her office is large and mirrors the spartan feel of the reception, but in contrast to metal frame benches, she has two white leather sofas forming an L shape in one corner. I'm pleased to see she's avoided the temptation to hang bonkers art, instead favouring classical scenes of Venice. A silver pot of coffee and three red espresso cups are on a low glass table in front of the sofas. As Valentina invites us to take a seat, I have no idea what is going to happen next, but my nerves are back, so tight my hands are shaking to the point I decline coffee, because I'll probably fling it all over the sofas.

Without wasting any time, Erskine kicks off

the meeting. "Lovely coffee, thank you Tina. Now, for the sake of clarity, I will fully outline the purpose of today's meeting, mostly for the benefit of Peter."

Leaning forward to pick up her coffee, Valentina's amber teardrop sways in front of her cleavage. Bloody hell... Sorry, Jayne Renton, I hope you're the forgiving type, because I know my eyes are going to be wandering.

As Erskine explains the details in accordance with my understanding, Valentina's reaction gives me no cause for concern. After a few minutes, Valentina takes over from Erskine and begins outlining the paperwork process but with her eyes locked on mine, her soft and musical accent, and that sodding amber teardrop dancing between us, it's difficult to concentrate. But I keep my shit together just enough to realise that everything she says, just like Erskine, is in line with my expectations. Having spent much of the last few days worried about intangibles and feeling out of my depth, as the minutes tick by, beginning to feel more settled, I brave the coffee.

Just over an hour later, and still no cause for worry, I'm helping myself to more coffee when Valentina finishes tapping at her computer. "Well, that's everything done and emailed. I expect to have confirmation back from the German authorities within twenty-four hours and the jewels in the bank vault within two to three weeks." Behind her desk, it's as if she's just ordered a take-away. She shows no emotion whatsoever. Mr. Outrage would be delighted.

The events of the last hour or so have been mainly orchestrated by Valentina, with Erskine playing second fiddle. Lots of computer forms, photocopying and signing of documents. All the time my radar sweeping for any hint of a blip, barrier or bombshell between the two of them, but so far, it all seems wonderfully seamless.

Walking together back into the reception area, Erskine is the cool cucumber he was when we met Valentina a couple of hours ago. "Well, Tina, thank you very much. Always such a pleasure to be working together."

"I'm pleased we've been able to help. It's really a great story.' Valentina's dark eyes turn to gaze into mine for a moment. "I am sure your grandmother's inheritance will bring you much happiness. We will keep Mr. Erskine updated on developments. I hope you enjoy your last night in Bologna." This time, she smiles and for the first time, I detect a little bit of emotion. I'm not going to mention Mr. Outrage, he's had enough exposure. But unlike during the meeting where she seemed a little robotic, Valentina is quite different as we say goodbye.

"Not so bad after all, eh?" Erskine says, shaking my hand as our cab darts its way back to the hotel. "I reckon that went about as well as could be expected. Fantastically efficient girl, Valentina. No fuss. Just gets things done."

I smile and nod. As far as I could tell it was a perfect afternoon, bringing me one massive leap for mankind closer to my inheritance. "She's quite a girl." I say, interested to know if he ever lets his guard down.

"Hmmm. Damned attractive woman, as my father would have said." Erskine is doing his best to keep his feelings buttoned up, but maybe Valentina Russo has loosened his collar just a little.

"Well, I'm quite happy to go on record as saying she's possibly the most gorgeous woman I've ever seen." I mean it. It's not the sort thing I'd normally share, but my world is changing by the hour and with a new sense of confidence, the words just flowed out.

Erskine smiles, "More gorgeous than say, I don't know... Jayne Renton for example?" He winks mischievously. Then, as if with a heavy heart he sighs. "These things are sent to try us."

I assume it's another one of his father's philosophical gems, but whatever thoughts rattle around Erskine's sizable head, I know that when it comes to women, I'm not going to get anywhere near them.

10

Back in London, I'm feeling on top of the world. After the trip to Bologna went without a hiccup, it seems everything is going to plan, just as Erskine had said it would. With a cash advance in the bank and the prospect of millions more just a few weeks away, I now have the luxury of killing time.

When we went our separate ways at London City airport last night, Erskine had reassured me not to be concerned about any radio silence from his end. There simply wasn't much to be done until Valentina Russo got back to him. He expected an update from her in the next day or so, to confirm that the paperwork had been accepted by the German authorities. But after that, it would be a couple of weeks before any significant news was likely to come through.

So, what do you do when the daily grind of life is taken away and you are suddenly faced with a new reality? Staring out of my window, I look out over the Walworth Road. Light drizzle is falling on the young and old as they trudge through real life against a backdrop of fried chicken take-aways, betting shops and London buses. Until a few days ago, that was my life. But now, it looks so bleak, I wonder why they're not all screaming. From nowhere, the abstract art in the Italian office enters my mind, suddenly making more sense, the vibrancy and vitality saying something about seeing things from a different perspective. As I look out over the unrelenting grey of London in the rain, just the thought of it radiates light.

I think about what I could do over the next few days until we hear back from Valentina Russo. Go to New York or Sydney? Why not? I could go wherever the hell I wanted. Still looking out of the window, I question if it would be nice to share the experience, but I don't have any close friends. Being a loner means keeping a few acquaintances, but not choosing to let them into your life. Maybe I should grab someone off the street and share a bit of my luck, a thought that disappears as quickly as it comes. Then I think about women and how money could, to some eyes, suddenly transform a Mr. Average like me into George Clooney. It might happen, I suppose. Then I begin to fantasise about Jayne Renton and Valentina Russo, trying to decide which one I'd choose, assuming I had the luxury. Putting their unquestionable beauty to one side, they're very different people. Jayne is an order taker, Valentina is an order giver. Jayne is softer, Valentina is tougher. Jayne is younger, Valentina is older. Jayne is oozingly gorgeous, Valentina is oozingly gorgeous. Fuck it, if I were lucky enough, I wouldn't turn down either of them!

In a bid to fill my head with fresh and realistic thoughts, I decide that going away for a few days would be a good thing, settling on the idea of travelling around the UK by train. I'd recently read about a ticket that gives you unlimited access to all rail networks and it makes sense to stay in the country, in case there's news from Erskine meaning I need to get back to London quickly.

Within two days I'm heading north, cocooned in first class with books, newspapers and headphones as towns, villages, canals, farms, rivers and people rip past, going through places I've never been before. Apart from deciding each morning where I'm going to stop that day, I have no grand plan, booking a hotel online from the train. The time away is useful, helping me to concentrate on something else, despite the welcome distraction en route of Erskine confirming that the paperwork is approved in Germany, and that he would call me when the jewels were safely received in Italy. After spending nights in York, Edinburgh, Aberdeen, Glasgow, I head back to London, and although it's been enjoyable, it's had the surprising effect of seeding my first thoughts of moving, possibly to Italy, after the money arrives. Something in Bologna had stirred me more than anything I've experienced in the last few days and it feels like the break has inadvertently helped clarify a new direction in my life.

Since getting back home, the idea of living in Italy reenters my head several times, but I'm snapped out of it when my phone rings at 9:30pm and the name 'Erskine' flashes on the screen. Suddenly worried again, that this is well out of office hours, convinced it's a problem, I answer it.

Erskine is straight in. "Peter, I hope you're well. Listen, fantastic news. Everything has been processed much faster than expected, and Valentina received the jewels this morning. They are safely under lock and key in a bank vault. I'll have all the official documentation tomorrow. She will begin organising the auction - it'll probably be several weeks away, but all the major hurdles have now been jumped. It's really great news. Oh, and do let me know if you need a further cash advance before the auction."

Thanking Erskine profusely, my heart is thumping as the call ends. It's more proof – proof I need - that this is all actually happening.

Feeling pleased as punch when I wake up the next day, I decide that I'll drop into the pub for lunch later. There are usually a few familiar faces to catch up with over a pint, even on a weekday, though I'll keep my imminent fortune a tight secret. I certainly don't want it to be public knowledge among some of the more colourful locals. But now that I'm somewhere on the journey between relative pauper and millionaire, it'll be interesting to see if anyone notices a change in me.

It's still quite early and before going to the pub, I decide to walk to an art supply shop I've found online. It's a couple of miles away, but it's a nice morning and I'll get a cab back. Having never been in an art shop before, I randomly buy two large canvases, three brushes – thin, medium and thick, a tube of black paint, and a tube each of orange, lime green, yellow and red, adding a lightweight easel for good measure.

Back at the flat, I pile the art materials in the spare room in readiness for my own Bologna-inspired abstract art, deciding the first one will be called 'Wild Fortune', into which I'll do my best to commit the joy I'm feeling onto canvas. As it will also be done after a few pints at the pub today, it could end up being seriously abstract.

Stopping at the hallway mirror, the confidence I'm feeling inside seems to have permeated my outer layer. I'm convinced I look healthier than the last time I stopped here, bright eyed, with smoother skin and less tension in my expression. Whistling as I walk the couple of hundred meters to the pub, it's difficult to imagine how life could be better.

"Here he is, look!" Standing up, Bruce Browning points a chunky finger in my direction. Then as the pub door slaps shut behind me, it's immediately followed by about half a dozen locals who all stand up cheering and applauding me. Dumbfounded, I'm literally lost for words. I know I've not been in the pub for a couple of weeks, but that's not especially unusual and I've never seen anyone get a reaction like this.

Looking behind me, I half expect Paul McCartney to be there. But it's actually me they're cheering. Trying to process the reaction, as I walk slowly towards the group of smiling flushed faces, I rule out anyone knowing about the inheritance. There's no way any of them could have found out. "What is this?" I'm confused.

Bruce Browning signals for everyone to calm down, which they do. Not many people ignore Bruce. Still standing, he holds up a newspaper and points to a headline. "Nazi Little B*****ds!" Then underneath, "Englishman inherits fortune from jewels stolen by WW2 Nazis."

Burning with anger and embarrassment, I can't take it in. How the fuck could this have happened? I need to read the article, then speak to Erskine. He must know the story is out there.

I utter some words to the locals, feeling sick, unable to bear the thought of my name being splashed all over the place. "It's not quite what it looks like. I haven't actually received anything." It's the best I can do in the heat of this weird atmosphere, and in any case it's true. I haven't got a penny of it yet. As Bruce passes me the paper, I feel myself slip into a parallel universe as the words sink in. There is my name, Peter Foster-Fewster, for the whole world to see, while the article tells the story in accurate detail. Erskine and City Law Partners are named. Even my grandmother, Giovanna, is mentioned.

Uncertain about how to react to the meltdown in front of them, the locals watch me. Feeling the need to throw them off the trail, I suggest the story is total bullshit and that I need to make some urgent phone calls.

Outside the pub in Walworth Road, I dial Erskine's number immediately.

He answers quickly. "Peter, I'll call you back. Everything has kicked off here after a story in the London News this morning. I've got about three phone calls going simultaneously. Will be back to you within fifteen minutes."

Standing in the street, I feel sick and paranoid. The only shred of good news is that there is no photograph of me, or my address, although it does mention Camberwell. As I wait for Erskine to return my call, unable to think straight, I pace restlessly, constantly checking my phone. Feeling my anger build with each second, it hits me that I'm going to have to move away. It won't be long before the jungle drums beat a track to my front door. There are some desperate people out there who will do anything to get their hands on a slice of other people's good fortune.

Twenty minutes later, when Erskine still hasn't called me, I've had enough. Quickly returning Bruce's newspaper, I apologise for being a bit random and leave the bemused locals to it. Outside again, I flag down a taxi and head straight for the Strand. After a couple of minutes, my phone flashes with a text message, but not from a number I recognise. Expecting another nasty bombshell, I open it nervously,

MATE, HOPE UR OK. IF THERES ANY KIND OF TROUBLE U KNOW WHERE WE ARE. A FRIEND IN NEED ETC. BRUCE BROWNING.

The message brings a welcome smile, and to my surprise, a lump to my throat as the warmth and good intentions seeping through the basic language have a powerful effect on me. Just the fact that the locals decided to contact me is brilliant and suddenly I don't feel quite so isolated. *Thanks guys*, I reply as my thoughts turn back to Erskine. Then as the cab nears his office, I spot him, on the opposite side of the road, deep in conversation with another man.

Getting out of the cab, I join a small crowd of people in a bus queue on my side of the road, so he doesn't spot me. All those questions and doubts I had before signing the papers in Italy are back. Do I fully trust Erskine or is this a scam?

While I watch his every move, it's now 45

minutes after he said he would call me. The Strand is busy with pedestrians and buses are filling the road between us, so that I don't have a clear view, though I think I see the other man hand something to Erskine.

As my paranoia grows, so does my anger, stressing me out as I wonder what I've got myself into. I can definitely now see the two men shaking hands, before Erskine turns towards his office. But instead of crossing the road, he pulls his phone from his jacket. Assuming he's calling me, I wait for my phone to ring, but it doesn't. But whoever he's talking to, Erskine is animated in conversation, repeating the same raised hand movements I saw in Bologna, open palm, arm jagging back and forth. Ending the call after a couple of minutes, he appears to try another number. This time, 'Erskine' flashes up on my phone and I answer it.

"Peter, I'm so sorry. It's been non-stop all morning. Are you OK to talk now?" Erskine sounds calm.

But I want to test him. I have to know if I can trust him. From the other side of the road, my eyes are locked on him. "It sounds like you're out and about," I say, fully aware of where he is. "I'm pissed off and I'm worried. I'd like to come over to your office. Are you nearby?" I'm giving him the opportunity to openly lie in front of me, should he want to put me off.

"Yes, absolutely… Just popped over the road to collect some hospitality tickets for next week's test match from an old friend who was passing. I'll be back in my office in a couple of minutes. Come up whenever it's convenient and we can review things. Try not to stress Peter, these things tend to blow over quickly." Erskine seems to be playing with a straight bat, which at least is something. Telling him I'll be there within half an hour, I slope off anonymously.

11

Before I go to Erskine's office, I buy a copy of the newspaper. I can't bring myself to read it again, but I want it in case Erskine hasn't got one to hand. As the lift clunks its way to the third floor, I'm so tight with stress that even Jayne Renton hasn't entered my head. Then it hits me. Erskine told me her boyfriend was a journalist. That must be it - she must be the source of the story. I have no idea how I'm going to react when I see her, but I need to speak with Erskine before I do or say something stupid. With Valentina Russo now firmly positioned at number one in my sexual fantasy chart, I'm trying to work out how Jayne Renton could be such a traitor. But then, it could just as easily be Valentina Russo who's leaked the story or been talking carelessly.

By the time I press the button outside City Law Partners, my head is well and truly spinning. But instead of Jayne Renton, it's a male Scottish voice that speaks. Within two minutes I'm in Erskine's office and for the first time I can recall, he looks tired.

I don't wait for the usual pleasantries. Instead of being pleased to be here, I'm sweaty, uncomfortable, wired. "Why has Jayne Renton taken the day off today?"

"Well, actually, she hasn't. She attends a legal secretary's training course every Wednesday afternoon. She was here this morning. Any particular reason for asking?" As ever, Erskine, has the perfect answer.

"Yes. Unless you've got an explanation as to how the story made it to the press, I'd say there was a very good reason for asking." My adrenalin is pumping, but I'm angry.

"Let me just set the record straight. We are at a complete loss as to how the story appeared. But I guess you're getting at the fact that Jayne's boyfriend is Jason Clarke, the tabloid journalist." From the way Erskine asks, I know he will have a correspondingly neat answer. Without waiting for my response, he carries on. "Well, firstly it's not the paper he works for, so that alone puts a line through that theory. But secondly, and more importantly, Jayne has absolutely no access to the details of your case. It hasn't crossed her desk in any way, shape or form. Even if she wanted to, she can't just go rootling through filing cabinets, either. We have security cameras in every room and she knows that. But probably more significant still, Jayne, although good at her job, is an absolute mouse. She simply wouldn't have the balls to carry out that kind of deception, then turn up for work like she did this morning and act the innocent. Excuse my language, but when we first became aware of the story at around ten this morning, the shit well and truly hit the fan. I was livid. We were all trying to get to the bottom of it and Jayne was fielding calls with her usual calm. She doesn't have the capacity to pull off that level of deceit. Believe me, as a lawyer, you develop a sixth sense for these things." In full swing, Erskine takes a long sip of water before picking up again. "So, who was behind it? I guess it either leaves the Italian office, or in theory... you."

"Me!?" I bark back, incredulous. "I seriously hope your sixth sense is telling you that is ridiculous."

"Of course, I don't really think it was you. I'm just establishing the point that in the heat of the moment, it's easy to jump to the wrong conclusion, especially without the facts." He takes another sip of water. "I've thought it through as much as I can today, and my hunch is that someone in Germany got wind of the story and found an investigative journalist to fit the jigsaw together." He shrugs.

"Well, whatever's happened, it's a major problem as far as I'm concerned. The last thing I want is my name in print associated with inheriting a fortune." I return Erskine's shrug.

Raising his palms, he holds them facing me

to suggest we calm things down. "I sympathise totally. It's been a horrible day for you, and frankly not much better for us here. But what I really want to do is review where we are, because actually this won't affect the auction, or your inheritance. Indeed, it could even attract more interest to the auction and by association, increase the price. And by the time the auction happens, this story will be long gone, and I suspect, forgotten."

Erskine's words calm me a little as I try to lend some perspective to the events of today, more so when he suggests that I book into a hotel for a few nights while the story and my stress levels die down.

I leave his office after twenty minutes or so, still pissed off but satisfied we're on the same side and that he doesn't seem to be hiding anything. Jumping in a cab, I look up hotels on my phone and find a room at the Cumberland near Marble Arch. Within ten minutes of arriving I'm spread-eagled on the bed, this time missing any chocolates, as my head plunges into the soft pillows.

12

"Cheers." Two pint glasses clink together. Sitting at a table in The Sportsman pub, Gerald and Thomas **Bassinott** looked out over Reigate common, its stretching green swathes bathed in evening sunlight. It was approaching 7pm and the brothers were enjoying freedom after their recent release from prison. Serving two years for defrauding several wealthy international bankers in a very nearly well executed scam, had done little to dampen their spirits.

Checking his watch, Gerald baited his brother. "Ten quid says he'll be here before 7:15."

Thomas considered Gerald's offer for a few moments before nodding his acceptance.

"You're brave for taking that, our research shows he's normally here around seven."

Thomas didn't react. Watching eagle eyed over the common beyond the pub car park, the twins were awaiting the arrival of one particular car, its registration number written in the notebook in front of Gerald. At 7:16, Thomas handed Gerald a £10 note, the bet lost. It wasn't until

7.26, the car they were waiting for pulled slowly into the car park and reversed into a vacant space.

Nodding to each other, the twins headed behind the pub, to the beer garden, out of sight. Quietly reentering the pub ten minutes later, their target was sitting at a table reading a newspaper, his back turned towards them.

Stopping behind him, seeing the headline about the jewels, Gerald bent down and whispered into his ear. "Interesting article that, isn't it, Mr. Erskine?"

"Jesus, you could give someone a heart attack doing that. What's going on? Can I help you?" Turning around to see two men standing behind him, Erskine's initial shock grew more palpable.

"Help us? Interesting. But actually yes, we think you can," Gerald said brightly, giving any onlooker the impression all was well. "Let's sit over by the window and have a chat."

Getting up, Erskine followed them towards the window. "What's this about?" Erskine asked, looking slightly disconcerted as they sat down. "If it's help with legal matters, then you really need to go through the London office."

"I could beat about the bush Mr. Erskine, but it comes down to one word." Gerald spoke quietly but firmly. "Blackmail."

"Who are you? And what is all this, virtually ambushing me? I don't like it at all. I'm calling the police." Flustered, Erskine reached for his phone.

"That really would not be in your best interests, Mr. Erskine." There was more than a hint of menace in Gerald's words.

"We'll see about that." Standing up, Erskine ran a hand over his head to return a fallen shock of grey hair, before starting to punch the number into his phone.

"Duke Pyecoe." Gerald stared up hard into Erskine's eyes. "Or as you might remember him, Harry Pyecoe. But always Duke in our circles."

Erskine's face was emotionless as he returned his phone to his jacket pocket, before sitting down again. "What the hell has Duke Pyecoe got to do with anything?" he demanded. "Yes, I remember the name from a few years ago. He was a witness in a court case when I was a lawyer at Cooper Braithwaite. But why has his name popped up now?"

"You remember Duke Pyecoe as a witness? Are you sure that shouldn't be... *false* witness?" Gerald's words were now loaded with the same menace that was in his eyes. "It seems Duke was paid rather a lot of money to provide some, well, very unhelpful information to the defendant's case in that trial. Information that was cooked up. Or to put it another way, a whole lot of bollocks given under oath which helped the prosecution team snatch victory from the jaws of defeat." Gerald and Thomas both stared hard at Erskine.

"As far as I can recall, he seemed a completely

reliable witness. The jury obviously thought so. If someone did get to him, I don't see what that's got to do with me." Erskine kept his cool. "And in any case, who's feeding you all this nonsense?"

Gerald leant forward. "We've had a very interesting couple of years, spent at her Majesty's pleasure under lock and key. We went down trying to defraud some very wealthy people out of relatively small amounts of money. It was an international fraud, people with money in off shore tax havens, a few hundred grand here, a few hundred grand there. But it added up to a couple of million. It was quite a case. We were known as the Fraud Twins."

Shock consumed Erskine's face. "My God. I'm face-to-face with a couple of notorious, bungling criminals," he said condescendingly. "Tom and Jerry, I remember the press calling you." He carried on, talking down to them. "I wasn't involved in that case at all, so I don't know where you're going with that."

"We're not here to talk about our court case. We have no complaints about that. We were rumbled fair and square, and we served our time. But as a consequence of being sent down, I met Duke Pyecoe in Pentonville. He was in for theft. He'd recently run out of money and was desperate." As Erskine shrugged a 'so what' gesture, Gerald carried on, his voice measured. "He had a little nest egg that had kept him going nicely before that.

Quite a few grand in cash, under the bed. But when that ran out, he got into debt, then trouble and eventually prison."

"Well, that's a beautifully touching story, but I ask again, what has any of this got to do with me?" Erskine spoke sarcastically.

"I'll tell you exactly what it's got to do with you. You gave him the cash. Duke told me everything. Cons share a lot of information. There's a lot of time to kill in prison and it rarely goes any further. Honour amongst thieves and all that... You paid him to lie under oath when you needed to sway the jury. And it worked. Your career and standing benefited considerably as a result, paying you back way more than the cash you gave to Duke. Cash you probably got from the people you were defending."

Smiling ironically, as the brothers stared at him, Erskine shook his head. "And assuming all this eyewash is true, what next? Let me guess. You're going to tell me that unless I give Pyecoe some more cash, he's going to squeal to the police about been paid by me to be a false witness. Why would he go to the police? If they believed him, which is unlikely after he's just come out of prison for theft, he'd be arrested for perjury. Not great thinking there, lads." Any trace of his earlier bonhomie had vanished.

"Not quite that simple, I'm afraid." As Gerald spoke, his and his twin's eyes were riveted on

Erskine's. "Firstly, Duke is not long for this world. Three months max. Advanced pancreatic cancer. But he wants some help to look after his old mum when he goes. He's got nothing to lose by going to the police and squealing, as you call it. Just think about that, Erskine, a leading lawyer paying for a bent witness. You'll be the one rotting in jail. Your reputation, your family, your career. All down the pan. Forever."

Pausing before replying, Erskine lowered his voice. "Even if there was a shred of truth to what Pyecoe's told you, he wouldn't have a leg to stand on. No proof, no credibility, no money to defend himself. It's a hopeless effort to corner me. You need to move on. You're wasting your time, both of you." Erskine stood up again.

"Sit down, Mr Erskine." Gerald's voice was quiet, his eyes like little lasers. "There is proof."

"Proof of what?" Erskine chipped back, as he sat down.

"Proof of you paying Duke Pyecoe the money. You met him by the Ornamental Canal in Wapping. Quiet, pretty little place. But Duke is a wise old bird and he got his brother to photograph the exchange. Long lens camera. In fact, there are lots of photos, and we've brought them along especially for you to see. Exhibit A, please Mr. Bassinott." Gerald turned to his ever-silent brother who placed a brown A4 envelope in front of Erskine. "Take a look."

As Thomas pulled out a large black and white photograph, Erskine stared at it. There it was, as clear as day, Erskine in a baseball cap and dark glasses passing a backpack to Duke Pyecoe by the canal.

"Not sure that proves very much. Could be anyone." Erskine was defiant.

"When you add in the other fourteen photos, it proves everything." Upturning the envelope, Gerald allowed all the photographs to cascade onto the table. "I've always said those old press cameras give more detailed photos than digital ones." He fanned out some of them. "They show a detailed sequence. Duke is by the canal feeding ducks on the water. You then appear in the background, walking along the towpath from the east with a backpack. When you get level with Duke, you brush past him, holding the backpack out slightly and he takes it - that moment is caught on the image you're holding. You then carry on heading west and luckily for us, towards the camera. So, we have some lovely shots of you, especially when you removed your cap and sunglasses." Gerald placed that photograph carefully on top of the others.

Erskine took a few moments to gather his thoughts. "I'm not admitting to anything. But I need time to think. What's he after? A few quid to look after his mother, did you say?" For a man who'd just been skewered, he was holding up well.

"It's really a question of what *we* want. It just so happens that we were with Duke and his old mum for a cup of tea this morning. We like to keep in touch, especially as he's in a bad way. Mum was stuck into the paper and she read out the story of the jewels stolen by the Nazis. Some lucky chap is going to inherit a fortune. I've got the piece here, you've got it there." Gerald tapped the paper on the table in front of Erskine. "You feature quite prominently. Looks like you'll be doing alright when you get your cut. Duke got quite upset when he read it. Here you are rolling in all this cash and he's dying in a council flat. He's also very upset that the £25,000 bent witness money you agreed to pay him was never fully honoured. You ripped off the man you relied on in court. The deal was, £15,000 up front, £10,000 after the trial if Pyecoe's testimony led to a successful outcome, which it did. He tried to contact you several times after the trial, but you had no interest in him. So, we reassured Duke that we'd find you and give you every opportunity to set things straight."

Erskine remained calm. "Again, I'm not admitting to anything, but you're saying I owe him £10,000 in cash. Is that what he wants?" He scanned the Bassinott brothers.

"No." Gerald's reply was blunt. "What we want needs to be discussed in a lot more detail. Tomorrow, at your office. We'll be there at 11am. If that clashes with another appointment, cancel it. If there's any funny business, remember we can get you arrested on a charge of perverting the course of justice on the strength of the evidence we have now. And although Duke's ill, he's not gone yet. He can corroborate everything. Who knows what else you've been up to? These things have a nasty habit of escalating when the lid comes off. I'm sure you've worked it out, but in case it's not obvious, you have every reason to keep all of this to yourself." Gerald paused. "We'll see you tomorrow at eleven."

13

I wake up early in the Cumberland Hotel, the events of yesterday still clattering around my head, with no idea if the news story has died down or been picked up by other papers. Deciding I'll call Erskine later to find out, I wander over to the large window and open it slightly, letting in the sounds of early morning London, the odd bus and delivery van, but at 5:30 am, not much else.

Lying back in bed, I replay everything that's happened since meeting Erskine, trying once again to work out if there is another agenda somewhere that I'm missing. Am I just some innocent patsy who isn't bright enough to work out that I'm being taken for a ride? Despite thinking through it over and over, I can't hit on anything concrete, except for the occasional uneasiness I sometimes feel when I'm with Erskine. It doesn't happen often and it's difficult to put a finger on it, but despite his polished debonair exterior, there's something in his manner. Unable to resolve anything, I try to get some more sleep. Whatever else is going on with him, he was right about the hotel. Feeling safe and comfortable here, I decide it will be my home for the next few nights.

After a shower, then breakfast downstairs, just after 9am, I'm back in my room ready to call Erskine. There are a few things I need to speak to him about. Firstly, the press and whether there are any further developments. I also want to know if he's spoken to Valentina Russo since the story appeared. He didn't mention her yesterday, which in retrospect, surprises me. I also want to arrange another cash advance, urgently as it happens. He's mentioned several times that will not be a problem. If I'm going to be living in the Cumberland for a while, I need to make sure my bank account is healthy.

My paranoia is never far away when I call his mobile number, which this morning, rings several times before going to answerphone. Immediately I think he's avoiding me. If he was on another call, his answerphone would have triggered straight away. I decide to leave it ten minutes then call him from the phone in my room, so that he has no idea it's me who's calling.

Clearly, he had been avoiding me. This time, he answers after a couple of rings, but instead of his trade mark, "Hello, Erskine," he sounds cautious. "Who's calling please?"

"It's me - Peter Foster-Fewster. Is everything alright? Only you don't sound at all yourself."

"So sorry, Peter." Erskine suddenly sounds

more like the man I know. "The phone was under some papers and I was scrabbling around a bit. All fine. How can I help?"

"I'd like to pop in and see you. You did say you'd clear the decks if I needed to. But I've got a few things I'd like catch up on. How about 11am?"

"That's actually going to be tricky this morning, I've just had something come up that I can't rearrange. It's a personal matter. Erm, I'll be out of the office from about ten for the rest of the day. Can I call you later and arrange something for tomorrow?"

Erskine is clearly distracted. I assume his personal matter is a problem he could do without. "Sure, I'll wait for your call later. Incidentally, any further developments on the press story yesterday?" I ask before he goes.

"Not a sausage, as far as I'm aware. Hopefully, it's already blown over as I said it would. Look, I'm sorry Peter, I'm going to have to be very rude and let you go. I have a short meeting here before I leave the office this morning. No rest for the wicked."

"So it seems." I say with more than a hint of innuendo.

With my wavering levels of trust in Erskine under strain again, I'm becoming obsessed with the man. It's 9.15am now and he reckons he's leaving his office in 45 minutes. That gives me plenty of time to get a cab to the Strand and spy on him. It sounds crazy as I think about it for a moment, but I have the time and I need to know if he's fobbing me off. That uneasy feeling is bothering me. If I see him leave the office, fair enough. He probably does have an external meeting, as he said which means he's being straight with me. But if he doesn't appear through those shiny glass doors and walk down the steps, then I reckon he'll have spun me a whopper.

It's 9.40 when the cab drops me near Erskine's office. From the other side of the road, an Italian coffee shop provides a great view of City Law Partners. Getting a coffee, I take it upstairs to the first floor and sit by the window, waiting to see if Erskine emerges.

As the time approaches 10am, a few people come and go, but there's no sign of Erskine. He'd mentioned a meeting before that could easily overrun, so I continue to wait, my eyes locked on the steps opposite as the minutes click by. 10:15 becomes 10:30 and Erskine has definitely not left the building. I decide to give it until 11:00, my obsession keeping me rooted to the spot. Nothing remarkable happens until 10:55 when a private hire taxi stops right by the steps. Could this be to collect Erskine? I watch this last-minute hope intently, but it's not for Erskine. Instead two tall men, very similar in appearance and notable for their casual clothes, trot up the steps and in through the glass doors.

Satisfied that Erskine is still in the building, I'm pissed off. He's almost certainly lied to prevent me from seeing him today. Heading back to the hotel, I'm not really sure what I've achieved, as my trust levels in Erskine reach an all-time low.

14

"City Law Partners, how can I help?"

"Gerald and Thomas Bassinott to see Mr. Erskine."

"Just push the door open when you hear the buzzer and I'll come to meet you."

Doing as the voice instructed, the brothers walked through the door then down the corridor, where an attractive woman appeared at the other end to welcome them.

"Very pleased to meet you both. My name is Jayne Renton. Follow me and Mr Erskine will be with you shortly. Can I get you a drink of anything? Tea, coffee, water?"

Gerald took the lead. "Two teas would be much appreciated, milk, one sugar in mine, milk, no sugar in his." Sitting on the leather Chesterfield, the brothers waited silently, until Jayne Renton returned carrying their tea.

"I'm afraid Mr Erskine's running a few minutes late."

Gerald looked at his watch, showing nearly five past eleven. "Absolutely no problem." But he spoke through gritted teeth before whispering to his brother, "It's his pathetic way of exerting a bit of control, keeping us waiting." But after only a couple of minutes had passed, Jayne Renton was back. "Mr Erskine will see you now. Please follow me."

Leading the brothers to Erskine's door, she knocked a couple of times before opening it and showing the men in.

"Good morning, Gentlemen. Please take a seat. Thank you, Jayne." Standing behind his desk, Erskine was looking upbeat, giving no clue to indicate that all was not well. As Jayne Renton checked if any more refreshments were needed, the Bassinott brothers and Erskine were uber-polite as they declined, carefully keeping up the charade in front of her, before she closed the door on the three men.

Erskine started immediately. "The first thing I want to make absolutely clear is that I don't accept any of what you said in the pub yesterday. And I am certainly not admitting to any of it. But I am prepared to listen. Maybe there is a way to help your friend Pyecoe, if that draws a line under events. But my only commitment right now, as I say, is that I'm prepared to listen." Sitting back, Erskine waited for a response.

"Listen you most certainly will." Gerald was in no mood for playing games. "You can kid yourself all you want, but the three of us know you're a bent lawyer and we can end your career with one phone call. So don't crap on about not accepting it. That bit of our conversation was done yesterday in the pub. I'm not going back over it. Today is different. We're here to tell you what to do, unless you want us to make that phone call. Clear so far?"

Erskine didn't flinch, just moved a hand slightly, to suggest Gerald should carry on.

"The auction in Italy that's coming up - the one in the press yesterday for the Nazi jewels? For now, you will carry on as if we'd never met." Gerald remained calm. "You will make sure the auction goes ahead. Then when the cash comes through, there's going to be a re-distribution of wealth. In our direction."

As Gerald finished speaking, Erskine spontaneously erupted, coughing, laughing and blowing his cheeks out. "Well, I can assure you that isn't going to happen. Bloody hell, have you any idea how infantile that is? There are too many people involved. I can see why they called you Tom & Jerry. You're so far out of your depth, it's laughable. Why don't I throw in the crown jewels while we're at it? Or are you happy to act like your alter egos and tell me, 'That's all folks'?" Wearing an expression of condescension, Erskine looked at the brothers.

Gerald was unmoved. "This is no time for jokes, Erskine. This is the time for listening."

"I thought I would be listening to grown-ups. Not cartoon characters." Erskine quipped. "How on earth do you think you could hide that level of theft? Which is what it will be. Come on, give me the grand plan. I'm all ears."

"You don't need to know any more at this stage. We'll advise you at every step. The only thing you need to be crystal clear about is keeping this to yourself. Crystal. Clear. Not a word to anyone. Nothing to the Italian office. And certainly not a word to whoever thinks they're getting a lucky inheritance - Foster-Fewster, according to the press." Beneath Gerald's controlled manner, there was no mistaking he meant every word. "If he goes squealing now, we'll drop you right in it. And we'll be guilty of nothing. On balance, better to keep it all under your hat, I'm sure you'd agree?"

Staring at Gerald, Erskine took a sip of water before replying. "I'm going to the police with this. This is straightforward blackmail. The moment I tell them that the infamous Fraud Twins are up to their old tricks and have turned up in my office trying to defraud me, they'll be round here before you can say, Duke Pyecoe. No, I'm sorry gentlemen, this ends here and now. You have twenty seconds to apologise and get out of my office. If not, I'm picking up the phone and going straight through to the Chief Superintendent at Scotland Yard. A good friend of mine. So, I'll start the count down now and leave it up to you."

As seconds passed, all three men were silent, the brother's eyes locked on Erskine, his own eyes flitting between the two of them. With the time nearly up, Erskine reached for the phone on his desk.

He counted down the last five seconds. "Five,

four, three, two... sorry gentlemen, you've had your chance."

15

Waking up in the Cumberland, today is my second day in hiding. It's early again and I wander over to the window to watch city life awaken beneath me. No matter how much I try to distract myself, the need to see Erskine escalates with every passing minute. If he doesn't get in touch by 9:30, I'll call his office.

A long shower helps pass the time, before heading down for breakfast, grabbing a couple of free newspapers from the lobby to check I'm not front-page news. Fortunately, the story seems to have faded. Back in my hotel room just before nine, I'm surprised when my phone rings and its Erskine. After he fobbed me off yesterday, I thought I'd be chasing him all morning.

Since waking I've been building up to sounding irritated with him, but as always, he has the power to surprise.

"Peter, apologies for yesterday, unplanned events rather tied my hands. However, I've made sure I'm pretty much available to see you anytime today. 11am would be ideal, how does that suit you?"

"Sound's fine, although 10:30 would be better?" My inner impatience forcing a bit of control over events.

"That's absolutely fine. In the diary. Very much looking forward to seeing you then."

Now that I'm actually going to see Erskine face-to-face, I'm feeling fairly relaxed as my taxi joins the stop-start stream of buses, cycles and taxis strategically shunting along like chess pieces. Thinking about my call this morning, Erskine sounded as calm as ever so I'm optimistic that we're getting back on track. But I do need another cash advance and reassurance that the press story hasn't caused any problems with the forthcoming auction in Italy. Then there's Jayne Renton, who is apparently as pure as the driven snow, if Erskine is to be believed. I want to scrutinise her every move no matter what.

After Jayne Renton welcomes me into the reception, I'm surprised to see Erskine sitting on the Chesterfield reading his phone. It curtails my heightened interest in Jayne.

Jumping up, Erskine seems more animated than normal, "Peter, good morning. Lovely to see you. Come on through."

Having placed our drinks order with the smiling Ms. Renton, we head for his office. After Jayne delivers our drinks, Erskine gets down to business. "Well, the good news is that the press story seems to have been confined to the London News. Not sparked any other interest as far as we can tell. Gone and forgotten, except maybe for wrapping chips." Erskine looks pleased.

"Does that mean there is bad news?" I ask, re-playing his opening words.

"No, no," Erskine is amused. "It's just that, well... it's all good news."

"And so everything is still on track? The auction? And when did you last speak to Valentina Russo?" I know I'm coming across as frantic, but I've been bottling things up for too long.

"Auction is all in hand. I've been in regular contact with Valentina. She's very happy with everything, just waiting for a date confirmation from Gallo-Moretti - that's the name of the auction house they'll be using. They're in Florence.

The provisional date is 15th of September, so just a few weeks away. As soon as Gallo-Moretti confirm, the invites to potential buyers will be sent. They have a database of clients and people who have registered special interests. They'll advertise it as well. So not just on track Peter, some good way down it."

"That's really good news. But still no clue as to the press leak?" I ask, not wanting the major upset it caused to just disappear without another word.

"We're none the wiser. Our best guess is still that someone in Germany made it their business to try and sell the story. But we may never know. It didn't really work, if that was their plan." Erskine shakes his head. "Was there something else on your mind?"

In no doubt that he lied to me yesterday, when he invented his story about leaving the office, I'm desperate to ask him about it. I know for a fact that he didn't leave, so what was the real reason he didn't want to see me? Frustrated that I can't think of a way to subtly pursue the issue, in reality, I can see it's none of my business. And the upside is that so far today, he's given me no reason to worry and already my earlier concerns are dissipating.

Instead, I ask about having more money. "I really could do with another advance payment. Living at the Cumberland is expensive. I'm also thinking about going away for a couple of weeks. I want to get away from London. See a bit of the world. I assume an advance is still OK?" I study Erskine for the smallest hint of a problem.

But there is no delay. "Yes, of course. No problem at all. How about the same as before?"

I nod my agreement, delighted at how trouble-free that was.

"I'll get it transferred to your account this afternoon."

16

Back at the hotel, I take stock of the situation. The advance from Erskine is already in my bank account and apart from sorting a couple of things back at the flat, I'm free to travel until the auction. In fact, I don't even need to be at the auction, but I want to be there. Erskine has already told me he will be sorting out travel and accommodation for both of us.

So, where to go? It's an alien reality that time and money don't come into the decision making process. Now that I can go pretty much wherever I want, choosing somewhere seems surprisingly difficult. America has never really appealed, and Australia is too far away. Then it hits me. Italy, of course! I loved what I saw in Bologna and I've already had thoughts about moving there after the money arrives. This is a perfect opportunity to spend some quiet time there alone and check it out properly. Flicking through various travel websites on my phone, the list of stunning places seems endless. Rome, Florence, Milan, and Pisa are on my immediate hit list. But I'll start with

Bologna.

Before doing anything else, I send a text message to Bruce Browning. His concern touched me when the press story came out. Telling him that I'm OK and things have settled down, I also tell him that I'll be traveling for a few weeks and will catch up with the old crowd soon. Not sure if I believe my own words about going back to the pub, but for now I want them all to know I'm alive and grateful for their support, even though I know they'll have been gossiping.

I buy flights for the following day and book a couple of nights at a hotel in Bologna, deciding to make further plans when I get there. The rest of the day is given over to shopping for new clothes and spending a few hours at the flat in Camberwell, to collect post and check the place over. I'll end the tenancy when the inheritance money comes through, but for now it's needed as a base. Returning to the Cumberland quite late, the hotel restaurant is perfect for a light dinner before heading up for a relatively early night. Collapsing on the bed, I call reception and arrange a 5:30am taxi to Gatwick.

A fresh excitement fills me the next morning as I wait to board the plane. Its July and the majority of passengers are wearing shorts and t-shirts. There's a definite holiday buzz even if Bologna isn't exactly Ibiza. Taking my window seat, I relax for a few minutes before cracking open 'Discovering Italy', the book I've just bought at the airport. Colourful photographs of Italian architecture and landscapes fill every page, forcing a passion attack to rise within. My earlier excitement turbocharged, I can't wait to be let loose.

The flight passes quickly. From Bologna airport, the cab flits through the city suburbs before turning into Via Indipendenza, the street that first turned my head when I was here with Erskine a couple of weeks ago. In the sunshine and bristling with medieval charm, it's lost none of its magic. Via Indipendenza is long and straight and the hotel I've chosen is fairly close to Piazza Maggiore at the other end. I didn't want to stay in the nearby Grand Hotel Majestic. Even now, I can't justify paying ten times over the odds. And from the pictures online, my hotel looks more in keeping with the true atmosphere of Bologna.

We turn into a tiny side street and the cab stops. "Hotel Asinelli," the old taxi driver croaks, unfurling a crooked finger towards a tiny but smart hotel, squashed between a bakery and a wine shop. It looks perfect.

Paying the driver, I grab my bags and virtually step out of the taxi straight into the hotel. Inside it's cool, what it lacks in width is made up for in length as I see all the way through to the breakfast room. Behind the desk, the receptionist is a slim, grey-haired gentleman with skin the colour of Italian mahogany and a neatly trimmed white beard. Smartly dressed, he is picture-perfect as he fusses carefully over the paperwork in front of him, before giving me a medieval key attached to a weighty lug.

Avoiding the lift which looks like a dingy broom cupboard, I take the steps. My room is a decent size and the double bed performs well as I carry out my ritual of falling on it spread-eagled. No chocolates on the pillows, I realise gratefully, as my head sinks into the softness.

By lunchtime, having unpacked, I head for Piazza Maggiore, a five-minute walk away under Bologna's trademark porticos which line most of the city's streets, where the midday heat is pleasantly subdued.

Stepping out of the shade, I cross the road to the piazza. Surrounded by red medieval buildings, the open square is like a cauldron, stone masonry soaking up the belting heat and radiating it back, amplifying the already roasting sun. On the far side of the piazza, the obvious refuge is the massive church. Walking across, I pass groups of happy students apparently unaffected by the temperature, elderly folk with tiny dogs, buskers with violins and a couple of grim-faced activists who want me to sign up for some distant cause. With everyone safely sidestepped, I walk up the steps to the church and through the door.

Inside, the cool hits me immediately, as does the scale of the building. Wide, high, long and wonderfully echoey. In the shadowy atmosphere, it's unfussy until I reach the far end. As I gaze at the huge ornate altar, there's an atmosphere of tangible otherworldliness illuminated by pale beams of ethereal greenish light. Sitting on one of the many empty seats, I stare at everything, awe-struck, not just by the scale, but the calm. It feels like a good place to contemplate life, and so for the next hour, that's what I do.

As I leave the church, I head for another ob-vious refuge from the heat, a bar on the opposite side of the piazza. Nicely shaded under a parasol, with a carafe of icy cold rose wine, I gaze back at the church that captivated me this afternoon. My Italian holiday has got off to a good start.

17

The smell of freshly baked bread drifts through my open window and into my consciousness. What a wonderful way to wake up. After a day of walking and a little too much wine and grappa, I've slept like a log. The hotel curtains are thick, but it's obvious from the glow around them that the sun is already beating down and I'm excited to make the most of it.

The train station is a fifteen-minute walk from my hotel and from what I've read, connects directly with most major Italian cities. Thinking about a day trip somewhere, in search of inspiration, I reach to the floor for my Italian guide book, but at exactly the same moment my phone flashes up with a message. It's Erskine.

Butterflies always stir before reading his messages or taking his calls. Is this the moment I learn that this crazy fairy tale is over? Reading it with trepidation, I'm immediately calmed. It's confirmation that the auction date has been set for 2pm on Friday 15th September at Gallo-

Moretti in Florence. I chuck the guide book back on the floor. The inspiration has been inadvertently supplied by Erskine. A day trip to Florence, sorted!

After the hotel breakfast of coffee, toast and a slightly dry apple, I make my way to the station at the end of Via Indipendenza. It's a t-shirt and shorts day and once again, I'm grateful for the shade offered by the porticos. Inside the station, it's cool and busy, while the departure board reads like my dream wish list. From here you can get trains to Rome, Venice, Milan, Turin and the list goes on.

Florence is showing two options, and I overhear a posh English student explain the difference to her friend in upper received pronunciation, how one is cheap but quite grubby, darling, while the other is like sparkling and whizzes through mountain tunnels. Of course it cost more, but it doesn't matter because Daddy is paying for everything.

Joining one of the queues for the ticket office, I people-watch as it glacially edges forwards. Each ticket sale is painfully slow, seeming to involve too much interaction between buyer and seller. Made slower when an Italian in a skin-tight blue suit steps in at the front of the queue. I'm gobsmacked. Mirrored sunglasses, designer stubble and slicked hair do nothing to endear him to me. I twist around, hoping someone will punch his lights out, but no-one bats an eyelid.

Realising I have a lot to learn about Italian culture, with my ticket safely negotiated, I board the speedy, clean whizzy train to Florence. Gliding slowly out of the station, it slithers through the suburbs of Bologna, within a few minutes gathering speed; the open countryside replacing apartment blocks and business parks; before long the seatback speed counter showing 300 kilometres per hour, the train still remaining silent.

The blurring landscape of fields and farms suddenly disappears as the train torpedoes into a mountain tunnel. For the next twenty minutes we power through unrelenting darkness before being fired out of the other end into bright daylight and the serene countryside surrounding Florence, before I'm hit by my first view of the city, the Duomo rising above everything else, ridiculously familiar in the morning sun.

As the train pulls into the station, I head for the exit, noticing the queue jumper from Bologna walking towards me from the adjacent carriage. Quickening my step just enough to get the door before him so that I can get off first, it's a minor victory, but it feels good. *Take that, you cocky bastard*, I shout as he and his forcefield of Italian fragrance breeze past me on the platform. OK, the words might not have left my mouth, but it's the thought that counts.

The walk from the station into the city

centre is unremarkable and exciting at the same time, as the prospect of being immersed in so much history gets closer with each step. Then, almost without warning I'm in and among it. The roof of the Duomo visible between gaps in the buildings and suddenly closer than expected. A couple more streets and I'm face-to-face with the most iconic medieval building in the world.

The outer walls of the Duomo are much more ornate than I'm expecting, probably because most photographs only capture its famous dome. Passing a student violinist delivering a virtuoso performance on the steps, when I go inside, the scale hits me like the church in Bologna. Half expecting to see the queue-jumper appear from nowhere and elbow everyone aside, I head for the dome at the far end. Standing underneath is dizzying. A parallel to my recent life. All around me, camera shutters reverberate through the vastness, but no photographs needed. I just want to stand and stare, taking it all in, the image of beauty and human endeavour tattooed on my memory forever.

Ten vertigo inducing minutes later, I find a seat giving me panoramic views around the rest of the building, as I realise I have a new love in my life - Italian churches. It's their glitzy grandness combined with plain and simple. Their big echoey spaces that help me to chew the fat calmly. It occurs to me that this love affair is more real than my fantasies with Jayne Renton or Valentina Russo, but there's plenty of time to put that right.

Thinking of those two brings the auction house to mind, so I look on my phone for the address of Gallo-Moretti. Not sure if I want to go in, but I'd like to see the place. It'll give me another slice of mental security for those moments when I convince myself that I'm at the centre of an enormous scam.

Gallo-Moretti is about a ten-minute walk on the other side of the Arno river, which means walking over the Ponte Vecchio, very much on my list of things to do. By going to Gallo-Moretti via the famous bridge means I'll be hitting two birds with one stone.

Aware that it sounds rather too like a metaphor for my Renton-Russo fantasy, I leave the Duomo, following the tourist signs towards the Ponte Vecchio, but any beauty offered by the ancient bridge is neutralised by the throng gathered there. Forcing my way through to the other side, I reach the relative calm of the road opposite, following my map until I find Gallo-Moretti, at the far end of Via Crostini.

As I wander down the street of expensive antique shops and high-end galleries, I window shop, thinking how for most of my life, I could never have imagined being able to afford such things, but after the auction, how that will change.

One piece in particular catches my eye, a large leather settee, which thanks to some serious Italian buffing is luminous under the light cast from a huge retro angle-poise lamp. It reminds me of the Chesterfield in Erskine's office, but this one isn't oxblood. It's muted jade and quite possibly the most beautiful piece of furniture I've ever seen, its contours stretched and studded tightly to perfection. Subtle green leather darkens towards deeply plunged buttons and cushion edges. I reach into the back pocket of my shorts and take out my phone to photograph it, noticing the price as I zoom in. Nearly fifteen thousand euros! Even if I had the money, at that price I'd have to sit on it.

A reflection in the window causes me to freeze. On the other side of the street, there's a man looking exactly like Erskine, with a woman who could easily be Valentina Russo. Surely if he was here, he would have mentioned it? My suspicions rising to the surface, I follow cautiously for a few steps before the woman peels away and the man turns. It isn't Erskine. It's my overactive brain at it again, but deep inside, a part of me clearly doesn't trust him.

Continuing to wander down Via Crostini, ahead of me I see the auction house, or its name at least, written in white letters on a black background on what looks like an elaborate pub sign, hanging from a beam over the street.

Arriving in front of the building I'm surprised it isn't bigger. But I know from my hotel and the Italian churches I've seen, buildings here have the power to surprise. Intrigued to see inside, I have no idea what the form is and I try to make sense of the few words neatly engraved into the darkened glass doors.

Still none the wiser, the moment is made easier when two smartly dressed ladies, deep in conversation, glide past me and push the doors open, holding them for me to enter. Taking in their combined perfumes, I offer them my best "grazie" which is suitably ignored as they carry on their conversation at blistering pace, but now reduced to a whisper as they show respect for the grandeur of all things Gallo-Moretti.

And grand it certainly is. Up a few steps to an automatic sliding door, I enter a reception area that is hushed, low lit and plush with dark brown carpet. Five wide walls surround me, bronze coloured, slightly concave and decorated with simple golden architrave.

Where a sixth wall could have been, a wide staircase curls upwards out of view to what I assume will be the auction rooms. Wandering over to the information counter where I'm apparently invisible, eventually a tall young man of student appearance in an oversized pair of blue-framed glasses notices me and coasts over.

"Buongiorno." he says quietly.

"Buongiorno. Do you speak English?" I ask anxiously.

"A little, yes. I try, at least." Looking slightly embarrassed, he laughs, running a hand through a lustrous head of glossy black ringlets.

"When is the next auction, and can anyone attend?" I haven't come with any questions in mind. I just want to get a better understanding of the way things work here.

The young man slides a brochure along the counter towards me. "All auction dates are in here, but a new brochure is about to be printed. It's also online on Gallo-Moretti website, which gets updated when the brochure is out. If you want to attend auction as a buyer, you register your details online first. Or I can do that now if you have ID. Passport is best. You get a member's card, and you can download our app, you scan card or phone when you go into the auction. You can also register on the day. But it's better to do before. Without that, security won't let you in." The young man prods his glasses back up his nose, awaiting my response.

"I've got my ID with me. I'd like to register now if possible?" I reach for my passport.

"Sure. I just get the forms up on the screen here." Giving his hair another comb of his fingers, the young man smiles, before turning his concentration to the computer on the counter between us, taking my name, address, passport and a few other details, while I watch his glasses gradually slip down his nose. I feel like prodding them back up just to help, but he beats me to it every time. After it's done, armed with my membership card, I take a look through the brochure. It's too early for my auction to be listed, but I like the idea of attending a sale here before I go home.

Noticing there's a fine art and jewellery auction in two days' time, I check with the young man that I'm now eligible to attend.

"You're good to go," he confirms, with a final flourish of both hands through his tousled locks.

Walking back towards the Duomo, I'd intended to stop at the Uffizi Gallery, but the queues are enormous. Instead, I content myself by exploring narrow streets, some empty of life, others dotted with bars and trattorias where slices of medieval history are served all day long. Choosing a small bistro, I order a simple pizza and a half carafe of Italian red wine. Sitting outside at one of five tables, my only neighbours are a silent elderly couple spiralling spaghetti accurately onto their forks.

Before there is time to unfold the large red serviette, my wine is delivered by an efficient waiter along with a large empty glass. Taking a minute to enjoy the atmosphere, I slowly transfer the dark vino rosso from terracotta carafe to bulbous glass, swirling it gently before holding it up to the light. Admiring the blackish purple hue in contrast to the blameless blue sky, I'm again surprised by the speed of service as suddenly a pizza is lowered gracefully in front of me. But this is nothing like the frozen version I'm used to at home. Instead, aromas of wood smoke, warm garlic and fresh herbs rise up, while blobs of melting cheese seep into the orangey-red tomato base. I have no idea how an Italian would set about eating this. Finger food or knife and fork? I look over to my elderly neighbours for inspiration and watch their precise fork work and decide they wouldn't resort to fingers, not even for a pizza. So, I begin by cutting a smallish piece, no crust for now, just a neat square of Italian unctuousness, the flavour giving me butterflies as it hits my taste buds. Scientifically and symmetrically, working my way through the rest of the pizza, not wanting it to end, only pausing occasionally for a slug of the plummy wine. With not a crumb left and the carafe empty, I glance over to the elderly couple now silently sharing a pizza of their own, tearing into it ruthlessly with all four hands and not a fork in sight.

Tired after walking, I drift back in the direction of the station, half an hour in the relative luxury of the fast train seeming very appealing now that I know I'm coming back here in a couple of days, for Gallo-Moretti's next auction.

After an effortless train journey, I head for

my hotel along familiar streets that after Florence, feel homely and understated. There were some obvious highlights there - the pizza being one of them. Pulling back the bedsheets for a late afternoon nap, as my head hits the pillow, the auction house is forgotten, as instead, I'm thinking of the dozens of restaurants scattered around my doorstep. Starting tonight, I'm determined to find another where the pizza is every bit as good.

18

Erskine looked out across the Strand from his office window, his hands clasped behind his back. Glancing at the grandfather clock, he knew that within minutes, the Bassinott brothers would be here to give him further instructions. When they last met, Erskine had tried to bluff them with a threat to call the Chief Superintendent at Scotland Yard, but despite his ultimatum, he'd caved-in to the inevitable at the last moment, agreeing to do exactly as the brothers instructed. At that point, it was to do nothing but keep his mouth shut, carry on as normal and make sure Foster-Fewster had no reason to suspect that there were any problems. Erskine had been as good as his word, even when Foster-Fewster requested another cash advance just a few days ago. Erskine had no option but to happily oblige.

He didn't know what to expect from today's meeting, but Erskine knew he had to go along with their plans for now, convincing himself all the time that he would be able to outwit the Bassinots at some point and prevent them from taking all the cash from the auction sale. Still staring out of the window, Erskine was doing his best to relax when a couple of respectful raps on the door told him Jayne Renton was poised to enter, no doubt with his 10am guests close behind.

Taking a deep breath, he turned as she opened the door. "Thank you Jayne. Gentlemen, please take a seat. I trust Jayne is bringing you some tea or coffee?" His smile confirming what a capable performer he was under pressure.

"We've just had a coffee, so thanks very much, but we're OK." When it came to performance, Gerald Bassinott's skill matched Erskine's.

With Jayne Renton gone, Erskine started to speak, but Gerald raised an index finger to his lips. "Shhhhhhh. Let's keep this simple. We're running this. For the record, I'm sure we don't need to be threatening, unpleasant or feel the need to lay things on the line any more. You seem to be understanding your role in this. It's even conceivable that if you do everything we ask, there may be something in it for you. We know you like a bag or two of cash." Gerald nodded at Erskine with half a smile.

Erskine was thinking quickly. "The potential problem with your scam, very clever though it may be, is that it exposes me and City Law Partners to massive scrutiny when the money disappears - not that I have any idea how you are planning to swipe x-millions of euros. When the heist happens, you'll be relying on me to cover up for you – which is obviously why you want to pay me off. But the irony is you'll be investing all your trust in someone you clearly don't trust... me. Are you sure you've thought through the nitty-gritty properly gentlemen?" Looking more relaxed, a mild wind was beginning to fill his sails.

"Yes, we've got the whole thing locked down. The only thing that could spoil it now is if you blab or Foster-Fewster suspects you. But you've got every incentive to keep it to yourself because, as we said before, one phone call from us to the right police official would ruin your world forever. At least this way, you're going to come out a complete innocent in the eyes of the law and with a couple of very heavy bags of cash." Gerald sounded confident.

Erskine looked puzzled. "How are you proposing that I will be free from suspicion? If your plan works, you'll be needing me to somehow transfer the auction money to you or some other bank account."

"For now, believe me that all angles are covered. We'll be giving you instructions all the way. All you have to do is follow everything to the letter and you and City Law Partners will never be under serious suspicion. Just do what you do best - lie and keep a straight face."

Resigned, Erskine nodded slowly.

"So today, we need to you to confirm the

auction details. The date, time, location and a few other facts. We can find out for ourselves but it's better we work with you on the key details to make sure we're all singing from the same hymn sheet. So, let's start with the basics. What details about the auction have you got so far?" Gerald's tablet was at the ready to take down the information.

"The auction is on 15th September. 2pm. It's a Friday. Our partner agency in Bologna, Città Legale Italia, is coordinating things there. The auction house they are using is Gallo-Moretti in Florence. The new brochure with our sale items is due out any day. I'll have a copy within the week. It'll also be online when the new brochure is out." Erskine paused for a few moments then sounded more urgent, "Since you clearly have no intention of telling me how you are going to play your cards, can you at least tell me if you are planning to attend the auction?"

"I don't think that would be very sensible," Gerald quipped sarcastically, pulling an 'is he mad' face to his brother before continuing, "No. You'll be there obviously, and I guess Foster-Fewster, poor chap. Fancy expecting all that money, then… nothing."

"Well, exactly. Surely he is one of the biggest snags with your plan. He's not brain of Britain, but he isn't just going to sit there and accept that his inheritance has been stolen from under his nose. How do you propose all that will be managed?" Erskine sounded outraged.

"It won't be a problem. We have a plan for that, but again, it'll all become clear, as and when you need to know. Just keep us informed if he seems to be behaving strangely, or anything out of the ordinary. Do you have any concerns about him?"

"Well, I've given him two cash advances already. The last one was just a few days ago. I had no choice. He's been nervous right from the start, ironically without any reason. Now he has every reason to be worried, he's as happy as Larry. But he's an innocent, and that really is a low blow, even for hardened fraudsters. Don't you think it's time to reconsider all this again? Aren't there easier ways to con people? Foster-Fewster doesn't deserve to be treated like this, just as much as you don't deserve the money." Erskine looked angry.

"Just make sure you do everything to guarantee he doesn't suspect anything. Keep the advances going if he asks for more. If this all comes together as planned, we'll make sure the very least you'll get in cash covers those expenses." Gerald's clinical response showed no emotion towards Foster-Fewster.

"While we're on the subject of money, and seeing as you're blackmailing me, I feel I should ask what sort of pay-off I can expect?"

Erskine's question had clearly surprised Gerald. "Woah, open admission of involvement - that's progress, I suppose. We haven't decided figures yet, but it will be enough to prove your involvement in case you were ever to think about blabbing in the future. Sadly, for you it'll be nothing like the millions in commission you would have made. But that's part of the reason we're doing this. It's the perfect crime. You're a bent lawyer with cast iron proof against you. You can't run away. You've done bad things in the past and this is payback time, especially for poor old Duke Pyecoe and his mum. But do everything as we tell you and you'll get a dollop of cash along with the freedom to carry on your professional career. We may even add a bit for Foster-Fewster - you can tell him it's a compensation payment from one of your corporate insurance policies. And when it's all done and dusted, you'll be very pleased to hear that we'll quietly disappear into the ether."

"Well, that's a shred of good news I suppose." Erskine sounded disgruntled. "I'll be very happy never to see you again."

"Mutual. We have what we need for now. Let me know when the new Gallo-Moretti brochure goes live, and we'll put a date in the diary to plan the next steps." Gerald stood up to leave, followed by his brother.

Leaving his guests to see themselves out of his office, Erskine waited in silence until the door was closed behind them. Satisfied that the twins were out of earshot, he allowed himself just one word. "Fuckwits."

19

Waking up on my third day in Bologna, a familiar sense of optimism fills the air, the morning sun fringing the curtains with an aura of gold. Without further thought, the smell of fresh bread and the prospect of Italian coffee in the breakfast room downstairs urges me to throw back the bedsheets and jump into the shower.

Downstairs, an old Italian waitress shuffles non-stop across the breakfast room clearing plates and laying tables. I'd noticed her routine yesterday. Sliding up to a seated guest, she only needs to know one word to do her job. Nodding for my 'cafe' when she croaks at me, I head to the food self-service area where ham and cheese, bread rolls, yogurt and a banana look the most appealing, back at my table just in time for the returning waitress. The coffee is delightful, nutty dark and fresh tasting. Sipping it, I get out my guide book, looking for inspiration for things to do today. There are lots of options for day trips, but as I'm going back to Florence tomorrow for the auction, today I want to explore more of Bologna.

I decide on a relatively lazy day with a plod around the city, a classic Italian restaurant for lunch before maybe plodding some more, then an afternoon nap. Sensing it's already warm outside and going to get hotter, it's another shorts and t-shirt day. Leaving the bedroom and trotting down the stairs, I'm fantasising again about moving to Bologna. Dropping the clunky room key with the smiling receptionist, I head out into the new day thinking this really could be my new home soon. Walking towards Piazza Maggiore with a positive spring in my step, I decide a bit of estate agent window shopping would be a good way to spend the morning. Filled with a happy sense of freedom, thoughts return of how I used to dream of winning the lottery and then spend ages deciding how the money would be spent. It feels a bit the same today, assuming I end up with Erskine's estimated 2.5 million. With my thoughts of living in Bologna not fully formed yet, I'm still at the fun stage, day-dreaming.

Within a few minutes I spot the first 'agente immobiliare' and make my way to the large window front full of property details, each one displayed on an A4 sized card and slotted into a hanging rail. Most of the properties are small functional apartments in the suburbs and not what I'm interested in. But then as price increases, there are a number of reasonably central apartments. Then I notice an apartment a stone's throw from where I am now, situated at the top of Via Indipendenza. Overlooking Piazza Maggiore, it looks magnificent, two floors up and an integral part of the city's historic red architecture. As a genuine prospective buyer, I should feel comfortable about going inside but I'm in such a new world, I feel slightly awkward. But I quickly overcome it and push the door open, which seems to auto eject a young Italian man from behind his desk to right in front of me. "Buongiorno..." After a lot of pointing, hand waving, awkward laughing, nodding and eventual smiling he gives me a copy of the details displayed in the window, after which I try to beat a hasty retreat before he offloads an entire filing cabinet of other properties onto me. 'Grazie, grazie... ciao.' Apologetically, I tap my watch to inject a sense of urgency, waving the property details in my hand as I head back out into the street.

It seems a fun way to spend the next couple of hours and so I randomly criss-cross the city centre collecting suitable details from other agents, their reactions ranging from mumbling indifference to servile bowing and scraping, until one way or the other, I manage to gather details on around ten interesting properties.

With the time approaching midday I decide to switch my radar from bricks and mortar to meat and two veg. Down a little side street, I find what I'm looking for. A small trattoria with a few tables outside and a chalkboard offering simple pasta and pizzas, complete with a waiter of piratical appearance who stumps out with a menu and growls softly. "English?" Then adds, "Wine, beer, you want?"

Ordering a half carafe of locally produced red wine, it's delivered quickly by a younger waiter. After a lot of walking, I dive in without delay and pour myself a glass, savouring the velvety soft pleasure of smooth uncomplicated red wine. A few minutes pass before the pirate is back. "Please, you eat?"

Ordering a pizza which claims to be entirely constructed from local farm ingredients, I hope it's in the same league as yesterday's. Following my experience in Florence which included an almost implausibly quick service, I begin to wonder if the staff here have driven off to pick the ingredients themselves when twenty minutes go by without sight of it. But I'm enjoying just sitting here, letting the world go by while the wine gets to work. It's all part of what I love about Bologna.

The property details from this morning's search folded and squashed into my back pocket, I pull them out and flatten them on the table, beginning to stack them in price order just as the pirate clatters out of the restaurant carrying my pizza. Clumsily placing it in front of me, he stands back, looking at it admiringly for a few moments before grunting, "Masterpiece yes? Better than a Caravaggio painting."

And I have to agree. Right here, right now with a couple of glasses of wine elevating my senses, this is a masterpiece. It's huge with a rustic appearance, thanks to an uneven crust which has been perfectly blackened and blistered by the wood ovens. The centre is filled with a rich tomato sauce, sticky with various melted cheeses. Among the other identifiable ingredients are black and green olives, fried onions, thin discs of meat and a couple of fried quail eggs all arranged with mosaic artistry, a selection of randomly strewn chopped fresh herbs completing the effect, with little reservoirs of warm olive oil nestling among the topography.

Taking my knife, I dissect the pizza into eighths. This is going to be finger food from here on. Picking up the first section with two hands, the slice remains firmly connected to the mothership via a network of mozzarella guy ropes. After some inelegant moves to liberate them, I turn the thinnest point towards me and take a bite. It's messy and awkward but the payoff is incredible. My technique has improved by slice three. By slice four I'm adept at bending, rolling and ripping the pizza into manageable mouthfuls. By slice six I'm full. By the end of slice eight I'm not sure I ever want to see a pizza again. The property details covered in olive oil fingerprints where eating and reading have merged, my plate is surrounded by several paper napkins scrunched into balls. Drinking the last of my wine, I pay the pirate. He tells me if I eat one of those every day, I'll live to be a hundred. I shake my head, tap my tummy and tell him if squeezed one of those in every day, I'd be lucky to see my fiftieth.

He winks and taps his own sizeable girth. "Not years, inches!"

As I leave the restaurant, I decide on a quick walk around Piazza Maggiore before heading back to my hotel for a lazy nap. The sun is hot, the square vibrant with life and after only a few minutes, the walk seems suddenly less enticing and the temptation of a glass of chilled wine irresistibly tantalising. Taking a seat outside my favourite bar opposite the huge church in the piazza, I begin to enjoy the cold blush wine just as I spot the face of someone I know. Adrenaline pulses through me as for the second day running, I see a woman who looks like Valentina Russo. But this time, as she gets closer, I can see it is her.

I shrink into the shadows, instinctively not wanting her to see me, knowing how much I must reek of garlic and wine. She probably wouldn't spot me anyway, out of context wearing sunglasses in a piazza bar. My face may have slipped her busy mind, anyway. It was a couple of weeks ago when Erskine and I met her at her office to sign off the papers. Plenty of time to forget about me.

But I certainly haven't forgotten her. Dressed in the same style as before, today her green dress has been upgraded to pure white. In the warm afternoon sun and with her with her olive skin and lissom physique, Tina, as she likes to be called, looks fantastic.

As she nears, I'm suddenly compelled to play amateur sleuth and follow her - from a safe distance. I stand up, taking a final slug of wine with my back to her before sauntering in the wake of her distinctive scent.

I would make a hopeless spy, I realise, as Valentina walks ahead of me. It feels like the whole world is watching me and that she knows I'm a few steps behind. It's impossible not to feel self-conscious being randomly forced to window-shop every time there's a hint of being noticed. But I keep her in my sights as she crosses over the road and heads down Via Indipendenza, carrying on for a couple of hundred metres or so, before stopping at Grand Majestic Hotel.

I try to melt into the background as she stands outside and takes her phone from her bag, then swivels around while waiting for whoever to answer. On the other side of the road, I'm hopelessly exposed should her eyes fall on me, but fortunately they don't and after a few seconds she returns the phone to her bag, before walking up the steps into the hotel.

By following Valentina, I've managed to prove nothing, except to confirm that she completely captivates me. But I also realise, just like my paranoia when stalking Erskine from the café in the Strand, what either of them do privately is absolutely none of my business.

Back at my hotel, as I climb into bed for my long-awaited nap, thoughts return to yet another superb and simple lunch in shaded Italian sunshine, made even more pleasurable by daydreaming over potential property details, together with Valentina's surprise appearance. With all this in mind, my head sinks heavily into my pillow and my eyes close.

20

After a solid lunch and a few glasses of wine, I sleep heavily for an hour or so, on waking trying to work out if I dreamed about seeing Valentina Russo earlier. It prompts me to think of contacting Erskine for the first time since I left London, not just to share the news about seeing her here, but for a general catch up - he doesn't even know I'm in Bologna. Checking the time, - only four o'clock in the UK, I call his office number, on the off chance the object of my other fantasy, Jayne Renton, will answer. She does.

'Could I speak to Mr Erskine?'

"I'm afraid he's on annual leave this week, returning next Monday. Is there anything I can help you with in his absence?"

'Thank you, but it's nothing that can't wait till he's back.'

Making a mental note to call him next week, I lie back in bed, thinking about my afternoon and the chance sighting of Valentina Russo. Was it Erskine that she was meeting this afternoon in the Grand Majestic Hotel? After all, he isn't in the office this week. As usual, I can't think of a reason for my suspicions, but the thought of them meeting unsettles me.

As Erskine isn't going to know I've called his office, I try his mobile. More than anything, I want him to tell me where he is.

He answers after a few rings. "Hello, Peter... Lovely surprise, how are you?"

"I'm great, thanks. I thought I'd just check everything is ticking along as planned?"

"All good, Peter. Nothing to report as we speak. I'm actually away on holiday this week, so I'll give you a buzz on Monday if that's OK, just as soon as I've been through my inbox."

"Sorry, I had no idea you were away, apologies. Anywhere nice?"

"A few days with the family at my brother's place in France. It's a big old renovated farmhouse near Toulouse, lots of countryside, lots of family and very relaxing. Apologies, but I'm helping with dinner - a bit of a military exercise going on here carrying everything out onto the terrace. Unless its life and death, I'm going to have to be very rude and let you go. Call you next week?"

"No problem – enjoy!"

I guess that rules out Erskine being in Bologna, and why did I even suspect that, anyway? Valentina has to be somewhere, so why not at the Grand Majestic Hotel? She could have been meeting anyone, personal or professional. My busy mind needs to slow down and at the moment the best cure for that is wine.

After a quick shower, I'm out of the hotel and into the amber glow of a warm sun setting over medieval streets, heading straight up to the piazza for a chilled glass of rose wine and a plate of complementary olives at my now favourite watering hole, the imaginatively named, Bologna Bar. After a couple of hours people watching, snacking, reading Private Eye and savouring several glasses of wine, most of the women walking around Piazza Maggiore in the darkening light are beginning to look like Valentina Russo. Wine goggles and wishful thinking on my part, but I'd love to get to know her more. Maybe I could call her office in Bologna before I go back to London, but what would I say? It would just be obvious I fancied the pants off her. Or maybe she would like to meet up for a drink and a bite to eat. You never know if you never ask. Fuelled with wine, these are easy thoughts - that the cold light of day will temper, I remind myself, plodding along Via Indipendenza for a reasonably early night. I want a clear head tomorrow to see Gallo-Moretti in full swing.

21

In the afternoon heat, Valentina Russo stood in front of Bologna's Grand Majestic Hotel, her olive skin sparkling with the finest layer of perspiration after walking across Piazza Maggiore. Reaching into her bag and taking out a chilled water spray, she spritzed her face and arms being careful to avoid her pure white dress. Returning the spray to her bag and taking her phone, she called her office to check for messages. Then she slowly made her way up the steps, letting a hotel porter open the large doors leading to the reception area.

Valentina knew exactly where she was going. Café Marinetti, a stylish lounge and meeting place within the hotel serving every drink imaginable including its own brand of coffee. Her meet was already sitting in the lounge with a large glass of iced water.

Walking over, Valentina extended her slender hand. "Erskine, very good to see you again."

Taking her hand, Erskine stood up for a continental double kiss. "And you too Tina. Thank you for seeing me today at such short notice. What will you have to drink?"

"Does it need to be strong? I'm not sure what you are going to tell me." Valentina spoke with friendly suspicion. "I'll have a coffee for now, and keep you posted if I need anything stronger," she added, keeping her eyes on Erskine's and sinking into the armchair opposite his.

After ordering Valentina's coffee from a waiter caressing his gleaming trolley between tables, with a silent Italian flourish, it was placed on the ornate low table separating the two of them.

Erskine sipped his water, then took a deep breath, before beginning to explain the reason for the meeting. "OK, I need to tell you something that has happened since we last met in Bologna, with Peter Foster-Fewster. There's no way to sugar the pill, I'm afraid. So, I'll get straight to the point. Basically, I've been approached by some well-known criminals who are now blackmailing me. In short, they want all of the money from the auction when it goes through in September."

"Wait. What are you talking about? How can this happen? Blackmail? I am really confused. And why come to me? Why not the police - how can these people blackmail you? Who are they? I don't understand any of this." Clearly dumbfounded and angry in equal measure, Valentina still managed to keep her composure and volume appropriate to the grand surroundings.

"Well, the truth is these people can blackmail me because of some stupid misunderstandings from a few years ago. I'd rather not go into full details now, but the bottom line is I am going to lose all our commission, as are you." Erskine looked surprisingly in control considering the information he was offloading.

"I am not going to say anything just now," Valentina spoke slowly. "I'm going to let you talk. Tell me everything. And I mean everything, including how they can blackmail you. At the end, I'll decide whether I explode, kill you or something worse."

"Fair enough." Erskine took a lengthy slug of icy cold water. "About twenty years ago I did a regrettable thing. I was a very ambitious young lawyer and it was my first high profile prosecution. The case was on a knife edge. It was obvious the jury were siding with the defence. I needed to pull something out of the hat. I'd recently read a novel about a lawyer paying someone to be a false witness. It triggered something. Anyway, somewhere in the cut and thrust of the courtroom, I stepped over a line." He was silent for a moment. "Just like in the book, I found someone who was prepared to swear under oath and provide false testimony." He glanced at Valentina Russo but she was holding her tongue. He carried on. "Probably sounds easy getting a false witness, but in reality, it's almost impossible to find someone capable of performing the role effectively. The book made that very clear and I wasn't sure it would ever come to anything. Think about it. A false witness has got to be credible, obviously, and can't have any kind of criminal record. Or even be known to the police. They've got to understand and answer legal arguments from professional interrogators - the pressure in a courtroom is like nothing else. They have to perform like a trained actor, flawlessly, on different days, in front of forensic minds dedicated to finding inconsistencies. And they can't really have a moral conscience. Which is why false witnesses in complicated trials virtually never come to the surface. Except in my case. I was genuinely compromised when I met someone who clearly ticked all the boxes. Suddenly a remote possibility became a sure-fire bet." Erskine shrugged. "But finding someone with those abilities comes at a cost. I paid around £25,000 to a man called Duke Pyecoe, who took the oath in court and put across a version of events which was not entirely accurate. And it worked. I won the case and paid him off. Well, actually I still owe him a bit, but that aside, it advanced my career exactly as I'd hoped."

Leaning forward in her armchair, Valentina's elbows were on her thighs, her chin cupped in the palm of her hand, her head just perceptibly shaking from side to side, indicating total disbelief.

But she still didn't speak.

Erskine took another long sip of water and carried on. "Eventually, years later, Pyecoe was arrested for burglary in a completely separate case. When he was in prison, he met Gerald Bassinott, a clever, or not so clever as it turned out, fraudster. He has a twin brother, Thomas. The press dubbed them the Fraud Twins when they were sent down for a couple of years. It got a lot of publicity. On the face of it they were posh, well-spoken gentlemen." Finishing the last of his water, Erskine beckoned to the waiter to replenish his glass, before carrying on. "When Gerald met Pyecoe in prison, they got talking. It seems I'd angered Pyecoe, because the cash I gave him was short of the agreed amount. An oversight on my part. I'd always intended to correct that error."

Valentina nodded sarcastically, the look on her face suggesting she didn't believe a word he was saying.

Erskine paused, as if considering whether to continue with his confessional. "So, as Gerald's prison release date was before Pyecoe's, he said he'd find me and, in his words, give me the opportunity to put things right. But at the same time as the brothers finding me, the story of Foster-Fewster's inheritance broke in the London News. Unbelievably bad luck, because the Bassinott twins saw it as their opportunity to extort me. They had proof that I'd paid Pyecoe to be a false witness, and with that evidence, they demanded much more than the cash I owed him. They wanted one hundred percent of the sale price from the auctioned jewels." As Erskine cautiously glanced at Valentina, she was still silent.

After drinking more water, he picked up again. "My instructions are to carry on as normal and they will tell me what to do as the auction date nears. They've apparently got a plan for everything, including how the money will be transferred so as no suspicion will be placed on me, and how they're going to deal with Foster-Fewster. There's no stone unturned. They're thoroughbred fraudsters. And of course, if I don't go along with it, they will expose me as a bent lawyer, ruin my career, livelihood, personal life, family. I'll be finished." Erskine held his hands up.

"I sincerely hope you haven't come here for sympathy." Valentina's words were sparse and cold.

"No, I haven't. But depending on the final sale price of the jewels, if they pull this off, your agency could be looking at losing half a million euros."

"So, you really are a criminal lawyer. And your past has caught up with you. My first thought is I don't know how to process any of this. But the fact you're here suggests you want me to do something, no?" Valentina pulled her hair back, twisting it into a knot behind her head.

"Well, what are my options? Yes, its high risk coming here. You could go straight to the police. Obviously, I've thought through everything. But the upside from your point of view is, at least you know. If I hadn't spoken to you, the first you'd have known would have been shortly after the auction when your commission money wasn't paid." Erskine spoke more confidentially. "For now, I am certain they can be outwitted, and it wouldn't require you to do anything illegal. But I can't do it without being able to confide in you. Until I know how they're planning to execute the heist, I can't do any more. All I ask is that you will consider working with me on this. We both have a lot to lose. Or gain, if we outsmart the fraudsters. No one needs to know about this conversation and you've done nothing wrong. You are not, or ever will be, culpable of anything."

"Except you've told me a lot of information that automatically draws me into a blackmail scenario. Blackmail is not a word I like." Valentina was retying her hair, making sure any loose strands were firmly included in the tightened knot.

"There could be an incentive," Erskine looked slightly awkward. "I mean, we share a bit of history, you and me." As Valentina angled her head with disbelief, Erskine continued. "I really didn't want to go there, but we both know what happened five years ago."

"You bastard." Valentina seethed the words through gritted teeth. "You absolute bastard. You'd actually use that mistake, disaster, whatever you want to call it, you'd use it to blackmail me?"

"It takes two to tango, Tina. It happened, and to be fair to me, I didn't know you were engaged at the time. Certainly didn't know you were engaged to some third rate mobster who'd have killed us both if he'd found out you were pregnant. And I paid for everything to be sorted out, the termination and "the holiday" you had to go on with your girlfriends. All things I still have receipts for." Erskine was doing his best to make everything sound reasonable, running a hand over his hair and jutting his jaw a little, suggesting he still had what it took to turn heads.

"I don't believe this. You are not the man I ever thought I knew. One stupid drunk night at our company party in Bologna and it results in this, five years later. Being blackmailed to save your criminal arse." Valentina's face reddened with pure anger.

Erskine bit back. "You think I want to be having this conversation? I'm being pushed against a cliff edge with a knife against my throat. This is my only option. You think I want to let your secret out of the bag? I'm sure it would end your marriage and possibly much more. Think of it as more of an insurance policy from my point of view. I have no doubt I can outwit these idiots, and as I said, you won't have to do anything illegal. I just need a reliable confidante. Maybe this conversation guarantees your reliability, that's all." Erskine was back to making it all sound as rosy as possible.

"Dress it up how you want. But it's still blackmail." Sounding robotic, Valentina was looking at the floor as she spoke. "What did you say their names were, these twins?"

"Bassinott. Gerald and Thomas Bassinott. Why?"

"How do they spell their names? You said they had a famous trial. I want to research them. That's all." She watched as Erskine jotted the names down on a napkin.

"So, can I count on you to keep all this to yourself? For now, that's all that's needed."

Valentina lifted her eyes to meet his. "Do I have a choice?"

Erskine shrugged. "About as much as I do."

22

After Erskine's bombshell, needing to compose herself, Valentina headed to the lady's room. After paying the bar bill, as Erskine waited for her to return, he checked the time knowing he had a flight to catch later that evening. It was nearly four o'clock, giving him enough time for a bite to eat in Bologna before getting a taxi to the airport.

As she walked back, the redness in Valentina's face had now reduced to just flushed cheeks, while Erskine looked his usual unflustered self as they made their way in silence through the lobby and out into the fresh air. Walking down the hotel steps, they'd turned towards Piazza Maggiore, before Valentina spoke.

"What happens now?"

But before Erskine could speak, his phone rang and Peter Foster-Fewster's name flashed up.

He showed Valentina before answering. "Hello Peter... lovely surprise, how are you?"

As Erskine lied fluently about being on holiday at his brother's house in France, when the call finished, Valentina shook her head. "And you're asking me to trust you? I've never known someone who can lie so comfortably. Also, the fact that you're prepared to tell my family about getting me pregnant, it's unbelievable. You know abortion is a massive no-no in Italy, even today. It's pure blackmail. Nothing else. Just so you know, I have no respect for you at all. Zero."

"We've both broken the rules," Erskine insisted. "And it's brought us to where we are today. I paid a false witness, you slept with me and got pregnant, while you were engaged. Both regrettable incidents. Both with regrettable consequences. Both rebounding on us now. It might sound twisted, but the way I see it, we're in this together."

But Erskine's summary of events clearly hadn't impressed Valentina as they walked towards Piazza Maggiore. "Twisted? I agree, it sounds twisted. Twisted logic. Twisted, twisted, twisted. I feel like spitting on you." She paused for a few moments, thinking about the situation. "But right now, you need me. Arguably more than I need you. I need to regain some control and get my thoughts in order. I'm going to make a decision in the next two days. Meet me on Saturday night, here in Bologna. Book dinner at Camilleri's Restaurant. I'll be there at seven. So will you."

As they reached the piazza's fountain, Fontana Di Nettuno, Erskine shook his head. "I'm flying back to Toulouse tonight; the family holiday is actually going on - that much at least was true in my call with Peter. Can't I just call you?"

"No. Some of this needs to be on my terms. I will make a thoughtful decision and look you in the eye when I tell you what it is when we meet. You can easily fly back here from Toulouse – unless this isn't important enough to you."

"Saturday is when the family is flying back to London. I can't just abandon them without a plausible reason. Today they think I've got a business meeting, but telling them I've got an appointment on Saturday evening... well, it just won't wash."

Valentina wasn't interested. "If you're the great fixer, fix it. That's the deal if you want my help. Until I've made a decision, I need you to demonstrate some respect." As Erskine looked more and more discomfited, Valentina appeared to be almost enjoying herself. "Of course, if I decide not to go along with your plan, then I may not be alone at Camilleri's Restaurant. My husband loves great food."

"Hmmm. Let's think about that." Erskine bit back cockily. "In that scenario, you would have told your husband about the affair and your pregnancy, and of course he would have forgiven you to the point he'd be happy to go to dinner with the man who got his wife pregnant. I suppose you're inferring that he would take me outside and put his fist through my head?"

"It's all quite possible," Valentina replied defiantly.

"Well, I'll be sure to bring along the invoice for the termination and the other expenses that were needed to complete the full cover up. That'll make him feel really good, if I show just what lengths you went to, to deceive the man you were about to marry. That should pretty much guarantee he puts a fist through both our heads." He paused. "No, I'm quite happy that you're not going to say a word about it. It's a calculated risk on my part, I realise that, but it doesn't change my hunch. You have too much to lose."

"Maybe. Maybe not. I need to make my own decision and you will know what that is on Saturday." Valentina was holding her own.

"Out of interest, what will happen if I don't turn up?" Erskine sounded intrigued.

"I'll have a lovely meal all on my own and you'll be going out of your mind wondering what the hell I'm going to do."

"I still don't see why I need to be there. Surely when you've made a decision you just need to tell me what it is." Erskine was still trying to reason with Valentina.

"You have a lot to learn about Italian culture. It's about respect. If you respect me enough to be there, then that might be what I need to finalise my decision. Respect is important."

"You didn't seem to respect your fiancé that

night five years ago." Erskine spoke sarcastically.

"Different. Alcohol-induced sex is not about respect. God knows how much grappa you were pouring that night. Not only is it a night I do not wish to remember, it is a night I can't remember. Thank God."

Erskine stood up from the bench, "OK. I will let you know what I can do. I'll call you tomorrow."

"No." Valentina was uncompromising. "Don't call me. In fact, don't make any contact with me or my office, at all. I will be at the restaurant at seven on Saturday night. You'll either be there or you won't. Your choice. One hundred percent your choice. But remember, respect runs thick through Italian blood."

Without another word, as Valentina disappeared into the late afternoon bustle of the piazza, Erskine sat down on the bench and clasped his hands over his face. At that precise moment, Peter Foster-Fewster walked past the Fontana Di Nettuno, completely unaware of Erskine sitting only ten metres to his left, before disappearing around the corner to sit outside the Bologna Bar and order a cold rose.

Getting up, Erskine wandered off in the other direction towards Via Indipendenza to get a taxi to the airport, blissfully unaware that if Foster-Fewster had left the hotel a few minutes earlier, he could easily have witnessed Erskine and

Valentina demonstrating beyond any reasonable doubt that trouble lay ahead.

23

It's the day of the dry run auction in Florence and I wake up with a sense of purpose. With the auction starting at two o'clock, I have plenty of time for a leisurely breakfast and morning walk, before I head for the train station for around midday.

Breakfast is the usual fayre and I enjoy two cups of coffee from the monotone waitress. Then after, I'm straight out into the streets and gauging the weather, which looks set to be another cloudless day. During the hour's walk along interesting side streets, I discover five new churches, the calm they contain the perfect foil to the mad world I've been thrust into and I make a note to self to visit them again when I have more time.

Back at the hotel, despite today's warm weather and the likelihood it's going to get hotter, I decide on jeans, not sure shorts are quite the ticket inside the auction house, and I don't want to stick out like a sore thumb.

Setting off for the station, I go for the twelve-thirty train, which gets into Florence for one o'clock, giving me time for a light lunch near Gallo-Moretti before the auction starts. Like last time, the queues at the station are slow, but it's a queue-jumper free zone today and before long, I'm being silently whizzed into Florence.

As the Duomo comes into view again, it occurs to me how quickly we adapt to the new. When I came here a couple of days ago, Florence from a distance was a big deal, its history and famous buildings unknown to me, creating a sense of expectation. But seeing the same view today, already I feel like an old hand. I know the exact route to walk into the centre, how long it will take and what to expect at every turn.

Leaving the station and heading down the small hill towards the city, it takes less than twenty minutes to be reunited with the magnificence of the Duomo, where I allow myself a few minutes to walk around the outside and study the complicated architecture. From there past the Uffizi gallery, over the Ponte Vecchio and into Via Crostini, stopping briefly only to look at my fantasy sofa through the shop window. But the minor en-route sightseeing leaves me no time for lunch and I quicken my pace to the other end where Gallo Moretti is situated.

Inside the auction house, there's already a buzz, with around two dozen people chatting in small groups and a couple of smartly dressed staff pointing visitors in various directions. A small queue at the registration desk prompts me to double check my wallet and membership card. Pleased that mine was done in advance, I notice the same young man, now in full spectacle-prodding mode, helping others with their registrations.

As I look around, the whole atmosphere is tingling with expectancy yet still hushed with dignified calm. A minimalist bespoke clock built into the wall next to the wide staircase shows thirty minutes to go before the auction starts. Below the clock, a waist height pole of gleaming brass holds an arrowed sign, with the words, *Vendita All Asta* pointing towards the stairs. Guessing it must mean 'auction', it's a relief when I catch the eye of the bespectacled young man on the other side of the room, who sensing my uncertainty, gives me a thumbs up and nods towards the stairs - amazingly without touching his glasses.

The wide staircase sweeps around to the left, continuing up until what feels like a full circle has been completed. At the top and brightly lit with sunlight, a gathering area is busy, while on the far side are what looks like the entrance to the auction room, tall double doors guarded by two uniformed security personnel, hands behind their backs, humourless.

In front of them at two wide desks, a seated member of staff at each are swiping attendees' registration cards and handing out compulsory lanyards. Legitimatised with an official necklace, visitors head for the double doors between the all-seeing guards.

As I head for the registration desks, I'm expecting all kinds of Italian queue shenanigans, but my membership card is swiped effortlessly and in no time the lady dangles my lanyard towards me, before I push at one of the heavy doors.

Squeezing into the auction room, my first thought is surprise at how big it is. A mix of grandeur, functionality and no natural light create a sense of being in a very posh cinema, with gently tiered seats encircling a stage at the front, which has a large screen displaying the words 'Gallo-Moretti. Buon Giorno'.

There are other words on the screen, but apart from recognising the date and time, my Italian is so bad it could be Sanskrit. The back row of seats looking nicely anonymous, I make my way to a vacant area and ease myself down, amusing myself with a few minutes of people watching as the room fills, before an electric bell rings and a softly spoken message announces the start of the auction.

As two spotlights cast large white circles over the auctioneer's lectern and display area next to it, I'm enjoying the performance so far. After tapping the microphone, there are no lengthy formalities from the diminutive auctioneer, just a few Italian sentences machine-gunned quietly at the hushed audience. Thinking ahead to my auction in a few weeks, I'm grateful that Erskine will be at my side, should the incomprehensible need explanation.

I settle in for the first lot, a gold necklace, chunky and clunky to my eye. The auctioneer's pretty female accomplice lays it over a red cushion on the display table and automatically it's broadcast to the large screen above. Then as the bidding gets underway, starting at €5,000, I feel a flutter of excitement as I think how exceptional my inherited jewels must be if they are worth millions. The bidding steps up in hundreds before in less than a minute, the auctioneer respectfully taps the gavel down. Final price €6,200. After several more items are auctioned, I'm pleased to note that all of them sold for more than their guide price, some considerably more. Pleased I won't feel like a novice when it comes to my auction, after an hour or so passes, realising there's not much more I can learn from this, I slip away. Besides, at the back of my mind are thoughts of that wonderful pizza I had when I was last here.

As I head down the stairs towards the reception area, my world suddenly freezes as though I've hit a wall and been thrown into a parallel universe. Unable to take in the information in front of me, I stand and watch as Valentina Russo slowly walks up the stairs, texting, her eyes dedicated to her phone.

Automatically I blurt out, "Tina! What an incredible coincidence! How are you!?"

Clearly familiar with my face but obviously unable to place it, she looks happily puzzled.

I prompt her. "Sorry. Peter Foster-Fewster. I visited you recently in Bologna with Mr Erskine."

"Peter, of course. Sorry, I should have remembered. How are you?" Tina leans forward for the double kiss, but instead of exhibiting her normal confidence she seems flat.

I decide to sound upbeat. "I'm very well. I'm spending some time travelling before my auction in September. Reckoned this part of Italy was a good place to start. As I was in Florence, I thought I'd check out Gallo-Moretti - just so I know what to expect when my big day comes. What about you? Are you here for the sale today?"

Tina seems neither elevated by my buoyancy or particularly shocked to see me. "No, Gallo-Moretti are one of my clients." Her voice is lacklustre. "Apart from using them for auctions, we also act as their lawyers, so I'm usually here at least one day a week. I use an office upstairs."

"Lovely place, Gallo-Moretti." Her mood seems glum, so I have another go at sounding chirpy. "Must be a nice place to work. I'm really looking forward to my auction now I've seen how it all works. Will you be here for it?"

"I'm really not sure. It depends on what's

going on at the time." Tina is weirdly non-committal about anything as we stand awkwardly on the stairs, her body language, as they say, closed.

"Well, look, you're obviously very busy and bumping into me is enough to frighten anyone. I really ought to let you get on." I think about adding 'fancy a drink in Bologna sometime?' Somehow knowing it clearly wouldn't be a sensible thing to do.

"Yes. You must forgive me. Unfortunately, I have someone waiting for me in my office." Turning to continue up the steps, she stops momentarily to add, "Enjoy your time in Italy. You're staying in Florence, I guess?"

I'm surprised by this little jot of interest in my plans. "No, Bologna actually. For the next few days at least." It's impossible to read her reaction. Surprise, for sure; shock possibly.

A second or two later, she steps back down and double kisses me. "Rude of me not to say goodbye properly. Enjoy Bologna." And with that, she continues up the stairs and out of sight.

24

Inside Camilleri's restaurant on Saturday night, Valentina Russo was shown to her table. She had no idea if Erskine was going to show up, but she'd reasoned it was more likely than not. With around ten minutes to go before knowing if she would be dining alone, Valentina took a moment to admire the décor of the restaurant. Dark wood walls, a long wooden service counter in front of decorated mirrors, shelves loaded with bottles of aging liqueurs and spirits. With the dark oil paintings and the ceiling home to dangling kitchen frippery from a bygone era, the whole scene exuded traditional Italian culture, history and a sense of permanence. It was the perfect setting in which to meet Erskine. Ordering a glass of Rosso di Montalcino, she waited.

By the time fifteen minutes had passed, Erskine was officially late. But Valentina was expecting it. She knew there would be mind games tonight and by being late, Erskine would be showing he was not entirely beholden to her exact demands. She'd give him another twenty minutes, and if he didn't show, she'd find another strategy.

Sure enough, just before 7:30pm, Erskine appeared outside the restaurant, on his phone. From the street he looked through the window, raising a hand to Valentina in acknowledgement, then repeatedly clapped a thumb against his fingers to indicate he was stuck with someone who was jabbering endlessly, a further mime suggesting he would be another five minutes before turning his back, still animated on the phone.

Instinct told Valentina he was playing a game, no question. Calling his phone, she watched him as it connected immediately, clearly ringing loud enough in his ear to make him pull it away, before checking the caller name. Twisting around on the spot, he saw Valentina speaking into her mobile.

"Really Erskine. Inventing lovers on the phone? Isn't that what little children do?"

"Tina? How confusing. I'd just ended a call a second before yours came through. I'm coming in now."

"Whatever." Ending the call, Valentina knew she was right.

Looking relaxed as he entered the restaurant, Erskine was dressed suitably for a warm evening in a cream jacket over a short-sleeved blue cotton shirt. Shown to the table by a waiter, he shook Valentina's hand, double kissing somehow inappropriate, before he checked her preference and ordered a bottle of Rosso di Montalcino.

"Well, as you can see, I've made it. Not the easiest thing to arrange at short notice. But I've made the effort because, well, I understand it's important to you." As Valentina looked unimpressed, her silence forced Erskine to continue. "So, depending on what your decision is, I may have wasted a lot of time and this could be a very short dinner. But I'm here. To hear it from the horse's mouth. So to speak." He raised a glass to himself.

Clearly still unimpressed, Valentina spoke slowly. "From the horse's mouth? Interesting choice of words. Is that another one of those English sayings that could be... disrespectful? Depending on the way it's said?"

"No, no. Absolutely not. No innuendo intended. Apologies. It's a very common saying. Just means getting the information directly from source..." In full knowledge he'd used the phrase sarcastically, Erskine pretended to be bright and breezy.

"That's good, because if you are comparing me to a wild animal... I promise you I will turn into one. Right here, right now. Respect, Erskine. All I ask is respect." Valentina's mood palpable, she raised her own glass and took a large sip.

Before either could say anything, the waiter appeared. Handing over artfully designed menus, the couple reviewed their options while the waiter hovered, checking the condition of his fingernails. Just a main course each, both of them wanting this over with. Knowing she could have accelerated the process and given Erskine her decision, for Valentina, this dinner was about forcing Erskine to play by her rules.

With the waiter gone, Valentina took control. "Let's talk business over dinner. We don't want indigestion, so maybe a few minutes of calm first. I'm intrigued, what story did you come up with for your family? I assume it wasn't along the lines of you needing to visit Bologna to blackmail your former mistress?" Smiling ironically, she raised her glass again.

Erskine's face creased with incredulity. "That's your idea of calm?"

"I'm just interested. What did you come up with? You're a man under pressure. A man usually calm under pressure. Were you calm?" She was the model of calm as she spoke.

"In fact, I was. An emergency weekend meeting covered it. And say what you like, you'll have a problem trying to accuse me of lying on that one." Returning the ironic smile, Erskine raised his glass again.

"I see. A man of honour? Maybe you're turning over a new leaf." Valentina's irony turned to sarcasm, but before Erskine could respond, the waiter arrived with their dishes. A few moments of silence passed as they allowed black pepper to be crunched over their food from a grinder the size of a table leg. As the silence continued, Valentina began coiling spaghetti onto her fork, then with one elbow resting on the table, she upturned the fork with a nest of pasta tightly interwoven between its prongs.

Holding the fork in the centre of the table, she met Erskine's stare, speaking softly. "What a tangled web we weave when first we practise to deceive..."

"That's quite a good trick. If I tried that all the pasta would fall off." Erskine's attempt to divert failed.

Valentina held the fork motionless. "Have you ever thought how tangled your life is becoming? Just like the strands on my fork. Safe for the moment, but at risk of coming undone at any time. If you're not careful, your life will be like an entire plate of spaghetti bolognaise, Erskine. Spaghetti bolognaise - that's what you English call it, don't you?" Valentina turned the fork towards her open mouth, posted the pasta through her pale rose lips and slid it off between perfect white teeth.

Erskine's irritation was obvious. "To avoid us both being chopped up and served for dinner, I seriously hope you've decided to work with me on this. Can you tell me your decision, or are you going to string this out like one of those bits of pasta?" Grunting the last few words, Erskine started sawing aggressively at his costata di manzo, a steak so rare that blood haemorrhaged across his plate with every cut. Staring at mushrooms now floating in a scarlet pool, he added pointedly, "Maybe now is a good time to end the metaphors?"

"Maybe." Valentina sucked a single strand of spaghetti into her mouth. "I want to talk about Peter Foster-Fewster. He's the real victim in this mess. Do you know where he is right now?"

"Not a clue." Erskine replied, shrugging. "I think he's taking some time out to travel before the auction - which I'm bankrolling by the way."

"Interesting." Valentina was being mysterious. "I want to know what your plan is for Foster-Fewster. If the Bassinott brothers pull this off, he gets nothing. If you outwit them and keep the money, what will he get?"

"A lot more than he would have done under the Bassinott brothers' plan. Frankly I'm not that bothered. You and I would get our expected commissions, but there is an opportunity to rejig the contract in terms of Foster-Fewster. He's not that savvy."

"Unbelievable. Your criminal instincts are growing by the day. He should get exactly what's due to him as per the contract. Surely you can see that?" Valentina sounded incredulous.

"I'll have to look at all that, but what I do know is he'll be in a better position with my plan, even though I can't be certain how things will unfold until the Bassinott twits reveal their hand. Anyway, why the sudden interest in Foster-Fewster?"

"Would you be surprised if I told you I know where he is?" Valentina was back to her mysterious best.

"Yes, I would be surprised. Do you??" Erskine was clearly uncomfortable.

Valentina repeated her earlier performance with the spaghetti, twisting it onto her fork and holding it between them. "Well, as it happens, I do know where is. I spoke to him. In fact, we met. Yesterday." Valentina smiled. "Tangled web, Erskine, tangled web."

"You contacted Foster-Fewster, what on earth for?" Erskine only just managed to keep his fury under control.

"Did I say I contacted him? Anyway, right now that's for me to know. But he helped me make my decision. My decision of either helping you or facing the consequences of playing it straight. The latter option meaning you would rat on me, which I have no doubt you would do."

Erskine bristled with irritation. "God, this is a disaster. What did you say to him? You better tell me what's going on and what he knows. And don't give me any more of that crap about spaghetti bolognaise, webs, forks, tangles, any of that shit. I'm pissed off. I need to know what's going on."

"I'll tell you very soon. But how about guessing where he is?"

"Tim-buk-fucking-tu for all I care right now. I'm not in the mood for games." Erskine was properly rattled.

After a few moments of silence during which he refuelled his glass and chewed his way through a sizable slab of steak, Valentina spoke. "OK, he's here. In Bologna."

Erskine looked shocked. "What?"

"He knows nothing. We met in Florence yesterday. By chance, at Gallo-Moretti. He was checking out an auction sale and I was working there for the day. We bumped into each other on the stairs." Erskine listened as if he was in a fairy tale, as Valentina carried on. "I felt awful and had to get away because of what I knew about you being blackmailed, and you blackmailing me. I felt sick he didn't know any of it. There I was talking to him knowing the Bassinotts are planning to rob him. It made me feel ill that he is an innocent pawn. Afterwards, something clicked. I realised I needed to see your threat to blackmail me in a different light. Although I can't stomach the thought of giving in to your blackmail, I'm seeing this as helping Peter Foster-Fewster. He needs me involved if he's going to get his inheritance, even if he doesn't ever have a clue about what happened. I am not prepared to give you the opportunity to screw him over, which is what I think you would do if you outwit the Bassinotts. You admitted as much a few minutes ago."

"You've lost me. Are you saying you'll help me?" Erskine looked puzzled.

"I'm saying the conditions of my involvement are that Peter Foster-Fewster gets his rightful inheritance if you, or we, outwit the Bassinotts. I'm doing this for him, not you, Erskine. To my mind, it means I'm not being blackmailed by you. That's critical for me. I need your agreement to this condition before we shake on it. And believe me, I will bring you down if you renege on it."

"Well, of course I agree to that. That's really no big deal in all this. Foster-Fewster will get everything he's due if we pull this off, I can confirm that. Can we shake on it?"

"We can. It will look good on my little video of this evening." Valentina tapped the top of her clutch bag next to her on the table. "As *you* might say, look on it as my insurance policy."

As Erskine stifled his shock at being filmed, he held his hands up. It was a fair cop. "Fair enough." He gracefully shook her hand.

"You know, you need to be very grateful to Foster-Fewster." Valentina spoke confidently. "If I hadn't bumped into him on the stairs yesterday, I certainly wouldn't be shaking your hand. And you better be careful you don't bump into him here. He's almost certainly walking around these central streets tonight. I live here, I can explain my reasons easily enough. But you? Even you might struggle to come up with something plausible, if you were to come face-to-face with him."

"After you saw him yesterday, why on earth didn't you just call me with your decision? Why run the risk of me, or you, bumping into Foster-Fewster? I don't get it." Erskine sounded exasperated.

"It's a calculated risk. But one I like. I wanted you to hear it 'from the horse's mouth', so to speak. To leave you in no doubt that you are not blackmailing me. So that you know I'm doing this for Foster-Fewster. And bringing you here means you know I'm serious, despite the risks. It gives me a sense of control, which feels good - like adding a bit of piccante to the spaghetti bolognaise." Valentina smiled insincerely.

"OK, well I'd love to say it's been a lot of fun, but that would stretch even my skills. I'll organise a cab from here to take me straight to the airport hotel. If you want to slip away first, I'll pick up the bill. In terms of next moves, I'll keep you up to speed with my instructions from the fraud twits." Erskine sounded matter of fact.

"You better be careful there, too. Serious fraudsters have a sixth sense when it comes to detecting lies and liars. It's one of their best survival instincts. I've been reading about them. You had better hope they don't smell a rat." With that, Valentina gathered her belongings, insincerely thanked Erskine for dinner and headed out into the busy street.

25

It's Monday morning and after a weekend exploring Bologna, I'm enjoying a lie-in. Lots of walking around museums, galleries and churches has left my leg muscles in knots, while a combination of tourist information overload and grappa means my head is hurting. Giving myself another lazy hour in bed, followed by coffee, I decide maybe after that, I'll call Erskine.

After an hour and a shower, I'm enjoying coffee in the breakfast room, but no shuffling waitress this morning. The coffee is delivered by the smart gentleman normally on reception, who darts a nod at me when I thank him, then disappears.

Daydreaming and people watching over breakfast, thoughts of Valentina Russo come to mind as they have done many times over the weekend. But it was her manner and body language in Florence that's puzzled me the most. She seemed so different when Erskine and I first met her in her office. But after thinking it through, I convince myself that she was just wrong-footed by meeting me out of context. It's a feeling I know well. That day I saw her walking across Piazza Maggiore, I didn't want her to see me. OK, my reason on that day was because I was embarrassed at the thought of huffing a heady cocktail of red wine and garlic over such a subtly fragranced sophisticate. Had she caught me unawares, I'm sure I would have seemed extremely uncomfortable and probably tried to get away as quickly as possible. People don't always like being unexpectedly pounced upon.

It's time to get out into the sunshine. After leaving the hotel, I decide to give Erskine a call from Piazza Maggiore, a five minute walk away. It's about 11am in London, which seems like a good time.

After a few rings, he answers. "Hello, Peter. You are on my list of people to call today. How are you?"

"Fine thanks - enjoying some time away from London. How was your holiday in France?"

"Oh, usual stuff, too much wine and food. But nice to be with family and friends. Tell me about your travels, where are you?"

"I'm actually in Bologna."

"Really! How lovely."

"Been here for a few days, doing a bit of day tripping on the train. So much to see. You'll never guess who I bumped into in Florence a few days ago!"

"No idea. The Pope?"

"Very good. No, much more interesting…" I pause for dramatic effect. "Valentina Russo."

"That's extraordinary. Where? Did you speak?"

"I was at Gallo Moretti to view an auction, to get a better idea of how these things work…"

Cutting me off, Erskine takes over. "And she works there sometimes, of course."

"Absolutely, we bumped into each other on the stairs!"

"There are certainly worse people in the world to bump into!" Although Erskine sounds surprised, he doesn't quite hit the peak of astonishment I was expecting. "How did she seem, pleased to see you?"

"She didn't recognise me at first. I think she was just fazed at seeing me out of context."

"Of course. Can be odd meeting someone in unexpected circumstances."

"I saw her a couple of days before that as well, in Bologna, going up the steps into the Grand Majestic Hotel where you and I stayed. She didn't see me that time, I just happened to be walking along Via Indipendenza a few metres behind her."

"I suppose she does live in Bologna, so it's always going to be a possibility that paths will cross."

I shift the subject slightly towards my auction. "When was the last time you spoke to her?"

"Oh, crikey. When was it? Before my holiday, obviously. I'd say about ten days ago."

"And everything all on track?"

"Well, it so happens that Tina is also on my list of people to call today. I'm not expecting any issues and she certainly hasn't communicated during my break, but part of the reason I need to speak to her is because we'll need to organise things for the trip soon. There's a registration process at Gallo-Moretti, hotels, flights and so on. Jayne will organise most of that, and Valentina will manage things with Gallo-Moretti."

"I've actually registered at Gallo-Moretti, I have my membership card," I tell him, feeling slightly proud of my pro-activeness.

"OK, I'll let Valentina know." Again, Erskine doesn't seem to match my mood. But then he brightens up a little, "I'll make sure she reserves good seats for all three of us. Working there means she can pull a few strings."

"Oh? When I spoke to her on the stairs the other day, she was very non-committal about attending. I think she said it depended on what else was going on at the time. I have to say it did surprise me. Slightly concerned me, if I'm honest."

"Oh, that's just lawyer speak. It's a kind of stock line when you're overloaded with different demands. She probably has a list of tasks as high as the Tower of Pisa."

Erskine's comment almost tempts me to quip about the precarious nature of the tower, but I resist. "She did seem a bit more like herself by the time we said goodbye, so you never know, if I bump into her again, I might ask her out for dinner!" I say the last few words with a laugh in my voice.

Erskine again fails to follow my mood. "I wouldn't recommend doing that. Best to keep work and personal matters separate. At least until after the auction." He sounds distinctly disapproving.

"I wasn't really being serious. There's always the hope she'll ask me out for dinner. I reckon it would be rude to turn her down!"

Erskine's mood is unchanged. "Same answer as before, if you want my advice. The Italians can be tricky to deal with. Far better you leave all those relationships to me. After all, that's what you're paying me for."

I honestly can't tell if Erskine is seriously trying to discourage me from seeing Valentina. Then it hits me. The dirty old bastard… he's got designs on her himself! That must be it. He can cut an impressive figure at times and I bet he fancies his chances. I'll be watching those two, I tell myself. "OK, message received. She's all yours," I add with a hint of playfulness. It's met with Erskine's professional laugh, a skill he's honed better than most.

After a few meaningless pleasantries, the call ends and I'm left to reflect on a rather strange conversation. But Piazza Maggiore is a great place to let thoughts run freely, and while I replay Erskine's words, I admire the Fontana Di Nettuno; a magnificent sixteenth century bronze fountain where Neptune himself stands proud on a central block, four sculptured ladies sitting below flaunting their top halves, their water-spraying nipples very much on display to the piazza. Quite a distraction when thinking about Valentina Russo.

But it's not enough to take my mind off the phone call with Erskine and as I set off for an amble around the city, I'm unsettled. Erskine seems odd. Valentina seems odd. Are they up to something? Of course not, I remind myself. I'm just a paranoid innocent abroad.

26

Inside the reception area at Gallo-Moretti, the young man on reception prodded his glasses into place as he looked up to the businessman on the other side of the counter.

"Buongiorno," the young man said quietly.

"Buongiorno. Do you speak English?" The businessman spoke quietly.

"A little. I try at least." The glasses slipped slightly.

"Excellent. Peter Hobday to see Marco Spinetti."

"I let him know you are here. Please go up the steps opposite. There are seats at the top. You can wait there."

Upstairs, seated, the businessman opened his wallet, making sure the calling card for '*Gerald Bassinott, Business Consultant*' was left firmly in its place. Instead, he prized out a card showing '*Peter Hobday, International Entrepreneur*'. With his alter ego set up, Gerald Bassinott was ready.

Within a few minutes, "Peter Hobday" as he wanted to be known today, was being welcomed into Marco Spinetti's office.

Taking seats, Spinetti spoke slowly. "Mr Hobday, thank you for visiting Gallo-Moretti today. I understand you may be interested in selling some items through our auction house. I think you make a good choice." With his husky voice and thinning black hair slicked back over a head the colour of a conker, Spinetti wouldn't have been out of place in a mafia movie.

"Thank you for seeing me today." Pushing his Peter Hobday card across the desk, Gerald got down to business. "There are two main reasons I wanted to visit Gallo-Moretti. Firstly, I wanted to get a sense of the place. I do a lot of business on intuition. Or gut instinct, as we English call it. I like to know who I'm dealing with and understand the modus operandi."

"I trust you like what you see so far, Mr Hobday?" Spinetti smiled.

"Very much so. An impressive set up."

"Can I ask what sort of value items you would be looking to auction here?" Spinetti was clearly keen to establish how much energy to apply to his sales effort.

"High end fine art, mostly. Value anywhere between fifty thousand euros and on a good day, possibly half a million." Gerald sounded intentionally blasé.

The sum high enough to invigorate him, Spinetti sat up. "Well, after we talk, I'll show you around the main auction room, meet some of our people. I think you'll like us even more."

"That would indeed be useful, thank you. So, apart for just wanting to get a feel for all things Gallo-Moretti, I want to fully understand how the payment process works. If I'm interested in putting some items in the auction, what do you need from me?"

"We will need your contact information, including your bank details, so that we can pay you once the sale has happened. I have an information sheet on it here." Spinetti slid a piece of paper across the desk to Gerald. "This tells you what to do. You need to email the address here, as it says, with the subject title *New Seller Details*." Spinetti circled a finger vaguely over the bottom half of the paper. "They will email you back with what's needed. But really, it's just your name, address, phone and bank account. Oh, and of course, passport details. We're discreet here, but we do need to know the money is going to the right person!" Spinetti weaved a mild chuckle through the final sentence.

"Of course. All makes perfect sense." Folding the information sheet, Gerald slipped it into his inside blazer pocket.

Armed with the information he wanted, Gerald might have left Gallo-Moretti there and then, but he wanted to underline his plausibility as Peter Hobday. Feigning interest and going through the motions sincerely, is a fraudster's skill and as Gerald excelled himself, Spinetti rhapsodised over the company's history whilst showing him every room in the building.

Opening the door into one of the offices, a handful of staff were working, their heads buried in their computers. As Spinetti quietly described what tasks were undertaken here, Gerald nodded sagely, but he wasn't taking in a single word. Instead, he'd noticed a woman looking towards them from her desk. He looked away several times, but every time his eyes returned, she was still focussed on him. Or that's how it seemed.

After a comprehensive sales pitch, which seemed to involve demonstrating the workings of everything including the contents of the stationery cupboard, the two men ended up back in the reception, where Spinetti ordered a taxi to be called. Then with Spinetti-Hobday pleasantries done, Gerald headed outside.

Away from the auction house, Gerald was straight on the phone to his brother, Thomas who had been waiting nearby while the erroneous Peter Hobday was doing his work. Within a minute, just out of sight of the Gallo-Moretti building, the brothers were reunited.

"That was easy," Gerald boasted. "Got the lowdown on how they operate and checked out a few other things too. We need to get to Erskine as soon as we get back to London tomorrow. By then, I'll have worked out what we need him to do. Should be a piece of cake." As Gerald spoke, he noticed their taxi pull up outside Gallo-Moretti. "Don't want anyone to see us getting in the cab together. I'll go first, and you follow me in a minute."

With Gerald in the taxi, Thomas sauntered the short distance to join him. Fastening their seat belts, as they confirmed the hotel address, Gerald stared up at the overhanging sign. Then as they pulled away, he thought he could just make out a face looking down at him from a first-floor window. Was he being watched? The moment had gone before he could be sure.

27

Erskine was in Strand staring mode again. It was a place to be quiet; a birds-eye view over hectic London life, silent from his wood-panelled cocoon. It was just before 7pm and he was obeying orders to make time for an evening meeting with the Bassinott brothers. With Jayne Renton rarely straying from her nine-to-five obligations, Erskine was alone and had wandered through to the reception area in readiness to let them in. Waiting on the oxblood Chesterfield, as usual he had no idea what their agenda would be.

He didn't have to wait long. Punctual and polite, after coming through the door, the brothers followed Erskine to his office. Sitting down, and making sure the door was closed, Gerald was straight in. "OK, firstly, we just want you to confirm that you've kept all of this to yourself. It's a question I'm going to ask you a lot over the next few meetings. And I'm going to ask it slowly whilst looking into your soul. If I detect a flicker, it's game over." This time, Gerald sounded menacing. "I really want to make that clear. Game over. So, here it is. Have you spoken to anyone about our involvement? Anyone at all?"

"Ask as many times as you want. You'll get the same answer. And I'll say it slowly while you're looking into my soul. Ready?" Unintimidated, Erskine held Gerald's stare for a moment. "Absolutely not. One hundred percent no."

The staring continued, before Gerald eventually broke the peace. "Keep it that way." A few more seconds passed before he continued. "I need some specific details. Assuming the auction was going ahead normally, who gets the payment from Gallo-Moretti - you or your Italian agent?"

"We are Gallo-Moretti's client, so the money comes to us. We then pay Città Legale Italia, our Italian agent. Then we pay, or would have paid, Peter Foster-Fewster, less our commission."

"Good. If you're the client, it makes the plan much easier to execute. I now know how they operate at Gallo-Moretti. Have you registered as a seller on their system? To do that, you'd have provided their admin team with your contact information, bank account numbers and passport details." Gerald passed Erskine the information sheet he had been given by Spinetti. "This shows the process. Has that been done yet?"

"My word, you have been busy digging around." Erskine spoke sarcastically. "But to answer your question, no. I'm waiting for Gallo-Moretti to contact me. Our Italian agency have been liaising, but I'll send the bank details as per this sheet to Gallo-Moretti when requested." Erskine wafted the information sheet nonchalantly at Gerald.

"Good. Not done yet. Again, makes things much easier. As soon you get that request from Gallo-Moretti, contact us before responding. We'll give you further instructions. Is that absolutely clear?"

"Crystal."

"OK, that's all we need right now. We'll see ourselves out." The Bassinotts stood up in unison and with little fuss slipped away leaving Erskine alone to ponder and unpick the brothers' thinking. Wandering back over to his window to stand and stare, he still didn't know exactly what they had in mind. He was just glad that he'd got a confidante, albeit a reluctant one, in Valentina Russo.

As he thought about the flash meeting he'd just had with the twins, deep inside Erskine was as pleased as punch that he still had the ability to convince serious fraudsters he was being honest, when he wasn't. The fact that he'd been able to lie under intense pressure, without producing so much as a bead of sweat, gave Erskine a twisted sense of satisfaction, along with the mental, if not physical, smile on his face.

28

A few days after the meeting with the twins, back at his desk in his Strand office, Erskine was reading a text message from Foster-Fewster.

Hi there, just wanted to keep in touch. Enjoying travelling around Italy by train, Ravenna, Ferrara, Parma, among the highlights. Not bumped into Valentina since we spoke!! Just enjoying the freedom. Will be back in London next week. Could we catch up then? Cheers, PFF.

Erskine read the message a couple of times, before leaving the phone on his desk, moving to the window as he contemplated his reply. Hands in his pockets, as he began writing the reply in his head.

Dear Peter. All tickety-boo here. Summary as follows. I'm essentially an appalling unprincipled criminal who should really be in prison. But the only reason I'm not is because I'm being blackmailed by two famous fraudsters who are forcing me to divert the cash from the sale of your inherited jewels. They can do that because they have proof that I'm a bent lawyer. By going along with their plan, I get to save my arse, but sadly, you lose everything. But don't worry, I'm on the case and I'm blackmailing Valentina Russo, who I got pregnant five years ago when she was already engaged to be married. I paid for the termination and have threatened to tell her husband if she refuses to cooperate. She's agreed to cooperate, not surprising when you think her husband acts like an Italian mobster at the best of times. All clear so far? Good. So, with Valentina playing ball, I reckon the fraud twits can be outwitted and I'll get the cash. Assuming we did get the money, I wanted to swindle you, so you got less than you were expecting. But Valentina made me promise I'd honour our agreement and pay you in full. No doubt plenty more news to come in the next few weeks, but for now, as you can see, nothing at all to worry about. Ersky.

In the time that it took to walk back to his desk, Erskine had mentally edited the main thrust of his message. He began typing into his phone.

Hello Peter. Sounds great. Nothing to report from here, all going to plan and everyone happy. Call me when you're back and we'll meet up for a spot of lunch. Auction date coming up fast – exciting times! Best, Erskine.

Taking a deep breath, he pressed send.

Later the same day, as he prepared for a 3pm appointment in his office, Jayne Renton's trademark knock preceded her entry, along with a fit, tanned man dressed in jeans and black polo shirt with the collar upturned. Guessing he was in his early forties, Erskine already knew from his research that the man was ex-services.

Jayne spoke. "Mr Erskine. Mike Reynolds to see you."

"Thank you, Jayne." Erskine pointed to a seat with one hand, whilst shaking Reynolds' hand with the other. "Pleasure to meet you, Mike. I assume Jayne has your drinks order?"

"I'm just fine. Thank you." Reynolds' voice conveyed a hint of Irish heritage as he held Jayne's gaze for one or two seconds longer than necessary. Slightly blushing, Jayne slipped out.

"So, Mr Erskine, how can I help you?"

"Well firstly, thank you for seeing me at such short notice." Erskine paused as Reynolds nodded in acknowledgement. "I need some help to get a better idea of someone's movements. Or more accurately, two people's movements and any plans they may have. They're twins - elusive but not dangerous. Not violent dangerous, anyway."

"So, find them, follow them, possibly overhear conversations and report back to you, scenario?" Reynolds was unfazed by Erskine's requirements so far.

"Yes, that sort of thing. I want to know where they live, who they meet, what they do during the day. And probably more, but that would depend on what you turn up... and your fees. You don't need to know why I'm interested in them at this point, except to say it's personal. I've prepared a profile with as much basic information as I have on them. Any significant gaps can hopefully be filled in from the information you come back with." Erskine handed Reynolds a print out with the Bassinott's names, photos and a brief outline of their criminal tendencies.

"So, they're fraudsters. Shouldn't be a problem." Reynolds' eyes scanned the stapled sheets.

Erskine sounded relieved. "I can probably help to get things going for you. The twins will be here in the next few days for a meeting with me. Not sure when exactly, but I can let you know. They won't stay long. You could track them arriving from outside somewhere, then follow them when they leave."

"Makes sense. As for my fees, I charge by the hour. A hundred plus expenses. Minimum contract is a grand, which obviously gets you ten hours. Half upfront in cash, the rest including expenses when those hours are done. So, if you want me to start in the next few days, it'll be five hundred now. In cash."

"Is that negotiable?" Erskine's voice was sharp.

"Not at first. But if things develop and there's a need for an extended investigation, then it's possible we could negotiate."

Erskine pondered Reynolds' words for a few moments. "OK, I'll dedicate a thousand to it and see what you find out. I'd really like some sort of overheard conversations if possible."

"Anything's possible given enough time," Reynolds said pointedly.

Nodding his agreement, Erskine opened his desk drawer and unlocked a tin, his hand lingering on the wad of fifty-pound notes inside it. "What about an invoice?"

"It usually suits my clients to pay cash and have no paper trail. An invoice can certainly be done, but it'll add fifty percent to my fees."

Again, Erskine pondered. "OK, cash it is. No invoice." He placed ten new fifty-pound notes in front of Reynolds, who taking them, raised a buttock to slide the folded notes into his back pocket.

Both men stood up. "The café opposite is a good place to watch people come and go from here." Erskine suggested.

Reynolds surveyed the view from Erskine's window. "I'll do a bit of digging before your next meeting with them. But for sure, I'll track them when they leave here. I'll be on my motorbike - set up like a courier. Gives me the perfect cover. I use a body cam for reference if anything interesting happens."

"Sounds good to me. I'll be in touch as soon as I know what day the twins will be here." Shaking hands, Erskine showed Reynolds out of his office.

29

Having spent nearly two weeks in Italy, I'm happy at the prospect of getting back to London and starting to think about the new life I'm going to build after the auction. With less than a month to go, I'm also looking forward to catching up with Erskine.

With one more day in Bologna before my flight tomorrow morning, I take a last look around some of the places I've enjoyed the most here. Big churches, towers, Piazza Maggiore, the Fontana Di Nettuno ladies spurting water proudly from their nipples and of course lunch at my favourite pizza restaurant, where I'm now on first name terms with the piratical waiter. All in all, after what has been the perfect break, my tentative thoughts about making this place my home have been replaced with definite intentions.

Back at the hotel after a few early evening glasses of wine in the square, I'm healthily exhausted and ready for an early night. The moment my head hits the pillow, it feels as though my alarm clock activates, but several hours of delightful unconsciousness have passed. Pushing the window open, I let the unmistakable atmosphere of early morning drift in, watching below as in the warmth of the rising sun, Bologna street life unfurls. The relative silence is broken only by echoey reverberations from occasional cars and buses, contrasting with the looming thrum of daytime. I may not know how my life will play out after the auction, but I'm determined that this place will be part of it.

Down in the breakfast room I'm pleased to see that after several days away, the shuffling waitress is back. She looks rested and for the first time, her "café?" inquisition comes with a brief smile. The coffee is superb and the breakfast adequate, much better that way round I decide, savouring every sip from my second cup. Then after breakfast, I settle my hotel bill with the smart man, looking happier returned to his role in reception. With the staff back in their familiar positions and bright sunlight casting in through the hotel's open front door, it feels like I'm leaving everything in perfect order.

Waiting in the tiny street for my taxi, I decide that when I get back to London, I should be safe enough to move back to the flat in Camberwell, at least for now. If I come and go quietly, no one will really notice me, though I'll chat it over with Erskine, just to make sure nothing else has popped out of the woodwork.

After my taxi arrives, an effortless twenty minutes later I'm at the airport and checking in, with about an hour to kill before it'll be nine o'clock in London, a good time to catch Erskine. Finding an English newspaper and a café with views over the runway, I settle down to some reading and plane watching, on alert for more displays of Italian queue jumping.

After an hour passes, I call Erskine, who as usual, answers before I get the chance to speak. "Good morning, Peter. You back in London yet?"

"I will be in a couple of hours! Just at the airport. I'll be quick, I know you're busy. When's good for lunch?"

"This week is looking a bit tight now - not sure I'll be able to do lunch. But if you wanted to pop by for a coffee and a quick catch up, tomorrow at midday would work. We've got all the tickets and hotels sorted for the Florence trip, by the way. I'll bring you up to speed when I see you."

"Tomorrow's fine. All sounds good. Look forward to seeing you."

"Great. I'll block out half an hour in my diary. Have a good flight. I'll see you tomorrow."

As the call ends, I'm left somewhat disconcerted as I head for my boarding gate. Like Valentina was when I saw her last, Erskine seemed a little lacklustre, certainly more so than when last time I spoke to him. Not unfriendly exactly, but it would be a stretch to describe his manner as enthusiastic.

After an uneventful night at the flat in Camberwell I'm on my way to see Erskine. The cab feels grimy compared to its Italian equivalent and London exudes a greyness I'm not used to. Still daydreaming about the vibrancy of Italy in hot sunshine, I arrive at the Strand early, feeling the need to not only see Erskine but also to top up my Jayne Renton memory bank. After my chance meeting with Valentina where she seemed keen to get away from me, that fantasy at least has lost its shine.

The clanking lift hauls me up to the third floor where Jayne Renton welcomes me into reception. I'm fifteen minutes early and Jayne has lost none of her allure as I watch her bring me a cup of tea, confirming that Erskine's current meeting is overrunning and that hopefully he will be free by midday.

I pretend to read my phone for a few minutes, while my eyes are swivelled to their fullest extent towards Jayne. Before long Erskine's door opens and a man comes out. In a black leather jacket, blue jeans and trainers, he's carrying a crash helmet. I watch Jayne obviously admire this vision of virility heading towards her as she rises to open the door and he confidently thanks her. Detecting the faint blush of her cheeks, I study my phone and wait for Erskine to see me.

30

Two days after the Bassinott's last visit, Erskine had received the anticipated email from Gallo-Moretti requesting his full contact and banking details. Having given much thought to the twins, and what they might be planning, he felt better knowing that Mike Reynolds was going to be tracking them, giving him hope that some light would be shed on their activities.

After Erskine had called Gerald Bassinott as instructed, telling him the email had arrived, having been reminded by Gerald, with appropriate emphasis, not to reply until he gave the go ahead, Gerald had suggested meeting later that evening. With little or no choice, Erskine had reluctantly agreed.

With Reynolds tipped off about the Bassinott twins arriving that evening, when the time came, Erskine was alone. Letting them in, he showed them into his office.

Once seated, Gerald spoke slowly "OK. First things first. Same as last time. Have you spoken to anyone about our involvement? Anyone at all?

Connected or not connected with this case? Does anyone know about us as a result of anything you've said?"

Aware of both brothers scrutinising his every move, Erskine stayed cool. "And just like last time. No - to all those questions. You really don't need to ask me repeatedly. Your message is... how shall I put it... engraved on my mind." Bending the truth one hundred and eighty degrees, Erskine was fully at ease.

"And again, just like last time, make sure it stays that way." Gerald threatened, as Erskine nodded.

"OK. Show me the email from Gallo-Moretti."

Having already printed it out, Erskine pushed it across the desk to Gerald.

He read it carefully. "Right, it's actually very simple." Gerald looked at Erskine. "All you need to do is send them all the normal details, except the bank information. Instead of your bank account details, put these details in the email." Taking a folded piece of paper from his inside jacket pocket, Gerald passed it across the desk to Erskine.

Unfolding the paper, Erskine read it, then turned to Gerald. "That's it? That's your plan? To divert the money straight into your account, instead of ours? That's ridiculous. Completely traceable. You'll be identified immediately and it's not just me involved. You may think I won't go to the police, but what about our Italian agents and Foster-Fewster? Once they realise they've been shafted, they'll be straight onto the authorities."

"We're not that stupid, Erskine. You don't need to know any more at this stage, but rest assured, it will not be traceable. For now, you just need to get those details emailed to Gallo-Moretti." Gerald tapped the piece of paper as he spoke.

"Fair enough. I'll do it first thing in the morning." Erskine placed Gerald's piece of paper in his desk drawer, as the Bassinott twins looked at each other before returning their gaze to Erskine.

"I'm a tenner better off for that." Gerald smiled. "I had a little bet with my brother before we got here tonight. It was just a hunch, but I guessed you'd prefer to send it in the morning. Or put another way, when we're not here. Well, that's not going to happen. So please get the piece of paper out of the drawer, turn on your computer and write the email. We'll double check it, before giving you the go-ahead to send it." Gerald's smile gave way to a more menacing grimace as he spoke.

"OK. But you do realise this is where the fraud starts? There'll be no going back. From this moment on, you're in it up to your necks. I thought it would be wise to sleep on it. Just in case you came to your senses overnight. But if this is the way you want it?" Employing his best withering tones, Erskine turned his computer on.

"Thank you for the concern, but no need to worry on our account." Gerald spoke sarcastically. "Let's get it done and sent now. Then we can leave you - until the next time we need to give you more instructions."

In a few minutes, Erskine had composed the email to Gallo-Moretti, turning the computer screen to face the twins.

"Good to go. Send it." Gerald ordered, after reading it carefully. "We have a plan to double check that those details are on their system just after the auction, so please don't get any ideas about asking them to amend them. We'll be on it."

"Why am I not entirely surprised?" Erskine was back to his withering delivery. Then he remembered that Mike Reynolds was waiting somewhere outside to follow the twins when they left. The meeting had gone on for longer than he expected, a quick glance at the grandfather clock confirming the twins had been in his office for just over half an hour.

"Well, if that's all for now, I really need to get going." Erskine stood up, his abruptness causing the twins to look at each other.

"You seem rather keen to get rid of us suddenly?" Gerald's loaded comment surprised Erskine.

"I thought we were done. I've actually got a

train to catch. That's all."

"Which station?" Gerald probed, narrowing his eyes.

"Charing Cross, why?"

"As luck would have it, that's on our route. Why don't we all walk there together"

"Not possible tonight. I've got a couple of calls to make here first." Erskine wasn't liking the way the conversation was going.

"We can wait, no problem." Gerald insisted. "We'll make use of that nice Chesterfield in reception until you're ready."

"There really is no need." Increasingly uncomfortable with this unexpected angle, Erskine was realising he had to shut this down. "Sorry gents, you'll have to manage without me."

Gerald stared into Erskine's eyes. "You wouldn't be hiding anything from us, would you?"

"Not at all. I just can't get away right now. Is that really so hard to understand?" Erskine was beginning to lose his poise. A diversion came to mind, "Oh, one other thing. Gallo-Moretti's online brochure is now live. Just saying."

Gerald ignored Erskine's last comment. "Don't worry. We had no intention of going to the station with you. I was just interested to see how you'd react."

But as he spoke, Erskine suddenly remembered Valentina Russo's comments about serious fraudsters having a sixth sense for detecting lies. Had he given anything away? Relieved the twins weren't going to wait, Erskine regained some cool. "Well, I assume I reacted as anyone would in the circumstances? I can't leave the office just yet. Simple as that."

"You're obviously a man in demand, so we better leave you alone. Looks like you've had enough for one day." Gerald spoke with a mischievous grin. "Don't worry. We'll see ourselves out."

Alone in his office, Erskine headed to the window to see if he could identify Reynolds in the street below. It wasn't long before he could see the brothers crossing the road and hailing a black cab. But there was no sign of Reynolds. Before long a cab pulled over and the twins got in, heading off towards Aldwych. Then a few moments later, a black motorbike with courier style paniers came into view and streaked away in the same direction.

Turning away from the window and heading out of his office, Erskine was already agreeing with the twins. He'd definitely had more than enough for one day.

31

"Italy??" Erskine was incredulous. "And they're going tomorrow? Are you absolutely sure?"

"One hundred percent. They were sitting closer to me than you are now." Mike Reynolds was unequivocal as he reported back in Erskine's Strand office. "Started off with basic surveillance. I tracked them to an address they've visited a few times since I've been on them. Council flat, near Peckham. Chap called Harry Pyecoe lives there with his mother. One night, the twins and Pyecoe went to a pub about five-minute's walk away."

Erskine interrupted. "I heard Pyecoe was gravely ill. Was it definitely him?"

"I can't be certain, but it was his address. It could have been someone else, but I wasn't specifically tracking the third person. Assumed it was. Maybe it wasn't. Do you want me to track him too?"

"Not just yet. This is already costing an arm and a leg. What happened next?"

"I followed the three of them into the Bugle

Horn pub. Didn't want to stand out from the crowd, so I quietly ordered my trick drink for this type of situation. Soda water with lime cordial in a pint glass. No ice, few drops of angostura bitters, quick stir and it's a dead ringer for lager. I got a seat as close as I could to the twins. Looked like I was in a little world of my own, reading my paper, phone earplugs in and apparently slugging beer. Expensive bit of kit, those earplugs - directional microphone helps pick up conversations from a few feet away."

"Was the third man in on the conversation? The possible Pyecoe character?" Erskine chipped in eagerly.

"No, he was off playing the pub quiz machine while the twins talked. Discreetly. I'd say they never fully let their guard down." Reynolds' debrief was solid. "They didn't talk about anything of real significance, until Gerald mentioned the flights to Bologna tomorrow. I didn't get everything. There was a football match on the pub TV and judging by the collective oohs and ahhs, there seemed to be a missed goal every ten seconds. They mentioned a hotel and they chatted about the best way to buy train tickets. But I didn't get where the train was going. They talked a bit about you, too. Left me with the impression they don't like you very much. And, the name Fester-Fowster, or something similar popped up a couple of times. They were also talking about 'the Baileys', whoever they are? Something about the Baileys being safe in Pyecoe's mum's flat."

"The Baileys? Means nothing to me. Probably some lowlife villains who need a safe house for a few days. Or more likely they've robbed an off licence and need to hide some boxes of Irish whiskey. Did you pick up anything else of note?"

"By that point the football was drowning out most conversation. I reckoned I'd got enough to report back to you and the twins were eyeing everyone in the pub. I left them to it. I've made a note of all the London flights to Bologna tomorrow. Fairly limited options, but my guess is they'll be on the 11:40 flight from Gatwick. The other flights are very early morning, or late night and much more expensive. Let me know if you want me to track them any further."

"No need at this point. The Italian pointer is relevant to my interests. I have a contact in Bologna I can follow this up with. You can stand down for now. I'll be in touch if I need your services again." Standing up, Erskine went to shake Reynolds' hand.

"That's fine. I'll slip away. Just the other half of the cash payment due before I go." Reynolds remained seated.

"Yes, of course. Not like me to forget something like that. A lot of information to take in. Apologies." Opening his drawer, Erskine removed an envelope with exactly the right amount inside.

Taking the envelope, Reynolds stared at Erskine. "Any particular reason the Bassinott twins don't like you?" His eyes dropping to the envelope, he flick-counted the cash.

"Oh, it's nothing serious. Friendly rivalry. We're always trying to outdo each other. I like to be one step ahead of the game." Erskine's trademark smile of insincerity lighting up his face.

"Well, I'd look out if I were you. They're serious players."

"Really?" Erskine responded sarcastically. "They're known as the fraud twits. Or Tom and Jerry in some circles. Bungling cartoon buffoons both of them. But I appreciate the concern." Erskine smiled again, making a second attempt to shake Reynolds' hand. With the correct cash in his pocket, accepting the handshake, Reynolds picked up his crash helmet and let himself out of Erskine's office.

32

"Working with superheroes now?!" I say as Erskine welcomes me into his office.

"Sorry? You've lost me." Erskine wears a friendly frown as we shake hands.

"The super fit guy with the crash helmet who's just left your office - looks a bit, well, I don't know. Handy?"

Erskine smiles. "Clients come in all shapes and sizes these days. Take a seat and tell me about your travels." Sitting down opposite Erskine, I give him a brief rundown of my Italy trip, including how I'm interested in buying a property there when the auction money arrives.

Small talk over, I turn to the subject of the auction. "So, what's the plan for going to Florence?"

"Right. All flights are booked. Two nights in Bologna, either side of one night in Florence. It'll be you and me going from London and we'll meet Valentina on the day." Erskine tapped away at his computer. "I'll email you the details, but a quick rundown is, we're flying out of Gatwick on

Thursday 14th September to Bologna. Jumping on the train to Florence early on Friday 15th for the auction and staying in Florence that night. Celebrating at the hotel! Back to Bologna on the Saturday for the last night there and flights back to London mid-afternoon on the Sunday. We could fly back on the Saturday, but I think it's wise to hang on one more night in Bologna, in case of any unforeseen requirements popping up from Gallo-Moretti. Jayne's got all the tickets etcetera. Not much else to do now - other than get excited!"

"Well that's great." I'm delighted, not only that everything is in place, but that Erskine seems bright and focussed. It seems a good time to ask about the money.

"How long after the auction will the money reach my account?"

"Not long, a day or two at the most. Incidentally, I'll send you the details of the independent financial advisor I use. John Portman. He's very good and he'll take you through the best options. I expect he'll recommend opening a new bank account, possibly off-shore, for tax reasons. His clients are a bit A-list, so he's not the cheapest but he'll make your money pay back far more than his fees. But you're free to do what you want. You could put it all in the Post Office where it'll be as safe as houses! But I would recommend getting advice. And Portman is about as good as they get."

"I'll certainly check him out." I take the business card Erskine hands me, on which Portman's name is embossed in gold letters.

"Well, I think that's everything from my end." Erskine sounds keen to wind up the meeting. "I suggest we put a date in the diary for the beginning of that week we go to Florence. How about ten on the morning of Monday 11th September?"

"Yes, that's good with me." Checking my phone calendar, I input the meeting time.

"Excellent." Smiling broadly, Erskine stands and offers me his hand. "Sorry to be a stickler, but busy schedule today."

But I'm aware we've overrun the half hour he allotted me. "No problem, I understand. Thanks for fitting me in. I'll see myself out."

Closing his door behind me, I'm interested to see what shape and size his next client is. Heading towards Jayne Renton, I'm slightly surprised to see no one is waiting on the oxblood Chesterfield.

As Jayne Renton gets up to let me out of the office, I conjure a reason to win a few more seconds with her, "So, Mr Erskine's next client is running late?!" I say light-heartedly, nodding towards the Chesterfield.

Jayne whispers confidentially. "Looks that way, but actually, he doesn't have any further meetings today." Even though she smiles sweetly, her words activate my worry buttons. No more meetings today? So why did he say he had? Last week he suggested we should go for lunch but he's apparently too busy now? Why is he pretending his diary is full? But I already know the answer. He's fobbing me off again, the same way he downplayed me seeing Valentina Russo in Italy. I refocus on Jayne. Holding the door open, she's obviously aware I'm lost in my own world.

"Is there anything else I can help you with?" Jayne looks puzzled.

"No. Sorry." I attempt a laugh. "Miles away, not worth explaining!"

Slightly embarrassed, after thanking her, I'm on my way. By the time the lift has rattled me down to the ground level, rational thoughts have replaced the worries. Just because Erskine doesn't have any more client meetings today doesn't mean he's not busy. He could be dealing with a hundred and one things. Feeling the self-imposed stress lift, I decide to head back to Camberwell.

Taking the 176 bus I used to catch when I was working, I get off in Walworth Road, a five minute walk to my flat. Within a minute, I come face-to-face with a familiar broad smile.

"Hello, stranger. Where've you been hiding?" Bruce Browning stands in front of me, arms outstretched apparently inviting a man hug.

"Bruce!" Is all I can say before he lunges

forward and subsumes me into his considerable mass. Eventually releasing me, but not before a period of constriction during which my feet leave the ground while my nose is forced to take in the earthy aromas of diesel, sweat and beer.

"Bloody hell, Bruce." Shaking my arms, I try to get the blood circulating again. "You nearly squeezed the life out of me!"

"Sorry chap. All the guys in the pub have been worried about you. What's been going on?"

Quickly I think about my options. I know he means well, but do I really want to broadcast news about my upcoming fortune? In the end, I decide to play it straight. "Well, I'd rather you kept it to yourself." I watch as Bruce nods and forms an expression suggesting he is the model of trust. "The newspaper story was broadly right. It does look like I'm going to come into a fortune. It's an inheritance. But boy, is it complicated!"

"D'you know what? Good for you mate. I'm really pleased for you. Bloody good job it's not me that's getting a fortune. I'd piss it up against the wall in ten minutes!" Bruce barks a laugh before turning more serious. "But the boys in the pub would love to hear your news. I'll keep it quiet if you want, but it might be worth letting them know if you ever need some mates. It won't go any further, we're a pretty tight little huddle."

Despite their rough delivery, his words are heart-warming. "Would you mind sitting on it for now? I'm not getting any money for at least a couple of weeks. I'll drop you a message when things come good. Maybe tell the guys then? We can all head up to the West End for the best restaurant and pub crawl ever. I'll pay for everything. And I'd be happy to share a bit of my good fortune. I'll think about what I can do."

"Sounds like a plan, mate. Mum's the word. Not a squeak from me until I hear from you. And in the meantime, any bother from anyone, just you let me know." Bruce places his hand on my shoulder.

"Great, appreciate that, Bruce."

"Come here," Bruce demands, opening his arms and drawing me into another stranglehold, this time downgraded sufficiently so that I don't leave the ground.

Reassured after my chance encounter with Bruce, safe in the knowledge that I still have one foot in the real world, I head back to the flat, making a note to self to make sure I keep it that way.

33

"Tina, it's Erskine. Have I called at a good time?"

"I don't think it will ever be a good time. One thing, though. From now on, I'd like you to call me Valentina."

"Don't tell me *Valentina*, it's about respect?" Erskine sounded anything but respectful.

"It's mainly because I don't want any hint of intimacy between us. And yes, respect. Far more than you've just shown, so that changes right now or I hang up."

"Fair enough. Noted. Look, I've spoken with the twins and I've got a better idea of what their plans are. They've forced me to send an email to Gallo-Moretti, with their bank account details instead of mine here. So, what I need you to do is change it back to mine while you're working there. But not yet. The twins are going to get me to check that it's their bank details Gallo-Moretti have after the auction, precisely to make sure it hasn't been amended back. You'll probably have to switch the information on the Monday morning after the auction. I'll let you know nearer the time. They obviously haven't told me everything, because as it stands, the money would be traceable back to them. But they assure me they have that covered. Is that making sense so far?

"I suppose."

"Right. The other thing is that they're heading to Bologna. Tomorrow."

"Really, why? And how do you know that?"

"I hired a private detective to find out more about their movements. Not sure what flight they'll be on. Apparently, they're going to get a train somewhere. I'm guessing Florence. No idea what they're up to. Can you be at Gallo-Moretti tomorrow, in case they turn up there?"

"Possibly. But what am I supposed to do if they do turn up?"

"It would be good if you could at least let me know. Also photograph them in the building."

"Why would you want a photograph?" Valentina sounded irritated.

"Well, you may have wondered why I'm not worried about them carrying out their blackmail threat *after* the auction - when they realise they've been shafted, and the money isn't in their bank account."

"It had occurred to me, yes."

"I'm building a comprehensive file against them. It may be useful to have a photograph of them there at the auction house. The file I'm working on includes secret video evidence from their meetings in my office, and recorded phone calls. It will show the worst of their demands and behaviour, and it won't incriminate me. As soon as the money lands in our account a day or two after the auction, the comprehensive file will be delivered to my contact at Scotland Yard. An international arrest warrant will follow immediately. Basically, the file will demonstrate beyond any doubt, that the famous Fraud Twins have been trying to pull off a grand heist and in doing so have broken the terms of their parole agreement. A beautifully simple charge, but it will stick. And they can scream and shout all they want about me having been a bent lawyer, but breaking the terms of a parole agreement will trump their claims all day long."

"But what about the evidence they have? All the photos you said they have of you paying the false witness, Pikkow or whatever his name is?"

"Pyecoe. It's a risk. If asked, I will claim the whole canal scene was staged with someone resembling me. But by the time any of that comes out, they'll be banged up and no one will be listening. That's why I need to strike first. If they drop me in it before I approach the police, it's game over."

"Couldn't you go to the police now? Why wait until after the auction?"

"It's too risky. Even without the photographs

they could still cause me serious problems. I need to make sure they're locked up before they start squealing. Equally important, I want the money in the bank before any spotlight is put on me or the auction. Once the file against them is bulletproof, the sale has been completed, and the money in my account, that's the time to drop them in it."

34

After the call with Valentina, Erskine was uncomfortable. No matter how much he tried to tell himself otherwise, the likelihood of the Bassinott's photographic evidence coming to light at some point was an uncomfortable reality. The fact that Valentina had mentioned it only served to heighten his sense of unease. He needed to contemplate the situation, think through every angle and see if there was an elegant way to overcome it. The twins claim against him could potentially end his career, even without the photographs. But at least if there were no photographs, it would make his position much easier to defend.

Wandering over to his office window, Erskine assumed his deep-thinking stance; upright posture, shoulders back and arms folded with the one hand clasping his chin. Playing everything over and over, he realised how inadequate his response had sounded when Valentina asked about the Bassinott's evidence coming to light. How had he managed to let this massive fly in the ointment sink from view? Kicking himself, he paced around the room, thinking through the twin's comments and actions, but no closer to finding a way around the fact they had conclusive proof that he'd paid off Pyecoe.

Then, just as the name Pyecoe ran through his brain he quickened his pace. "Pyecoe. Pyecoe," he muttered. "Maybe it's Pyecoe I need to focus on. What did Mike Reynolds say? The Baileys… what was that about? *The Baileys will be safe at Pyecoe's mum's flat.* Baileys, who are the Baileys? Or *what* are the Baileys?" The only Bailey Erskine could think of was David Bailey - the photographer. *The photographer*! The Baileys could be the twin's code name for the photographs - the David Baileys. The Baileys – or photos - are safe at Pyecoe's mum's flat.

Certain that his hunch was right, Erskine tried to apply some additional science to his theory, with the aid of an invisible lawyer, mentally questioning himself.

Surely the twins would have a duplicate set of photographs? *Maybe not. In fact, almost certainly not. Why would they run the risk of having that sort of material in their possession when they're on parole after a major fraud conviction? Could look very bad if they had a visit from the boys in blue no matter what it was in connection with. Also, these images implicate Pyecoe in something that he would need to explain, so he's got every incentive to ensure that there are no random sets of duplicates floating around anywhere. All in all, much better to keep one set of originals in anonymous safety, such as Pyecoe's flat where their whereabouts is only known to the three of them."*

Could there be more stored digitally? *The photos were taken using 35mm film before digital cameras were commonplace, so very unlikely they are stored on a memory stick or similar. The same point about Pyecoe not wanting other copies applies here. He's not going to want digital images circulating anywhere.*

Surely there are negatives? *They could well be stored with the photos. In fact, they almost certainly are for all the same reasons.*

So, for the Bassinots and Pyecoe, the best option is to have one set of original photos stored secretly, probably together with the negatives. *You make a very persuasive case Mr Erskine."*

Pleased with himself, back at his desk in a flash, he scrolled through his phone, stopping at Mike Reynolds.

Suitably anonymous, Reynolds answered the call. "Hello, who's calling?"

Recognising the slight Irish lilt, Erskine was straight in. "Mike, it's Erskine from City Law Partners. How are you?"

"Well now, there's a surprise. I was just thinking about you."

"Good thoughts, I hope?" Erskine laughed at

his own words, then after an awkward silence, carried on. "Listen, I might have another job for you. A bit more involved, so I'd need to discuss it face-to-face. When could you pop by for a chat?"

"You're lucky as it happens. I'm free pretty much anytime tomorrow morning. Tennish good with you?"

"That'd be fine. See you then."

Feeling an immediate release in tension, Erskine returned to his window. He couldn't be certain about the Baileys link, but at least he was doing all he could to eliminate that particularly troublesome strand of spaghetti from his plate.

The next morning, Mike Reynolds took a sip of tea from the delicate china cup just as Erskine's grandfather clock began ten dull chimes. After a flash of her eyes, Jayne Renton made sure that Reynolds required nothing else before she dutifully slipped out of Erskine's office.

"OK, so how can I help?" Sitting opposite Erskine, Reynolds looked relaxed.

"This job requires a bit more than just surveillance. I need something of mine retrieved from someone's property." Erskine sounded business-like.

Reynolds frowned "I'm not a burglar." He took a sip of tea. "But go on and I'll tell you if I can help."

"I've thought it through and I think it should be relatively straightforward for a man of your skill and experience."

Reynolds didn't look impressed. "Flattery will get you everywhere."

"Well, I mean it. Just hear me out. I'm sure there'll be nothing to cause any real concern. It's a place you went to when you were tracking the Bassinott twins. Duke Pyecoe's flat. There's a package in there somewhere. A large brown padded envelope with fifteen A4 photographs inside, and quite possibly a set of negatives."

Reynold's frown deepened. "And you want me to break in, search the place, find the package and bring it to you? Not really my line of work." Sipping his tea, Reynolds was keeping his thoughts to himself as he watched frustration fill Erskine's face. Placing his cup on the desk, after an extended silence, Reynolds' frown gave way. "But everyman has his price. What's it worth to you - if I pull it off?"

"Well, it'll involve a bit of surveillance to establish Pyecoe's and his mum's routine. Maybe they go shopping together at a certain time, or to the pub. Then, when you know they're out for a couple of hours, it's a matter of letting yourself into their flat - an easy task for you, I imagine. After that, some good old-fashioned rootling through drawers, under beds, tops of wardrobes etcetera. If you find the envelope, I'd like the contents replaced with some A4 photos that I'll give you. The replacement photos are blackened as if they've been damaged by damp, age or whatever. The point is, they'll be indecipherable. You will then return the original photos from Pyecoe's flat to me here." Erskine studied Reynolds face before continuing. "I have a budget of five grand."

Reynolds rubbed his chin. "I'm not touching it for less than ten. There's serious risk involved here."

"Well, that's obviously more than I was expecting. I might be able to up the figure, but only if the job is completed as I've described." Pausing, Erskine gathered his thoughts. "The best I can offer is two grand for taking on the job involving the surveillance and entering the flat, ten grand in total if you successfully return all fifteen photos to me." Waiting for Reynolds who was now in perpetual chin rubbing mode, Erskine tried to sugar the pill. "Look, there must be enough guaranteed to get you interested? Two grand. And then there's plenty of incentive to see the job through. If it goes well, you could have all the money in your pocket in a matter of days. Done and dusted."

Nodding thoughtfully to indicate he understood Erskine's offer, Reynolds remained silent for a few seconds. "I'll take the first part without any commitment to finish the job. If I think I can do it safely, I'll see it through. If something spooks me, I'm pulling out. But I want the two grand up-front."

It was Erskine's turn to be silent and contemplate his options. Ten grand was a high price, but he knew the real value of wiping out this evidence. The photographs being there was still only a hunch, but he was backing himself. "OK, I'll go for it. How long do you think you'll need to do the job?"

"I'll check out their movements over the next couple of days. I might be able to tap their phone. I wear contractors clothing with fake ID when I need to hang around somewhere without raising concern. I'll give you some feedback when I've got a feel for things."

"That's fine, but this is urgent." Erskine leant down to open a desk drawer, pulled out a brown A4 envelope. "These are the fifteen photos and negatives I want putting in Pyecoe's envelope. It's important that the contents are swapped, not the envelopes. His one is padded and has a lot of felt pen handwriting on it and a couple of stickers. I don't want anyone to notice anything has changed. Pyecoe has no reason to open the envelope all the time he is certain the contents are as they've always been. Obviously, you need to be careful to make sure the envelope is replaced exactly where it was and that nothing else is out of place when you leave Pyecoe's flat."

Reynolds took the envelope and studied

the contents. "Looks like these were taken in a deserted coal mine."

"That's the idea. Anyway, you're crystal clear about what's needed to be done?"

"Yep, make sure Pyecoe and his mum are out of the flat for a good hour at least. Let myself into the flat. Find the envelope with photos in. Swap the contents for these ones you've just given me and return his envelope to exactly the same place. All the time making sure nothing is disturbed in the flat, before bringing Pyecoe's photos to you."

"That's it. Perfect. Actually, just thinking about it, if you're watching Pyecoe and his mum, you could also let me know what his state of health looks like. I heard he was knocking on death's door. I'd be interested to know how he looks."

"I'll let you know. But some people carry on pretty well when they're seriously ill. My brother had cancer for four years and you wouldn't have known anything was wrong until a couple of days before he died. So, I may not be the best judge on that. But if he's crawling on all fours or something strange, I'll make a note."

"Any feedback on that would be useful." Standing up, Erskine went to shake Reynolds' hand. "Good, well, keep me posted."

"Just the small matter of two grand upfront." Still firmly seated, Reynolds hadn't budged.

"Yes of course. Really not like me to overlook something like that," Erskine blustered. "We did agree, apologies. I'm not used to paying up front in business."

At Erskine's words, a trace of a smile ran across Reynolds lips. Lips he wiped with the back of his hand. "Not like you at all, Mr Erskine. Apart from the last time we did business."

35

With ten days to go until the auction and the arrival of my fortune, I decide to find a pleasantly busy pub and enjoy a few anonymous pints. Newspaper in hand, I jump off the bus near London Bridge and walk along the newly developed plaza towards Tower Bridge. The iconic structure looks strong, solid and symmetrical in the early evening sunshine and although none of those qualities could be applied to the equally iconic Ponte Vecchio I recently crossed in Florence, they both have their own beauty and rightful place in the world. As if to make the point to myself, I try to imagine Tower Bridge plonked in the river Arno, as disastrous an image as my next, of an extruded Ponte Vecchio stretching across the east end of the Thames.

Such thoughts run wistfully through my mind as I pass hundreds of tourists meandering and posing in front of the here and now's perfect selfie backdrop; the London skyline in evening sunshine. Then I leave the open pedestrian space behind, slinking into Shad Thames, a narrow cobbled street dotted with high class restaurants, cafes and boutique shops. Steeped in Victorian history, the area is immortalised in old photographs displayed in occasional shop front windows. Studying the images, I try to imagine the harshness of life here in the wharfs. In those days, the cavernous warehouses were home to mountains of hessian sacks full of exotic spices, each one manfully offloaded from ships and hefted inside the multi-floored depots. Long after that industry faded, the bleak desolation of empty buildings and deserted docks provided the perfect backdrop for gangster movies in the sixties and seventies. Walking passed those same buildings today, the contrast could hardly be starker. Above the smart new eateries, large and luxurious apartments fill the spaces where Victorian workers once toiled for little reward. And instead of avoiding the area for fear of bumping into the mob, these days you'd be more likely to step on the toes of a resident celebrity.

Turning left at the end of Butler's Wharf, it's just a few feet to the edge of the Thames and a riverfront full of modern bars and restaurants bathed in sunshine. With world beating views in every direction, these are easy places to enjoy a drink.

The first bar I walk past looks pleasantly lively, but I amble on for a few minutes, checking out the others before committing. But not finding anywhere that matches the buoyant atmosphere, I head back there, happily taking in the sounds of al fresco socialising all around.

Inside the bar, I order a pint of Italian lager which looks impossibly enticing as the slender schooner fills under the barman's gaze. Placed on the counter and into a beam of sunlight, I watch myriad shoals of tiny bubbles rise through the chilled amber, in thirsty anticipation of my first sip.

Taking the pint, I head for a vacant space on a bench seat against a wall between two large tables, the one to my left occupied by studious individuals and quiet couples, the one to the right with animated office workers noisily crammed in. As I sit between both scenes, I focus on the busier table where everyone seems to be enjoying their release from whatever cage they've been confined to all week. It's interesting to watch them. Liberated from spreadsheets and targets, this is how they want to be, in this natural state of happiness, communicating and laughing together, their shirts untucked and hair ruffled.

As the first slug of cold lager hits my throat, I look at this crowd of normally sensible people, their positive energy growing as the shackles fall away, feeling sudden sympathy for them that they'll be back at their desks in the morning, full of dread for the day ahead. But as my pint goes down, I start to feel happier for them. They're enjoying themselves and none of them look like they'll starve tomorrow.

After a couple of pints, I contemplate my options. Home or another pint? The latter easily wins out partly because after time in Italy where I hardly understood a bloody word, I'm enjoying the easy to follow theatrics at the table beside me. But as I return with my new beer, the riotous cabal is gathering itself to leave, one-by-one rising, laughing, until the huddle of arm-linked workmates shuffles out towards the riverside, not exactly swimming synchronised, but swimmingly happy.

Taking my seat again, a shape flashes in front of me. "This table free, mate?"

"Certainly is," I reply, earning myself a double thumbs up and a ludicrously wide smile, before he signals the way to the rest of his crowd with exaggeratedly beckoning arm signals. Opening my newspaper, I bury my head, ignoring them as they descend around the table, assuming they're all installed before a couple of minutes later, a final member tries and fails to squeeze past me.

Standing, I let an orange haired girl through, then feel her wriggle into a tiny space available between me and the edge of the table as she ends up sitting sideways, her bony buttocks pushed hard into the side of my thigh and the back of her carrot plumage occasionally tickling my face.

Happy that this pub version of musical chairs is over, I angle my head away and return to my newspaper.

After ten minutes or so, apologising for having to turn in early, a couple of people leave. But it liberates the rest of the group who immediately spread out more comfortably, with grunts of relief as if they are all loosening overtight belts. As the girl with the orange hair repositions herself leaving plenty of space between us, she spins around to put her hand on my upper arm.

"Sorry to crash into you like that earlier. My colleagues are a little crazy... me too!"

You're not saying!? I think to myself, trying to work out the origin of her European inflection. "It's no problem." I actually say, wanting to add more, but finding myself stuck for words.

Nodding an appreciative smile, she returns her attention to the animated table, while I watch her. She's an unusual looking girl. Mid-twenties possibly, wearing vibrant clothes that hang loosely over her lanky frame. From our five second conversation earlier, I noticed the orange hair is not universal. She has an immaculately cut fringe of shiny pink framing her face like open theatre curtains. With a rather long face and pale complexion, she isn't what I would call classically good looking, but she's interesting, nonetheless.

"You're sad, no?" She's talking to me again, leaning closer due to the pub noise.

"No, not at all! Quite happy reading my paper with a beer." I'm flattered, if not a little surprised that she's apparently concerned about me.

"I can usually spot sadness. Feel free to join in with us. There's nothing special going on. Just people who know people who know people. We're all connected somehow, though I can't always remember how or why. Any old excuse for a drink, really!"

"That's very kind, but I don't want to intrude. Incidentally, I'm trying to work out your accent. It's faint but I can hear something - can't I?"

"Ooh, very good. I'll give you three guesses." As she turns more emphatically towards me, I'm asking myself, is this young woman with orange and pink hair chatting me up?

"I think I'd have to go with Scandinavia somewhere. Just as a first stab at getting the right hemisphere." As I speak, I close my newspaper, enjoying her attention.

"Impressive. Two more goes." Arms still folded, she tilts her head in expectation.

"Sweden?" I suggest with an upward inflection. She shakes her head with closed eyes.

"Norway?" My inflection even stronger. Still shaking her head, she slowly opens her eyes.

"It's actually Finland. I'm Finnish. Well, was. Not entirely sure what I am these days! But I'm Fin, by the way - my name." And with that declaration she flops an outstretched arm with a hand for me to shake.

"Hello, Fin. I'm Peter!" Shaking her hand, I notice the cat's cradle of thongs and charms around her wrist.

"So, was I right, Peter? Are you sad?" Fin looks interested rather than concerned.

Shrugging, I genuinely have no idea what to say to her.

But Fin seems unconcerned with the awkward silence and it isn't long before she fills it. "My friends tell me I have a special talent for spotting sadness. And also, for helping people to be happy. I like to help - even if it's just joining in around a pub table. It costs nothing and makes the world a better place."

"That's nice, but I don't think I'm sad!" I say, increasingly bemused at this bizarre interest in me. But when her stare suggests she isn't buying my response, I feel slightly unnerved. Then someone at the table buying a round shouts across to Fin to take her order and she's back to the chaotic girl that nearly squashed my nuts when she arrived earlier.

"Ooh, bloody hell! Yes, more to drink! Another one of those crazy green things I had before, what was it called, Betsy?" She calls to one of her group. "Betsy?!" She turns back. "Oh she's pissed! Never mind. Here, take my glass. The barman will probably remember - it was quite unusual.

Thanks! Hang on a mo..." Fin swings her multi-coloured head round to check with me. "Peter, do you want anything from the bar?"

"No, no! But thanks for the offer." I mainly address the chap buying the round who's been involuntarily invited to spend his money on a complete stranger. With Fin now in deep conversation with the girl next to her, I return to my paper.

After a few minutes Fin turns around again and much as I might want to pretend I haven't noticed, it's not really a plausible option with this girl. Not that I want to avoid her. It's a nice feeling when someone shows interest in you even if they're not quite your cup of tea.

Sensing she's about to say something, I get in first. "Are you sad? I mean, after the earlier conversation, I just thought I'd ask. You don't seem to be, I have to say. But I'm thinking, if you see it in others, then, maybe... you see it in yourself?"

Fin ponders my words for a while. "Can I answer that in a minute? I'd like to ask you something first."

"Fire away!"

"Do you still have parents?"

"No." I say, humorously and suspicious at the same time.

"Were you a child orphan?" As she asks, the hairs on the back of my neck prickle and butterflies rip through my stomach. Strangely emotional, thanks to Mr Outrage I'm keeping it under wraps. Or so I think. What the hell can Fin see in me to even ask that question?

I answer honestly. "Yes." Unable to look at her, I'm confused, emotional and aware Fin is scrutinising everything.

"How old were you?"

"Fourteen."

"I can see the sadness. You carry it. It's an invisible weight, but I can still see it. And whenever I see it, I want to connect with it."

"And would I be a million miles off target if I guessed you were orphaned too?"

"You'd be bullseye." Fin's answer suddenly makes the evening's odd conversation more understandable.

Then thinking about the group she's with tonight, I wonder if these are members of a support group. "Are your friends here all the same, orphaned?"

She laughs. "Hell no! This lot really are a random bunch of mates. I don't think any of them know I was orphaned. I don't necessarily want them to, it's not that interesting, I guess. But for those of us who have been through it, like you and me... well that's different. We keep this sadness bottled up. I can spot it a mile away."

"Do you ever get it wrong?"

"I never get the sadness bit wrong. The orphan guess is ninety percent right, I'd say."

"What happens after you connect?" I ask,

fascinated.

"We talk, share, sometimes cry. Sometimes we stay in touch. Mostly not. It's just a special discovery. A moment that helps us to feel understood, because despite all the training and good intentions, no therapist can possibly understand the impact on a child of losing both parents. No book can describe the way we feel. No drink can take away the pain. No medicine can heal the scars. The end result is sadness. Deep internalised sadness. And I can see it as clear as day."

As she talks, I'm transfixed. Despite the drinks, she's clear eyed and laser focussed.

"Fin! Come on, we're heading off to the restaurant in a couple of minutes, but finish off your mocktail first. It cost a fortune!" The young ringleader is back in action corralling his troops.

"Mocktail?" I ask, wondering how she can be so lively without a snifter or two.

"I don't drink alcohol. It killed my father." She even says this without sounding downbeat.

"God, so sorry."

"Don't be silly, you couldn't have known. But I'm determined it won't kill me!

"Fin… come on were hitting the road now…" As the group stand up to leave, Fin raises her hand in acknowledgment and swills down the last of her drink.

"Peter, here's my card. Obviously, I have no idea what your life is like, and you might be happy to see me disappear forever! But if you wanted to talk some more about the orphan connection, well... send me a message. I live in New Cross Gate. Not paradise, but it's good for getting around town. You, where do you live?"

"Fin...Fin...Come on...You're holding us up!" As a voice calls out to her, Fin gets up to leave.

"I live on my own in Camberwell, but I'm about to move soon."

"Sounds exciting, anywhere nice?" Fin's voice is rising as she edges towards her exit.

I think about saying 'maybe Italy', but decide to keep my powder dry. "I'll tell you when we meet next time?" I say loudly with megaphone hands.

"Sounds like a plan!" she shouts with a thumbs up, before disappearing through the crowded pub and joining her friends outside.

36

"You really don't need to be here. I couldn't give a monkey's about the photos. Just saying, in case you're worried I'm going to get them copied and have a go at blackmailing you myself." Mike Reynolds gaze was firmly on Pyecoe's flat as he spoke, motionless inside his parked car.

"The thought never crossed my mind." Erskine was combining jollity with indignation. "As I said on the way here, I just thought it might be useful to have a second pair of eyes. Nothing to do with the photos being copied. And where's this idea of blackmail come from?"

As he turned to face his front seat passenger, Reynolds seemed nettled that at the last minute, Erskine had decided to chaperone him. "It doesn't take much to work out that someone's got you by the short and curlies. But it's none of my business. I guess I'm a bit pissed off that you felt the need to check my movements. I never rat on an employer. Come into the flat with me if you want to see it all with your own eyes."

"No, I'll stay here in the car. You're the pro.

Look, regarding trust and all that. The truth is I'm keen to see all this put to bed. Somehow it feels right to be here, not stuck somewhere else thinking about it. Also, you might come across something unexpected. If you do, you can call me from the flat. That's all."

Reynolds nodded slowly, the dark night hiding the expression on his face, that he was perfectly aware Erskine was talking bollocks.

After a few minutes silence, Reynolds and Erskine watched two figures emerge from the front door of the building, Reynolds lifting an index finger which Erskine took to mean it was probably Pyecoe and his mum. Illuminated by street lamps, they were clearly visible - an elderly lady, slightly stooped, walking arm in arm with a thin middle-aged man, hobbling awkwardly in a tired tracksuit. Walking slowly along the hand-railed path to the pavement, they turned left and in less than a minute slipped out of view.

"That's your Pyecoe chap and his mum," Reynolds confirmed.

"He looks terrible. Doesn't look like he's fit enough to go out and make it back."

"Not exactly the picture of health, but he's up and about so this is my opportunity. I'm going to wait two minutes to make sure no one returns to pick up a forgotten wallet or something. Then I'm in there." Reynolds spoke quietly with calm authority, Erskine admiring the lack of nerves on display.

"You seem in control." Erskine whispered.

"Training and experience." Reynolds looked at Erskine. "Balls of steel, that's all you need. But you can't buy them from Amazon. They come from years of miserable, painful, relentless training and experience."

Erskine instinctively tried to find something to say that had any related parity, but after opening his mouth, quietly failed. As the illuminated dashboard clock swept silently through the seconds, both men sat in silence. Then Reynolds leant around. Pulling a kit bag from the back seat, he unzipped the top, getting out the envelope of blackened photographs and negatives Erskine had previously given him, before easing open the driver's door.

"Right, I'm going in. Anything unusual I'll call you. But I'll be whispering, so turn your phone up. Any surprise visitors heading into the building, call me."

"So, I am useful after all!" Erskine joked, as Reynolds moved out of the driver's seat.

"I hope not. Certainly not expecting you to be, if I've done my homework properly." Giving Erskine a reassuring wink, Reynolds quietly closed the car door with the aid of a gentle knee push.

Reynolds walked towards the flats as if it was his home. There was no looking around or nervous movements, just confident strides to suggest he had every right to be there. Then as he went in, Erskine tried to build a mental picture of events inside the building.

He's walking up the stairs now. He's found Pyecoe's flat. He's opening the lock, that'll take a minute. He's in. His narrow beam torch is on. He's in a bedroom. Torchlight flitting under the bed, onto all surfaces and then into drawers. Nothing. Next bedroom. Same routine. Nothing. Into the lounge. Lots more drawers. Nothing. Shit. Come on, Reynolds, what about the nooks and crannies in those sorts of flats, like storage cupboards where they keep hoovers and crap like that? Or under carpets and rugs. Get it together Reynolds, use that training and balls of steel shit. What about behind pictures on the wall? Even a man like Pyecoe must have pictures on the wall? The toilet?

Dizzying himself, Erskine was starting to question the ridiculousness of his hunch about 'the Baileys' connection. Sitting there in a depressing darkened cul-de-sac, the reality of the photographs being in Pyecoe's flat suddenly seemed a million to one against. He'd invested so much trust in his own ability to outwit the Bassinotts, he'd abandoned all reasonable logic when he'd decided the photographs would be there. He hadn't even trusted Reynolds to do the job, which was why, at the last minute, he insisted on being with him.

Staring into the night sky, Erskine contemplated the expensive cock-up that was likely to be playing out in the flat across the road, beginning to realise that Reynolds would be demanding the full pay-out, even if there were no photographs to find. His mental slump in full flow, when the driver's door suddenly crunched open, Erskine was almost startled into bowel-emptying shock. But his panic was short lived as Reynolds slipped back into the driver's seat.

Erskine's heart was thumping. He hadn't spotted him leave the flats. He'd just seemed to come out of nowhere.

"Is this what you were after?" Speaking with understated confidence, Reynolds handed Erskine the brown A4 envelope.

"Jesus – really? You've got them?" Erskine could feel his excitement adding to the strain on his already compromised digestive system.

"You better check them. I glanced over them in there, looked like the sort of thing you described." Reynolds checked his appearance in the vanity mirror.

Flicking through all fifteen photographs, Erskine couldn't believe this was happening. "I knew they were in there, one hundred percent. Never any doubt," he lied.

"Well, obviously you did, otherwise you wouldn't have hired me to get them. I can tell you, I wouldn't have been very happy if they weren't there." Reynolds making a clear reference to the fact that Erskine had agreed to pay the full ten grand only if the photographs were retrieved.

Erskine realised the value of changing the subject. "Oh fantastic. The negatives are here too. Did you swap these?"

"Of course. That's what you told me to do. Hopefully you'll agree a job well done?"

"Absolutely."

"So, the eight grand balance. When can I collect?"

"Give me a couple of days. It can't go through the books obviously, so it'll take a little time to get the cash. I'll call you when it's ready to collect."

"A couple of days I can live with." Reynolds paused. "But any longer and I might get a bit fidgety."

"Now I have this, you have nothing to worry about." Erskine waved the envelope. "Nothing to worry about whatsoever."

37

It feels strange going to meet a girl for a drink when all I really know about her is that she looks quite odd and is happy talking to strangers. But then again, I also know she's an orphan. And she's intriguing. Maybe I feel a bit flattered, too. We've arranged to meet in Covent Garden, an area I know well from my work days and it's a nice evening. Her wackiness should be very at home here.

I jump off the tube at Holborn then take a short cut off High Holborn, down through Macklin Street and into Covent Garden, London still feeling incredibly familiar despite the time I've been spending away from here. It's the first time I've thought about work since handing in my notice at 'Just the Job' and I can't resist walking past the old place – though not too close. Almost certainly they'll know about my forthcoming fortune from the press story a few weeks ago and I'm not in the mood to be encircled by a crowd of ex-colleagues with questionable motivations for talking to me. By comparison, the thought of being with the random, bubbly and multi-coloured Fin feels positively welcome.

Limiting myself to a rapid walk-past of my old glass fronted office, I make sure that my face is no more identifiable than an oval with sunglasses. As I breeze by, enough office life and long faces are on display to confirm that wild horses couldn't drag me back there. I make a note to self to kill Erskine if this auction falls through.

Having got that little episode out of my system, enjoying the bustle and buskers of Covent Garden, I head towards The Cross Keys, a little pub in Endell Street. I'm a few minutes before six o'clock; the time we arranged to meet by message a couple of days ago. After craning around the pub's cubbyholes to make sure Fin isn't already here, I order a beer and wander outside.

Considering it's Covent Garden, it's a relatively quiet one-way street with a wide pavement perfect for the pub overspill, which tonight is cast in dappled sunlight seeping through lilac trees.

Outside, it's pleasantly busy, with several office workers unwinding after a day in the workhouse, slugging hard on their beers and drawing mercilessly on their smokes. A few minutes pass before "Peter!!" is shouted from the other side of the street. What a sight! Jogging across the road like an animated rainbow, Fin drops a couple of weighty shoulder bags by my feet. Lightly sweated from the warmth of the city, she swipes a bare forearm across her face, then runs both hands through her nest of pink and orange hair.

"Wowsers, it's warm tonight!" Slightly out of breath, she's wearing a beaming smile.

"It sure is. Let me get you a drink. What would you like? Not a beer I'm guessing!"

"Well, I might *like* one, but I'm not having one! Just tap water and loads of ice please." Fin peels off a tissue-thin powder blue cardigan. "Maybe a squirt of lime if they have it," she calls after me, only just in earshot as I head back into the pub.

Returning with Fin's limey water and my topped-up beer, we manage to grab a couple of recently vacated bum spaces on a low wall surrounding a raised flower bed around the foot of a tree. Squeezing between besuited drinkers, we both "oooh" with delight as the weight is taken off our feet.

"So, how's things?" I ask, still not entirely convinced if it's a good idea that we've agreed to meet.

"Hmm, well. Considering I lost my job recently and I haven't got another one, not too bad!"

I'm already working out that Fin is a glass half-full person. Most people would be pissed off in her circumstances, but there seems to be a relentless positive energy within this colourful girl. "That sounds a bit worrying. What did you do?"

"I'm an art teacher. Or was! Seems my ideas

for creative thinking and free expression don't sit too well with the national curriculum in this country."

I'm surprised and not surprised in equal measure. She looks arty but also too disorganised to be a teacher. So, a sacked art teacher is about par for the course, I guess. "I had you down as a campaigner of some sort, working for Greenpeace or something like that."

"Ha! Maybe I could paint their boat a new shade of orange!" Fin chinks her glass against mine, before sucking a large lump of ice into her mouth and lodging it inside her cheek, carrying on talking seemingly unaware that a horrendous boil appears to have formed on the side of her face. "So, you said you were moving? Anywhere nice?" Fin's subtle Scandinavian accent becomes exaggerated as she struggles to retain the melting ice inside her mouth.

"Actually, I have options. Interesting ones."

"Oooh, a man of mystery. Go on, you can tell me!" Fin elbows me lightly.

"I haven't decided yet, but possibly not in the UK."

Fin slurps her melting ice. "Wow, an internashional man of myshtery, I like it!"

"Mishtery? You sound like Sean Connery!" I return her friendly elbow jab.

"Shorry, itsh the eysh!" And with that, Fin unceremoniously jettisons the ice pellet to the bottom of her glass with catapult force. "My last boyfriend hated it when I did that." Finding it a strangely impossible statement to react to without sounding either sarcastic or dishonest, I shrug my shoulders, smiling meaninglessly.

Fin carries on. "Really, you can't take me anywhere! He used to get so embarrassed, my boyfriend. I'd like burp during his parents' Sunday roasts, fart accidentally when teaching - mind you, the kids loved it. Laugh at all the wrong moments, that's another speciality of mine - especially in the cinema. During a minute's silence at his grandmother's funeral, I sneezed so hard that my hat fell into the pew in front and into the lap of a little kid. He put it on and his little sister started screaming with laughter. It didn't take long for me to join in. If looks could kill... My boyfriend was always treading on eggshells, apologising left, right and centre on my behalf. I didn't really ever see what the problem was. It's just life."

As I watch Fin's face, there's not a flicker of embarrassment as she stares up into the lilac trees, amazing me at how comfortable she is at just being, well, her. It seems she is what she is, no compromises, take her or leave her.

Feeling I can talk to her with no agenda, I decide this is my moment to edge towards my future life. "I'm thinking of moving to Italy. Specifically, Bologna."

"Oh, wow. Amazing. You work there?"

"No, not really. I can't really explain very easily." Unexpectedly, I feel awkward about the subject, suddenly not wanting to be evasive or talk about my upcoming fortune. I don't know this girl well enough to share what's happened, and although she's undeniably magnetic, I still think there's a chance she's a bit unhinged. Then an idea hits me. "Look, you're an out of work art teacher, right?"

"Yes, and a bit of a nutcase!"

Not really what I wanted to hear, but there's enough humour in her voice to suggest she's very switched on. "Well, I have an idea. How would you feel about giving me some art lessons?" I watch as Fin pulls a face of pleasant surprise. "I recently bought some canvases, paints and an easel. I was inspired to give it a go after one of my visits to Bologna. I haven't got started yet, been too busy. But the next few days... well, I have some time on my hands. I'd pay you, of course."

"Fantastic. Without hesitation, yes." Fin whoops with delight. "Depending on where I need to get to, we could start tomorrow?"

There's something nice about the way she says "we" that feels instantly collaborative. "I have a small flat in Camberwell. Tomorrow would be great. Just let me know the normal teaching hourly rate you were getting, I'm sure I'll be able to better it as its private tuition. And it'll be cash!"

"That's so brilliant. The timing for me is

perfect. And while you paint, you can tell me all about your mysterious Italian plans. I'd love to hear them. Only if you want to... Just tell me to shut up, whenever. You really won't be the first!" Fin is in full fidgety flow as she talks, holding her hair up, squiggling it around at the back as if to form a bun, letting it fall before angling her head and plaiting a few random side strands.

But this all sounds good to me and I'm especially happy that we've deferred the bigger conversation about my future life until I get to know her a bit more. "OK, that's a deal." I confirm. "So tonight, did you want to chat about the orphan thing?"

Fin's look of elation persists. "The invisible cord of sadness that connects us? I'd love to. Shall I start with my story?"

"Let me get some more drinks first. Same again?"

Fin looks thoughtful. "Actually, could you get me a mocktail of some sort? Anything colourful would be wonderful. Let me give you some money."

I shake my head. "No problem, all part of the fee structure!"

When I return with the drinks, Fin is deep in conversation with a guy sitting on the wall next to her. I can't tell whether it's jealousy that flashes through me, but something happens. It's an odd image, a hot looking chubby businessman in a thick black suit, while Fin represents the polar opposite in every respect; cool, lithe and colourful.

"Here you go." I hold out a tall glass filled with an orangey red concoction resembling a lava lamp.

"Ooh, wonderful. This is my friend Peter, the guy I was talking about." Addressing her companion, Fin takes her drink, then turns to me. "I was just telling David about our art lessons and our interesting connection, being orphans."

"Oh, you know each other?" I raise my glass towards David. Patting the empty space next to her, Fin holds an affectionate arm out towards me.

"No, no. We've just met. Squeeze back in next to me." Suddenly from nowhere, I feel a warm rush of inclusion from Fin's friendship. Being a relentless social butterfly, she's been chatting with David but there's no doubt she's been talking about us. As Fin carries on, David obviously assumes I'm her other half and it feels surprisingly welcome. While Fin supplies 99% of the words, David does his best not to look totally shell-shocked, before apologising for having to leave because he's just remembered a prior appointment. Having extracted himself with this obvious lie, he trudges away at pace.

"OK, food!" I declare, in the hope that Fin has time for a bite to eat. I know she wants to talk about our different experiences of growing up without parents and I'd like to do that somewhere relatively civilised. But whatever we talk about, I'm not ready to talk about my inheritance.

But I'm becoming enchanted by Fin and I like the fact we seem to have an embryonic friendship based on shared interests, with no other considerations. When I think of the undeniable beauty and sophistication of Jayne Renton and Valentina Russo, both acutely aware of their own sexuality, Fin, by comparison is the complete opposite. But what she lacks in looks and refinement is more than compensated for in personality.

"Yes, food!" Fin sounds delighted. "I'm vegan."

"Well I'm..." I pause. "Not surprised!" My words cause Fin to shriek with laughter. "Apologies, but I'm a carnivore. Not sure if I could survive on vegan food. But it doesn't seem to be holding you back!"

"You wanna try some?" Fin's wide open eyes are surrounded by mascara-extended eyelashes, the only obvious make up she wears.

"Will it turn my hair orange?"

"Of course it will. And pink!" Speaking with mock indignation, Fin prods the end of my nose.

"Great, then I'm in."

When Fin tells me there's a really good vegan restaurant called *Meet & Chew Veg* a couple of streets away, I have to agree that the name alone is clever enough to warrant a visit. With the sun dropping behind Covent Garden's skyline, we finish our drinks and head off. As we enter the small restaurant, I rapidly begin to question my own judgement when we agree to take the only available table which is squashed into a windowless corner at the back. As I squeeze through tables crammed with people made from plants, I think about the prospect of comparing orphan stories over tofu burgers with an orange haired livewire. All the time not having enough room to swing a carrot. It's the last place I would have chosen if I'd been eating alone, but oh well, nothing ventured...

38

After the previous night's events at Duke Pyecoe's flat with Mike Reynolds, Erskine reached his office early the next morning. Making sure his door was locked, he removed the A4 envelope from his brief case, opened it and slid the fifteen photographs onto his desk. Splaying them out in sequence like stills from a movie, he scrutinised the negatives meticulously, making sure each one corresponded exactly with a printed photograph. Satisfied that they were perfectly matched, Erskine felt emboldened that it was his 'Baileys' hunch that had led him to the entire horde of incriminating photographic evidence. Returning the contents carefully to the envelope, he placed them in his office safe, then spun the locking dial.

Later the same morning, Erskine called Valentina Russo and after the not so pleasantries, he was straight in. "So, any sign of the Bassinotts, Fraud Twins, Tom and Jerry or whatever name they go by these days?" After his apparent success with the photographs, Erskine felt chirpy.

"No, I was at Gallo-Moretti all day on Friday, the day you said they might come here. But I didn't see anything."

"God knows what they're up to, but as long as we amend the bank details just after the auction, they won't be able to pull this off. And I have some especially good news. It's regarding the evidence they'll be relying on to sink me, when they realise they've been stung."

"And what's that?"

"The photographs."

"The ones with Pikkow, Pie-whatever?" Valentina sounded confused.

"The very same. Well, guess where they are?"

"Is this really the time for games? I don't know, surprise me." Valentina couldn't have sounded more loathing if she'd tried.

"Under lock and key, in my office. Not two feet away from where I'm standing."

"And how did you manage that?"

"The private detective I hired. He was acting on my intelligence." Erskine was keen to establish he was in control.

"And what if the twins have copies?"

"I'll be very surprised if they have. All logic tells me they kept just one set in secret. Much safer for them that way. I'm 99.9% convinced I have the only copies."

"What if they notice they've been taken?"

"The way it's been done, no-one would have

any reason to suspect the photographs aren't exactly where they've always been." Erskine was still upbeat.

"Well, let's hope you're right." Valentina paused for a few moments. "Incidentally, regarding next week's auction, it looks like there is a lot of interest in the jewels. There are rumours that they've drawn the attention of a couple of Russian oligarchs. Last time that happened at Gallo-Moretti, the sale price went over 50% above the reserve."

"Well, that's excellent news. Makes all this effort worthwhile. I've had to invest a lot in this since the Bassinotts started muddying the waters; Peter's advances, the private detective, travel – including coming to see you in Bologna, when it could all have been down over the phone," he said pointedly. "All sorts of expenses. Kind of shit or bust, as we say here."

"Don't talk about that Bologna trip like that again. It got you what you wanted. I'm playing along with the plan and it saves your stuck-up British arse. And don't forget it - unless you want me to think again."

"Well, in point of fact, it saves all our arses, as you put it. Pulling this off means the Bassinotts will be in the slammer and we'll all get our rightful pay off. Including Peter Foster-Fewster. No need to lose any more sleep over him."

Valentina considered her response. "I think

the Bassinots will try to drop you in it whether or not they get the money. You think they'll be in prison with your plan, but if they outwit you, I don't get why they still wouldn't drop you in it."

"Because, if they get the money, they'll need to disappear into the ether. They won't want to be dealing with international police investigations into me. They'll be guilty of stealing from the auction and they'll do everything in their power to literally become invisible overnight. The only saving grace if that happens, is that they'll pay me off to keep my mouth shut about what they've done."

"And me, and Foster-Fewster, what do we get if they get the money?"

"Oh, I dare say the pay-off will give us all something. But these are all theoretical worries. Their basic plan is so stupid that we can stay one step ahead. We switch the bank account back and as soon the money is with us, I hand my file to Scotland Yard, who'll see beyond any doubt that the fraud twits are back in action and breaking their parole arrangements."

"And if they become invisible, how will they be caught?"

"They can only become properly invisible if they have the money. In my scenario, they'll just go underground when the international arrest warrant is issued. It'll only be a matter of time before they're flushed out, probably when they're caught red-handed robbing an old lady's handbag because they need to eat. Desperate idiots, the pair of them."

"Maybe. Maybe not. Are you expecting to see them before the auction?"

"They're like dog shit on a shoe. They'll be back to make sure I'm trotting along with their plan. Also, apart from making sure I'm onside, they'll want to intimidate me. They'll need to be certain I don't have a grand scheme. When they leave, they'll be quite happy I haven't."

Valentina let a few moments of silence pass before reacting. "Picante, Erskine. Spaghetti Bolognaise Picante."

39

"Your Aunt Daphne sounds wonderful. A real character." After telling my childhood story above the lively clatter inside *Meet & Chew Veg*, Fin's response is sympathetic, her eyes flitting between me and the wholemeal wrap she's trying to construct like a huge spliff.

"She was. After life at public school, the freedom with her was just fantastic. Being an only child, I got a bit reclusive but that didn't bother me. In fact, I loved being alone. Living in that part of London was magical. I had time to myself, a lovely bedroom and the knowledge that I probably wouldn't ever be going back to school. The view from my window was of cherry trees and when the blossom was out, I felt like I was viewing the world from inside some magical film. It's hard to describe it, but it felt cosy and safe - a million miles from my old life. Aunt Daphne was properly dotty, mind you, but we made it work."

"This might sound like a weird question, but did you grieve for your parents?" Fin grapples with her spliff, taking angled bites from one end, then the other.

"Seems odd to say, but not really at the time. Not till much later in life."

"That's quite common you know. Children accept things much better. Everything is new up until we are older teenagers." Fin shrugs. "Almost nothing surprises us. As kids, we cry when we fall over and scratch our knee, but we keep our shit together when a parent dies. It's always fascinated me."

As Fin talks about bereavement, it's the first time someone is speaking a language I understand. No-one has ever talked to me like this before. "It's really interesting. And so. What's your story Fin?" I register with an exaggerated nod that the vegetable lasagne I've just started eating is surprisingly tasty.

"I was an only child, too. My mother was from a town near Helsinki. My father was from Rotterdam. We lived in Helsinki - where life was pretty good. My father had a good job with a tech company. My mother was an artist - she sold her work successfully in several galleries. We lived in a nice house in a nice area. Then one day at school, I was summoned to the headmaster's office. There were police and other people there. They told me.... sorry." Raising a hand, as she places it over her mouth, her eyes fill with tears.

Consumed with emotion, I reach for her other hand. It's ice cold. I hold it between my own.

"You don't have to go on. We can talk about this another time."

But Fin doesn't hear me. Still staring at the floor, she carries on. "They said... there had been an accident. A car accident. A serious one. And people have been killed." Fin looks up at me. "They told me they thought my parents were involved in the accident. That they had both died." Looking down at the floor, she whispers, "I don't remember anything after that." A few silent moments pass. Then she looks up at me through tear-filled eyes. "It seems my father had been drunk."

As I take in the metamorphosis unfolding in front of me, from colourful bundle of joy to pale tearful child, my earlier rush of emotion is heightened. All I want to do is hold and comfort her, strange feelings for me. A bit of a loner, I've never really been affected by the emotions of others, nor am I emotional myself. But this feels different. I have to say something to her. "Look, why don't I sort the bill and then we can get some fresh air. A walk along the river, or in a park. It's a beautiful evening."

Fin lifts her eyes as a bit of colour returns to her face. "You know what, that'd be perfect."

Outside, as we walk, I feel compelled to put my arm around her, an instinctive, protective act. As we thread our way through the blurring background of city streets, mutually deriving comfort from the connection of kindred spirits, our silence feels natural. Before long we're walking beside the Thames and as I point towards a bench, Fin nods.

Sitting in silence, we stare over towards the London Eye, admiring its almost chandelier quality as it casts its luminescence across the calm water, city life moving around us.

After a few minutes I try to change the mood. "So, has my hair turned orange?"

"What?!" Fin sits upright, seemingly back to normal.

"The vegan food, you said it would turn my hair orange. And pink!"

"Maybe it's just starting. Tomorrow, you'll wake up like me!" Fin thrashes her hands to-and-fro across her head, electrifying her hair to almost terrifying effect.

"You're not really selling it to me. But seriously, it might be a price worth paying. That vegetable lasagne was properly tasty. I'd definitely eat that again."

Fin looks impressed. "Maybe I should cook something tomorrow when we do the art lesson. If we start around ten, I could cook some lunch. I have to be away around two, as I have an interview at three for a teaching job near London Bridge. That will leave plenty of time. I'll bring the ingredients, nothing too involved. Just a nice lunch."

"OK. Sounds like a plan. Actually, I've just realised I don't know the official name of my new art teacher."

"Ms Sakala. Ms. Fin Sakala. And the name of my student?"

"Erm, it's a weird one. Mr. Peter Foster-Fewster."

"Quite rhythmical. Unusual - but rhythmical."

"Well, that's better than some comments I've had over the years." As we sit there watching river taxis and dredgers pass by, Big Ben chimes ten o'clock.

"Wow, it's later than I thought. Do you think we should head for our respective homes, Ms. Fin Sakala? I'll get Uber on my phone, it can drop us both. We're roughly in the same hood, as they say."

"That would be fantastic, I really don't fancy the tube tonight. We have a long day tomorrow. Thank you, Mr. Peter Foster-Fewster."

After dropping Fin, I reflect on our evening together and how sharing our experiences triggered something in both of us. Among the talking and laughing and Fin crying, I felt more emotional than I can remember. Aware of a developing togetherness between us, I still feel the need to keep my distance. I have a life changing event coming up in the next few days, when I'll become a very wealthy man overnight. It's important that I'm liked for who I am, not for what I have in the bank.

After the auction I'll never have the innocence I have now. Fin has come into my life at a unique moment. Will she be part of my future? She'll certainly be a part of my tomorrow. Beyond that, who knows?

40

"Here will do." Gerald Bassinott pointed to a bench under a tree in Soho Gardens. Being midmorning, in advance of the lunchtime exodus of staff from the surrounding ad agencies, the square was relatively quiet.

Once both men were seated, Gerald turned to Erskine. "So, exactly one week to go until the auction. I guess you're pretty pissed off about our little intervention?"

Erskine stared straight ahead and spoke quietly. "I can think of better scenarios."

"But you're still behaving yourself, I hope?"

Erskine made a hissing noise, "Do you really need to ask again?"

"I hope not." Gerald sounded more serious. "This is probably the last time we'll meet before you head off for Florence. So we need to go over what's going to happen. And for Christ's sake, lose that hurt kid look. Anyone would think I was about to shoot you."

As Erskine pulled an ironic smile as if to suggest that it might actually be a preferable option,

Gerald didn't react.

"Listen carefully Erskine. A couple of days after the auction, Gallo-Moretti will transfer the money to our account, as per the details they have on file. Just in case you're expecting all hell to break loose or alarm bells to start ringing, remember it will only be you who's aware that the money hasn't gone into your account. Gallo-Moretti will have no reason to question anything. And you need to keep it that way. *Do not contact them.* I will personally give you instructions about your next move, a week after the auction."

"A week? What sort of person waits a week before shouting about being ripped off for millions?"

"A person like you, Erskine. Again, listen carefully, because if you want to avoid being arrested, this is what you need to do. After the auction, you will take time away from the office. A holiday - so you're not working. When you get back on the following Monday, September 23rd, I will call at some point during the afternoon. It's then you'll make the 'discovery' that Gallo-Moretti haven't paid you."

"Surely once I raise the alarm, the authorities will simply trace you and the money through your account?"

"Not your concern. We'll be one step ahead."

"And what am I supposed to be doing while this pantomime plays out?" Erskine sounded disparaging.

"Logically, you'll be one of the first people the authorities will want to question. You just play the bemused lawyer. You're distraught because the money has disappeared and beyond that, you have no explanation. There will be nothing anyone can pin on you."

"Haven't you rather forgotten about the email that went from me to Gallo-Moretti confirming the bank account details? Obviously, they were your bank details, but it came from my email address."

"You were hacked. It's totally plausible. Especially with large scale theft. I checked Gallo-Moretti's email security when I visited a few weeks ago." Gerald had it all covered. "They have nothing specialist in place. Doubtless they will after this. So, again you play the bewildered lawyer who's suffered a terrible loss. Play it right and you'll get nothing but sympathy. It'll be a while before they focus on any emails, anyway, but when they do, you just keep telling them you supplied your bank details. Eventually, they'll agree that you must have been hacked. What other explanation can there be?"

"The real one. i.e. you were in my office forcing me to email your account details instead of mine."

"Well, it's your knob on the block, Erskine. You just better convince them that you have no idea what's happened, unless you want your criminal history to jump out of the bag. Lie for your life, Erskine. Your specialist skill."

"And Foster-Fewster, what the hell am I meant to tell him?"

"You'll have to fob him off for a few days, after the auction. He needs to think the money is still happening or he might get pissed off and do something stupid, like calling Gallo-Moretti to find out what the hold-up is. Tell him international payments can take several days and you'll let him know as soon as it arrives."

"And when it doesn't, then what?"

"When I call you after the auction, I'll explain everything, including the details of your pay-off. So, assuming you play this straight, there'll be some for you, some for Foster-Fewster."

"Our Italian office are going to be out of pocket on this, too."

"If you feel strongly about them, share your bit with them. That's up to you. Nothing to do with us."

Erskine thought for a few moments. "They can poke it. It's me that's in the firing line. I'm doing all the work here."

"As I said, up to you. Nothing to do with us." Gerald was unmoved.

"And what about the missing millions? The police and authorities aren't just going to let that go, are they?"

"You needn't concern yourself with that. Remember, if you haven't got a bank account with millions of pounds in it, they're hardly going to be wasting time putting you in the spotlight."

With the hour approaching lunchtime, the grass square was starting to fill with the lunchtime throng, picnicking in clusters and sitting on park benches. As Gerald wound up the meeting, there was no handshake or pleasantries of any kind, before he stood up and left, leaving Erskine alone.

Sitting in the midday sun, after his performance as the aggrieved party, Erskine allowed himself the smallest of smiles. Pleased that he'd prepared the ground thoroughly and with Valentina on his side, Erskine's smile moved to a chuckle. Idiots, the pair of them, even imagining they could get away with this. It was going to be the Bassinotts, not him, waiting pointlessly for the money to materialise after the auction.

41

I'm up and about quite early this morning, the low September sun streaming across the kitchen. In a couple of hours, Fin will be arriving and in the cold light of day, it's obvious that my flat could do with a layer removing throughout. More of an all seasons clean rather than just a spring one.

I also want to have a go at turning the spare room into a makeshift studio, with more clear space and the easel set up. So, after a strong coffee, I'm sleeves rolled up as I start washing, scrubbing, polishing, sweeping, tidying and anything else that's required to breathe new life into tired surroundings. Happy with the end result, I flop onto my sofa and fall asleep.

I awake to hear Fin rapping on my window. Scurrying to the front door, I open it. "Sorry, the bell is broken, and I didn't hear you knock." Trying to summon some dignity as I hold the door open, it's the best I can manage.

"And you were asleep on the sofa. Typical student!" Walking past me into the corridor, Fin prods me affectionately on the nose.

"Straight on to the lounge. Would you like a tea or coffee?"

"Do you have any herbal teas?" Fin calls back as I head into the kitchen.

"Got some green tea somewhere from a health fad I had a while ago."

"Green tea's perfect."

Bringing the tea into the lounge, on the sofa, Fin sorts through her sizable carpet bag. Even though there's an innately chaotic side to her personality, there's also an air of imperturbable calm, striking me as odd that these two characteristics sit so harmoniously within one person.

"Yuk." Fin pulls a face resembling an astronaut under extreme g-force as the calm side of her personality takes a backseat. "The tea tastes like shit! How old is it?"

"Oops. Sorry. Could be years, thinking about it." I reach to take the cup from her.

"You really are becoming a model student, getting up late and keeping things well past their sell-by dates." Fin slaps the back of her wrist as if to suggest I should be reprimanded.

"Sorry Miss, it won't happen again." I sound intentionally pathetic. As she prods my nose, we laugh. I like this girl.

After making two cups of normal tea, albeit hers without milk, I show Fin to my impromptu studio.

"This is perfect. Good light." Fin wanders around the bare room, studying it as if the walls were bedecked with invisible paintings. Then she spirals round to face me. "So, what do you fancy having a go at? Still life, or figurative?"

"Well, it might sound odd, but I quite fancy trying some abstract art. I saw some pieces in Bologna. I didn't get it at first. They were full of bright colours contained within thick black lines. All very random, but when I got back to England, they suddenly made sense. Everything in London looked so grey and boring, I really wanted something on the walls to lift my mood."

"Hmm. That's interesting. And you'd probably expect someone like me to say, 'great idea, go for it'. But good abstract art isn't accidental. It works for a reason. It draws the eye, not necessarily in an obvious way. Sure, some artists get lucky painting shit and getting millions for it, but most are classically trained before they turn to it. I think it's a basic requirement to get a handle on things like perspective, light, shade and colour mixing. When you understand the basics, *then* you can twist what you know into something abstract."

"Wow!" I'm impressed with this impassioned version of Fin. But then I remember why she was sacked. "Didn't you say you lost your job for encouraging free expression?"

"No, the opposite. I said my ideas didn't fit with theirs. As part of a module, kids were being encouraged to create artworks with no boundaries at all. I thought it was a terrible idea. Only when you can draw an apple, so it looks like an apple, or a bottle so it looks like a bottle, can you develop ideas properly beyond that. Otherwise, it just becomes an excuse for not being able to paint and draw, as well as an insult to those who understand the principles of good art."

Her single mindedness, almost intolerance, slightly shocks me. Why does she feel so strongly? Then I remember her mother was an artist. "What sort of work did your mother do?"

"Immaculate city scenes. People, buildings, rivers, cars, buses. Slices of life, could be Venice, London, Helsinki or wherever. She travelled a lot when she was younger. They weren't photographic, but she had her own style, and they were all believable images that told a story of real life."

And there was my answer, her mother's legacy to her daughter: take time to treat things properly, I'm guessing in art and life. Just as I'm thinking about the reach of parental influence, even years after they've died, my phone rings.

"Peter, it's Erskine. How are you?"

"Yes, all good thanks. I may have to call you back as I'm just with someone, unless it's a quick one?" I roll my eyes at Fin to suggest the call is unimportant.

"OK, no problem. It is very quick. I wanted to confirm we have a meeting in the diary for ten on Monday morning. I'd like to push it back to eleven if all good with you?"

"Yep, that's fine with me, gives me another hour's lie-in!"

"Great, see you then. Have a good weekend."

"Cheers. You too."

Ending the call, I return to Fin. "Well, as I haven't got any apples, how about you showing me how to make a bottle look like a bottle?" Now that abstract art is well and truly erased from the agenda, it's the best thought I can come up with.

"I have another suggestion. Why don't you have a go at drawing me? I find it can be a really good way for a new student to start. It means I won't be hovering behind you and it will give me a really good idea of your natural ability. I can then make suggestions at intervals. We can also talk while you work. It often helps to have a slight distraction. That would be my suggestion. But it's up to you!"

"Let's do it," is all I can say.

Within a few minutes, Fin is sitting on a kitchen chair in the middle of my makeshift studio. She's taken off a couple of layers to leave a loose vest top untucked over jeans. Bare feet, slender arms, and hair tamed under a beret, she crosses a leg and straightens her back - she's clearly modelled before. Sitting at a table a few feet away, I check she is ready before I begin my masterpiece.

Following her basic advice to 'keep the lines loose and free' and 'draw what you see, not what you imagine', I'm underway.

After a few minutes of silent sketching, Fin begins her inevitable interrogation, "So why Italy?" Widening her eyes, suggesting there's an exciting explanation.

"I had to go there recently on some personal business. I'd never been before. I immediately fell in love with the place. Particularly Bologna. I really can see myself living there." Hyper aware that she wants to know more, especially what I do for a living, I'm happy to believe she doesn't have any ulterior motives and is just interested in my slightly mysterious life. Close to cracking and spilling the beans, I still hold back. "I'm back there next week actually."

"How lovely! For long?" Even though Fin is modelling like a statue, her enthusiasm still bubbles through.

"No, just three nights this time." I become obsessed with a close detail in my drawing. Having made the artwork worse as a result, I step back and carry on talking. "I spent a couple of weeks there recently, looking at properties, just checking a few things out."

"So, can I ask what it is you do?" The rolling eyes are back and there it is, the question that has no simple answer. It's the moment I have to decide whether I potentially alter the innocence of our friendship.

I pretend to be interested in the sketch. "Erm, well…"

As I hesitate, Fin cuts across. "Ooh, you're not a spy are you!?"

Tempted to play along with this suggestion, I even go as far as saying, "I might be, but if I told you, I'd have to kill you." Or whatever it is people say when they try to be funny about being a secret agent.

"I'd be a good Moneypenny, don't you think?" Fin slides a pointed bare foot up the inside of her calf, holding her beret with one hand and throwing her head back in the style of a burlesque dancer, as evidently, I look a bit shocked. "Don't worry, I studied drama as well as art!"

"Maybe you should teach me drama." I close the drawing pad, embarrassed that my drawing looks more like a ball of wool than a human, dropping it on the floor beside me knowing this is the moment to talk about my inheritance.

"Should I be worried?" Fin melts out of the model's pose and into the shape I know.

"No, no, not at all. It's just that my story is a bit unusual. So, if I'm going to share it with you, I'd really like to know that you can keep it to yourself - just for now. There's nothing sinister, quite the opposite, in fact, but there are good reasons for the secrecy."

"You must only tell me if you feel comfortable. I don't want to lead you into saying something you'll regret."

"Thank you." Her words give me a warm feeling. What I'm about to say has the potential to change so much and as far as my relationship with Fin goes, I have no idea if that will be for better or for the worse. But when she releases her hair from under her beret and the sun seems to illuminate her aura, suddenly there's no going back. "OK, where to start? Well, up until a few weeks ago, I was working the normal nine-to-five for a company in Covent Garden. It really was nothing special - just a recruitment company, although over time I managed to shuffle off the lowest rung and attain the impressive rank of account manager." I watch as Fin smiles kindly, apparently hanging on my every word. "Then one day, out of the blue, I got a phone call from a law firm in the Strand. I didn't know what to expect – in fact to start with, I thought one of our clients was suing us. But anyway, as it turned out, nothing could have been further from the truth. I went to meet a lawyer called Erskine in his very fancy office. He told me his law company was part of a bigger company that got involved in heir-hunting and that I was the sole beneficiary of a large estate. In fact, very large. Like about five million quid large." As the last few words spill out of my mouth, I feel dizzy.

"My God! That's amazing! You lucky thing! So now the Italy mystery is cleared up. That's such a brilliant, brilliant story. You must be over the moon – the universe, even!"

I know the human capacity to convey ill feeling when faced with other people's good luck, especially when things aren't going so well, but Fin's delight on my behalf is joyous and comes without a beat of jealousy.

"So, when are you going to wonderful Italy? I hope you'll pop back for the odd art lesson!"

"Well, it's not quite that simple. I haven't actually got the money yet. It's all rather complicated. The estate I'm inheriting is a set of incredibly valuable diamond and gold jewellery that belonged to my grandmother, Giovanna. Until recently, I didn't know of her existence, but she was Italian and lived near Florence. During the war her home was looted by the Nazis. Lots of families suffered the same fate. Seems stealing valuable art and jewellery was a popular Nazi pastime. The jewels have been in Germany since the war. So, wind the clock forward a few decades and Erskine's company managed to identify Giovanna's stolen property and connect it to the rightful owner, who turns out to be me."

"Wow – that's quite a story. One thing, two things, actually... Why does this Erskine chap make money from this and why haven't you got your jewels? I hope you don't mind me asking, I'm just curious!"

"Ah! You probably think it's a scam. I did at first. To be fair, it still feels surreal but I'm happy it's all above board. Regarding Erskine, he charges a fee for his work. I'm OK with that. It was him on the phone earlier, he keeps in touch regularly. Without their detective work, I'd still be slaving away in Covent Garden, re-writing CV's for illiterate out-of-work hopefuls applying for jobs they're never going to get." As I talk, Fin laughs out loud, rolling her eyes. "Regarding the jewels, well, that's why I'm going to Italy next week. They're being sold next Friday at an auction in Florence."

"Wowsers trousers! That's so exciting for you! And your grandmother sounds interesting. Have you checked her out? I love ancestry and all that digging about. I researched all my family in the hope of finding something interesting. I found a great-great grandfather on my father's side who invented a special cog that went in windmill gears. He made a lot of money and was quite famous at the time. He died quite young and his wife married again. They spent all the money and ended up on the streets."

"Oh dear. I hope my story will have a happier ending!"

"It will. And by the way, if you're interested in checking out Giovanna, I could help. I have an online membership for an ancestry website."

"It might be a better use of time rather than

art lessons." As I say that, Fin picks up the drawing pad and opens it at the hours' worth of scribbles I've committed to paper. Holding it up, she tilts her head, turns the pad upside down, tilts her head the other way, looks at me, then looks at the drawing again, as if she's trying to work out if it's meant to be lifelike or abstract.

"I never want to discourage a student, but actually on this occasion, I think you could be right!"

We're both laughing, but arranging the lesson was as much a way to maintain contact, rather than any serious attempt to make great art.

Fin starts to make lunch from a bagful of fresh ingredients she brought with her. In no time, the kitchen has never smelled so good. As she cooks, we chat about the many things money can buy, but we avoid talking about Erskine or the process I'm involved in. Even though I don't believe she has any gold-digging traits or intentions, I sense she has worries about being perceived that way. In time, of course I'll be happy to talk in more detail, but for now I'm glad to have shared my news and even happier to be sharing lunch.

42

Watching Friday night television with nothing impacting in my brain, I dwell on my time with Fin today. How nice it has been to spend time with a vibrant and positive presence. For all her colourful chaos on the outside, she seems solid and smart - and now that I'm used to her unconventional looks, increasingly attractive. But it also feels more than that. There's a strength of connection between us I've never had with anyone else before, while astonishingly Fin seems attracted to something in me.

Waking up on a bright Saturday morning, as I think about next week, I feel genuinely on top of the world. I'm meeting Erskine on Monday morning to go through any last minute details, then to Bologna on Thursday, Florence and the auction on Friday - at which point I'll become a millionaire. And on top of all that is my fledgling, if slightly mysterious relationship with Fin.

It's ten o'clock before I get up and shower, full of hope that Fin will get in touch today. We were both cool with everything when she left after lunch yesterday, maybe trying not to appear too keen on each other - that was my inclination, anyway. But I have a desire to know her more; her wider interests and I suppose, whether there is a possibility of Peter-and-Fin. With Italy in mind, I think I'm quite sold on the idea.

As I make a pot of coffee, I'm delighted to see my phone flash up with Fin's name.

I let a few rings go before I answer, trying to blend excitement and normality. "Hello, how are you?"

"Brilliant! Fancy a bit of a London day? The Eye, Madam Tussauds, a couple of things like that? Crazy tourist season is over and its beautiful out there! How are you anyway?" Fin's bubbly personality transmits equally efficiently down a phone line as in real life.

"Love to! And I'm all good thanks. How was yesterday, the job interview?"

"Interview was great. They only need me to cover for a maternity leave after Christmas. It's something and I'll keep looking for a permanent position. But good that they want me, so that's worth cheering about!"

"Indeed, I'll get you some limey water to celebrate – with ice, obviously!"

"Ha! I like being spoiled. So, what time shall we meet, and where?"

"How about midday at the Cross Keys in

Covent Garden, where we met the other night? It's about a twenty minute walk from there to the London Eye. Nice day to take in the views."

"Sounds perfect, Mr Peter Foster-Fewster. See you there."

"Looking forward to it, Ms. Fin Sakala."

With a spring in my step, I walk from the tube through Covent Garden towards the Cross Keys pub. With next week's auction in mind, it's almost impossible to think straight. Every snazzy car that drives past makes me think, *I'll be able to buy one of those next week if I want. Or even ten of them.* Every gleaming shop I walk past I think, *I'll be able to buy the entire stock. And probably the shop next door.* Every fancy restaurant I walk past I think, *I'll be able to eat in there whenever I want. Every day for the rest of my life if I choose.* But I'm surrounded by potential wants, none of them needs and after the auction, I hope my head will stay screwed on, rather than be screwed up.

Thinking of Fin, I try and guess how she would deal with becoming a millionaire overnight. Better than most, is the best of my reasoning, as first serious thoughts of being together to share my good fortune come to mind. Rapidly, this unlikely Finnish presence in my life is beginning to represent a strength, something I've been missing in my life. Something I want.

As I approach the pub I see Fin sitting on the

low wall outside. In red skin-tight trousers, and a loose red vest, she looks relaxed and happy, a gold headband going some way to controlling her locks. Typically Fin, she looks refreshingly unconventional, and as always, oddly alluring.

"Hey-ho, how are you? I got you a beer. Here you go." Looking very happy with the world, she passes my glass.

"You shouldn't be spending your money. You don't have a job. I'm paying for everything else today. But anyway, I'm really well, and thank you!" Taking the glass, I move forward to kiss her on the cheek. But as our faces move closer, spontaneously, our lips touch for a fleeting moment. Smiling, Fin prods me on the nose, a sign of affection from which I take to mean she considers it a meaningful moment, as I did.

As we enjoy a drink in the early afternoon sun, we debrief each other on the morning's critical events so far, such as breakfast ingredients and the differing merits of particular bus and tube routes. Then with the drinks finished and this morning's dealings clarified, we head off towards Waterloo Bridge and the London Eye.

As Fin and I thread our way through the streets, it occurs to me how nice it would be to be holding hands with her. But no closer to knowing how she feels about me, I resist the temptation. Apart from anything else, I suspect she may feel awkward about my inheritance, which neither of us mentions, probably for fear of being misconstrued.

So, we walk, with no shortage of things to chat about, from life before we met each other to memories of our parents. Among other things, she tells me that after her parents died, she came to live in Cambridge with her aunt and uncle.

"Aunt Renna, my mum's sister, taught modern languages at the university. The trauma was felt by everyone, but she gave me a good home and oversaw my education. And I did OK at school - and university - thanks to her."

Her description of a fragmented childhood reminds me of my own. "Are you still in touch?"

"Oh yes. Here. I have photos." Fin flicks through several photos of her on her mobile.

Briefly we cover off religion, both having the same view that it all seems to fly into the face of evidence and reason, yet the monuments built to endlessly worship the never-present deity are often things of great beauty.

"And I'm passionate about animal welfare. You probably guessed."

I assume that's why she's a vegan. But although I'm a hardened carnivore, I at least get some admiration for accepting the argument that we should all eat less meat. "But you should try harder, Peter."

When I prod her on the nose, she bursts into laughter.

Arriving at the London Eye, we manage to board a relatively unoccupied capsule with only two other couples sharing the ride. As our glass bubble gently sweeps away and rises, each of the couples puts as much distance as possible between them and the others, forming a perfect triangle of 'mind your own business' separation. Safely isolated from the other humans, Fin and I watch the familiar London skyline morph and shrink beneath us, as a new perspective rolls out with increasingly spectacular views.

"These things would be fantastic in Italy. All those towers to see from up high like this."

Fin smiles in agreement. "It would. And you'll be there next week. But unlike now, you'll have both feet firmly on the ground!"

As she speaks, I know I have to say it. "Would you consider coming with me?" I turn to look her in the eye.

"Me?" As Fin laughs out loud, the two other couples in our capsule spin around briefly to see what they're missing, before quickly turning back to their respective views.

"Yes, you, Fin. I'm serious. How would you feel about coming to Italy with me?"

"Really?" She looks astonished. "I'd absolutely love to, but..." As she pauses, her laughter is replaced with serious silence. "This is unexpected. I know we're getting on well, but it's just that... are you kind of asking me out?" This time her laughter is less raucous, more nervous.

As she stares at me, I think of what to say. "In a weird sort of way, I suppose I am."

More silence follows, while it's her turn to think of what to say. "Well... in a weird sort of way... I accept!" And with that, clasping me around the shoulders, Fin plants a full-on kiss firmly on my lips.

Before I can decide if I'm embarrassed, she releases me, bursting into happy laughter, causing the other occupants to turn around and stare at us again.

"He's asked me to go out with him!" Fin announces loudly to them. After exchanging muted and somewhat awkward congratulations, I breathe a sigh of relief when mutual ignoring is restored.

"It'll mean flying out on Thursday and then back on Sunday. Have you got any commitments in London during that time?" I try to regain a bit of poise.

"Nope, none. I would love to see Italy again. I haven't been for years."

"I'll speak to Erskine at my meeting on Monday. He should be able to arrange the travel and hotels. But for now, we should enjoy today. Then how about dinner at mine afterwards? Maybe we could cook something together? I'll even have a plate of plants if it completes a perfect day for you! Maybe watch a film and take it from there."

Fin scrunches up her nose and prods the end of mine.

Looks like we're on.

43

"Mr. Erskine is expecting you. You can go straight through to his office." As Jayne Renton smiles professionally, she has a look of freshness that office workers rarely embody beyond a Monday morning.

Seeing Erskine's door is slightly ajar, I knock lightly as I enter.

"Good Lord, Peter, and... I don't think I've had the pleasure." Erskine stands up with more urgency than normal as he addresses my unexpected guest.

"This is my good friend, Fin." I say, knowing that her presence will bemuse Erskine. But having spent the *entire* weekend together, it feels right to have her by my side. And I guess I'm flattered to have a girl who wants to be with me.

"Fin, lovely to meet you. I'm Erskine. No Mr or anything like that." Shaking hands, I can see that the old boy really doesn't know what to make of either the fact she is here, or indeed her appearance. Although, I have to say she's made quite an effort to look less chaotic than normal. Clothes just as colourful but better quality, including knee length olive green leather boots over sheer black tights, a chessboard jumper and long suede purple jacket. Wearing more make up than normal, her blue eye shadow suits her surprisingly well and her pink lipstick goes nicely with her fringe. But as for the orange hair, there's no getting away from the fact it's either spectacular or monstrous, depending on your sensibilities. And the more time I spend with her, the more I favour the spectacular angle.

"You know this reprobate well!?" Erskine cleverly tries to steer her into a revealing answer with his cheery style.

"Well enough." Intentionally giving little away, Fin smiles.

"Excellent. Take a seat, all. Now, just in terms of client confidentiality, am I free to discuss everything as we have before?" Looking for my approval, Erskine's clearly trying to work out why Fin is with me.

"Absolutely. No secrets here at all." I'm quite enjoying the fact that Erskine is puzzled.

"No secrets! That's good. My apologies both, I have to ask that question. Now, did Jayne get you drinks?"

"No, we're fine. We had a coffee over the road. We got here a bit early." As I speak, Erskine looks mildly unsettled. "Actually, we saw you in there, chatting to that guy who was here last time

I saw you. The fit guy with the skid lid."

A look of enlightenment crosses his face. "Oh yes, Mike... thingy, I had some tickets to give him. A hospitality event we're organising. I needed to catch up with him, hence the reason I pushed this meeting back a bit. Easier to meet off-site sometimes."

"Sure. So, what's on the agenda today?"

"Well actually, as it turns out, very little. But I thought it would be wise, as it's such a big week, to keep this meeting in the diary. Final check of the itinerary and give you the opportunity of asking any questions that may have arisen. Incidentally, did you follow up with John Portman about his financial services?"

"I did. Interesting guy, seems to know what he's talking about. I also spoke to my bank, who put me in contact with their investment advisors. I'm going to invest the money with them to start with. I can always change things later. I'll get less return, even they admit that, but I like to sleep at night. Fin thinks the bank is my best option too."

"Oh? Well, your choice entirely, Peter, but keep him in mind. He's as good as they get." Erskine seems surprised with my decision, but I guess making money on money becomes hypnotic once you start getting good returns. But having never had any real wealth before, I'm not interested in gilding the lily. A few million in the bank with a bit of interest is a pipe dream and I'm not going to risk losing a penny of it.

After running through the itinerary one last time, Erskine mentions the upcoming weather in northern Italy this week. Apparently, there is a late heatwave passing through, meaning it will be hot and sunny while we're there. This seems like a good cue to mention Fin.

"Fin's going to be coming to Bologna and Florence with me. Or us."

"Oh, right! Lovely. A bit of sightseeing? Have you been before?" Erskine's still obviously confused as to her role in my life.

"Yes, but not for a while. I love Florence." Fin sounds assured.

But I cut in. "Could you organise adding Fin to the itinerary?"

"I don't see any problem with that, assuming flights are available. Let me make a note. Same flights as us presumably?" When I nod, he goes on. "And about hotels, you already have a double suite at the Grand Majestic in Bologna and the same in Florence. Let me know if we need to book any further accommodation." Erskine is the model of discretion as he tries to establish if we are sleeping together. But after the intimate weekend I've just had with Fin, which started in the London Eye on Friday and then consumed our lives until now, there's part of me that wants him to know that we're an item.

"No, just the one suite is perfect."

Nodding, Erskine is nothing but professional as he makes a note. "I'll get Jayne onto it. Make sure you leave your contact details with her before you leave. She'll be in touch for passport information, things like that."

"Fin has all that with her, we guessed it would be needed." I say, pleased that we sound organised.

"Properly prepared." But as Erskine speaks, I think I detect a note of sarcasm. Maybe the old boy is jealous. Fin does look exciting today. After a little more peripheral chat during which little is learned on either side, Erskine winds things up.

"Well, I think that's everything. I'll let you get on with your day and see you both at Gatwick on Thursday morning." Before I can speak, Erskine picks up again. "Oh, just one quick thing. Have you got two minutes Peter? I'd like to catch up with you on a personal matter. While I do, it might be a good use of time if Fin catches up with Jayne, with passport details and all that?"

"Of course." What else can I say? After asking Jayne to come into his office, Erskine introduces Fin. As both women leave for Jayne's desk in reception, I can only assume that Erskine wants to talk to me about money, maybe details of repaying the advances I've had, which he hadn't wanted to discuss in front of Fin.

Over by the window, Erskine waits until the door is closed. "OK, Peter, I'll come straight to the point. Am I right in assuming you only very recently met Fin?"

I stare at him, gobsmacked he's even asking. Where's he going with this? Does he know her? "Fairly recently, yes. Why?"

"Look, this is a bit tricky. Forgive me for asking, but I'm guessing she just popped out of the woodwork? Befriended you out of nowhere? A chance meeting? Told you about a common thread you share?" Wandering back towards me, he sits on the edge of his desk. "What was her angle, Peter?"

Suddenly I feel as cold as stone, a weird sense of embarrassment containing my anger. But then I remember our meeting was absolutely by chance in that pub. My choice of venue was completely random. I nearly went to an alternative bar as I walked along the Thames that evening. Still completely fazed by Erskine's intervention, I'm thinking of what to say, but it's clear he hasn't finished yet.

"It gives me no pleasure to be blunt, Peter. But I assume you know of the term gold-digger?"

I can't answer. Instead, my mind is racing as I replay everything that Fin and I have talked about and done in the last few days.

Clearly seeing my discomfort, Erskine goes on. "I'm genuinely sorry to say this Peter, but Fin has gold-digger written all over her."

Aware that Fin is just outside the office with Jayne Renton, I regain some composure. "I really don't think that's what she is. In fact, I know she isn't. She's a teacher."

"Is she? What do you really know about her? Have you met her family?"

"Well, no." Suddenly, I know how hopeless my next statement will sound. "She has no family. She's originally from Finland. Her parents were killed in a car crash when she was fourteen and she's an only child."

"And you still don't have any alarm bells ringing?" Erskine's tone is patronising. "This is text book stuff Peter. Straight out of volume one. Untraceable and unaccountable. Where does she teach?"

Again, I'm suddenly struck with how hopeless my next answer will be. "She lost her job recently. But she's just been offered a new position."

"When does that start?"

"After Christmas. And before you ask, I don't know which school - just that it's somewhere near London Bridge. She's an art teacher and I know for a fact she really knows her subject."

"I assume she's shown you lots of her work?"

"Not in that way, but she came to give me a lesson and it was obvious she knows what she's talking about."

"But she didn't actually show you anything?

Nothing online for instance? Like everything else she's told you, this could be just a story without anything to back it up." Erskine pauses.

As I listen to him, I can see what he's getting at. But it's the last thing I want to believe – the last thing Fin seems capable of. But Erskine's clearly met more tricksters than I have.

Erskine walks slowly over and places a hand on my shoulder. "Look, don't beat yourself up. You wouldn't be the first to fall for this kind of thing and you certainly won't be the last." Erskine can see that I don't know whether to punch him or thank him. "And ignore me if you want to, Peter, but you might want to check a few things out before the auction. If there's one benefit to getting older it's experience. Sadly, I have plenty." Erskine's last words are an attempt to lighten the mood.

But I'm still embarrassed that he thinks I could be taken in so easily; and angry with him, too, for causing me to question my trust in Fin. I keep my cool. "I can see why you'd jump to that conclusion, but I'm convinced you're wrong."

Erskine looks unruffled. "Look, we'll book the tickets anyway. The cost is small fry. If for any reason, Fin doesn't accompany us, then we haven't lost much money. I'll leave it with you. I just want you to know that I really wouldn't be able to sleep at night if I hadn't got that off my chest. I hope you understand that."

As I stand there, I don't know who I'm more pissed off with, Erskine for being suspicious, or myself, for being so trusting. Or on the off chance he's right, potentially Fin.

Studying the effects of his intervention on my body language, Erskine crumples his face into a sympathetic smile and moves to shake my hand. "All part of life's rich tapestry, Peter. See you at Gatwick on Thursday morning, either with your new friend, or flying solo."

44

"Valentina. It's Erskine."

A heavy sigh came back through the phone. "I hope this is quick, I have a meeting in a few minutes."

"Yes. Look, Peter Foster-Fewster turned up at my office this morning with some lunatic looking gold-digger. He's only just met her. At first glance, I'd say she's getting her claws stuck in. He's so naïve sometimes."

"If she's planning to syphon his money in the name of love, well, that's his look out, surely. None of our business."

"That's why I'm calling. I think there may be another scenario. The Bassinotts might have planted her."

"What? Why?"

"To watch the end game, as the auction approaches and happens. A direct line into me. She'll be tasked with treading all over Foster-Fewster as a means of getting close to me, before reporting back if I'm up to anything. Then should the twits get the money, which they won't, they'll pay her off."

"Why use Peter? Why couldn't she work on you directly?"

"Because the twits know I'm too smart for that. Look, I've already seen through her. No, much better for them if they can get her entwined with Foster-Fewster. Hats off to them mind you, he's fallen for it hook, line and sinker."

"But all this is nothing more than one of your hunches, surely?"

"Would it be churlish of me to remind you that my last hunch led to Pyecoe's photographs being located and repositioned to the safe I'm currently leaning against?"

"So, what are you going to do about this girl?"

"I've tried to frighten Foster-Fewster into seeing that she's an obvious gold-digger. But I doubt he'll do anything about it. My options are limited, but maybe you could check her out, see if she has any form internationally. She's supposed to be from Finland. So, she's laughably told Foster-Fewster she's called Fin. Her passport has her as Heidi Sakala. I'll scan it and email you a copy."

"If it makes you happy. But I'm not very hopeful of finding anything. I'll run it through the criminal records our office can access, but the phrase *needle in a haystack* comes to mind. Or maybe that should be, a grain of pepper in a bowl of spaghetti bolognaise?"

"Bloody spaghetti bolognaise." Erskine spoke disparagingly. "Anyway, it's worth doing some basic surveillance on her. If nothing else, it's important you know about her in case she does turn up on Foster-Fewster's arm. I suspect she's simply a smart operator hiding behind the cover of being a ditsy artist. We need to keep her at arm's length."

"What if she's genuine and is simply an honourable friend of Peter Foster-Fewster?"

A sound like a snort came from Erskine. "If she is, I'll eat all the spaghetti in Italy."

45

"He seems a bit up himself!" Fin's laughing as we trot down the outside steps onto the Strand.

"He's a bit old school, I suppose. But he knows his stuff." However much I try to ignore it, Erskine's warning is forcing itself around inside my head. While there's nothing I want more than to prove him wrong, I don't want Fin thinking that I suspect her of anything. "Actually, he asked me if any of your artwork was out there, online or anything like that?"

"Why would he ask that?" Suddenly at a loss, Fin sounded indignant.

"He was interested. We chatted about art a bit in Bologna. Nothing more than that."

"I keep meaning to put my work online, but you know what it's like. Somehow I never get around to it."

"He was also interested in the school you'll be teaching at in London Bridge. I was a bit embarrassed, I didn't know which school it was." But as I'm speaking, I'm aware my words sound like loaded questions.

"It's none of his business. Is he checking me out, or something?" Fin stops and looks at me. "What's he worried about? Does he think I'm bad for you? Or worse, he thinks I'm a fraud? Is that what your chat was about? He's playing daddy, looking after you?"

"No, don't be silly." Wishing I hadn't started this conversation, I try to reassure her. "He was genuinely interested in you."

"What was his interest? And what do you think, Peter?" Fin's eyes are still clamped on mine. "Do you think I'm with you for the wrong reasons? I can hardly bring myself to say it. Do you think I'm only in it for the money?"

"No, I don't." Suddenly I'm furious with Erskine, for causing me to doubt her. "Absolutely not."

"But Erskine obviously does. And he's planted a seed of doubt in your mind. That's why you're asking subtle questions - to see if he's anywhere near the truth." She's summed it up, tearfully, perfectly.

But it's Erskine's view, not mine. "If I told you he does have concerns, what would you say?"

"I'd say fuck off. In fact, I am saying it. Fuck off, Erskine." Fin's face reddens as her emotions take over. "I can't go to Italy with Erskine looking down his nose at me, judging my every move. This was supposed to be a fun trip. Nothing more than that. It's not about money. My aunt Renna in Cambridge owns a massive house and it's left to me in her will. I have money in the bank and whenever I've needed help, she's always supported me. If I was motivated by money, I'd be sponging off Renna and watching telly all day in one of her six bedrooms." Fin sounds furious. "But obviously Erskine thinks I am."

But it's important to me she understands. "Just because he has concerns, it doesn't mean I share them. Obviously I don't. You must know that."

"But it does mean I can't go to Italy with you." She looks terribly upset. "You can see that, can't you? It will be horrible."

Suddenly I feel sick that I've let Erskine get to me, that I've upset her. I try to calm her down. "Look, Erskine probably thinks he's protecting me. Can't we talk about this? I really want you to come with me. And all this has come from Erskine. Not me."

Fin's silent for a moment. "I think we both need time to think about this. I wasn't expecting a reaction like his and it's really upset me." She turns away, tears streaming from her eyes. "Just think how you'd feel if you were accused of planning a robbery. That's what your Erskine has done today. And he's made you doubt me." I try to put my arm around her, but she moves away. "Please. I want to be alone."

I try to speak, but Fin puts her hand over

my mouth. "Go to Italy alone. Maybe when you're back, we can have a drink by the Thames, again. I'll bring my ancestry records and my art books. You can bring Erskine and we'll look through them together over a nice drink. Sorry to be sarcastic, but that's how I feel."

The speed of our disintegration leaves me dumbfounded. "There's nothing I can say to change your mind?" But as I watch her, Fin shakes her head, more tears falling. "I'm so sorry, Fin." I stare at her, utterly wretched. "This was the last thing I imagined happening. I wanted Erskine to meet you, because I wanted you to come with us. And because, if I'm honest, I felt proud that you wanted to be with me. Won't you at least think about it?" When she doesn't speak, I break the silence. "The flights will all be booked - so if you change your mind, give me a call?"

As Fin's eyes meet mine, seeing the sadness in them, my insides twist. All I'd been doing was trying to be straight with her. The last thing I'd ever want is to hurt her. Raising a hand in farewell, she turns away, soon merging into the busy street, until she disappears from sight.

Feeling more lost than I can remember feeling, as I amble aimlessly along the Strand, I'm consumed with a sense of bewilderment. The more I think back over the short time I've known Fin, the harder it is to believe that she is anything other than the person I thought she was, before

Erskine weighed in. Right now, I feel like I could go back into his office and knee him in the nuts. But it's not my style and I know he'd smooth-talk me out of it, anyway.

Will Fin call me before Thursday? I genuinely hope so. I try to imagine going to Italy alone, suddenly realising, without her, even the thought of the auction isn't the same.

46

"I'm guessing she didn't put up much of a fight." Clinking his fluted glass of prosecco against mine, Erskine sounds conspiratorial. We're sitting on substantial deep cushioned bar stools at Gatwick Airport's London Bar, an opulent structure with food and drinks priced to edit out the backpacking community. This oasis of calm in the middle of the departure lounge is designed to heighten 'us and them' emotions and sitting here surrounded by gleaming silver fittings and mirrored white light seems to be the perfect metaphor for my changing fortunes, though I have to admit, more than slightly marred by the circumstances of Fin's absence.

Far from convinced he's right in his assumptions, I'm not sure I particularly want to discuss them further. "Let's just say it wasn't what I planned. I've told her to call me if she changes her mind." And she still could, I suppose. A kind of dramatic last minute dash to the airport, like in the movies.

"That's hardly likely, is it? It rather sounds

as though we flushed her out. I'm certain from everything you've said she was onto you."

I shake my head. "I'm not so sure. How can she have known about me? I mean, if you're right, she must have been stalking me, certainly on that first night we met."

Erskine smiled knowingly. "It's what they do. She's likely part of a team. When it comes to money, you'd be surprised the lengths people go to in order to make things look normal, accidental or whatever." Erskine is doing his best to be the friendly voice of reason but before I can think of a reply, he raises his glass and takes a respectful sip, followed by an approving nod and an expression of superiority to suggest he's chosen wisely from the impressive wine list. Following his lead, I let a puddle of gently fizzing bubbles settle momentarily on my tongue before letting them slide on their way.

As the wine curls into my brain, I think about mentioning Fin again, but Erskine beats me to it. "Hmm, that's rather lovely." He looks admiringly into his glass. "Look, I know you're upset about the girl... but it's time to focus on the future. We should be celebrating! We're off to Italy to get your fortune." He chinks his glass against mine again. "And I reckon my sixth sense, or lawyer's nose as I call it, has stopped someone else getting their hands on it."

I shrug again. "I should probably sound more

grateful. It's just that if you're wrong about her motives, I've lost, well, a good friend."

Erskine's ready with an answer for that, too. "A friend who ran away at the first sign of being rumbled? Sort of friend you could do without, I'd have thought. You gave her every opportunity to talk things through, *to back up her own stories*. But did she? No, of course not. She's disappeared into the ether and moved onto the next mark. Classic behaviour from someone who has a secret to hide."

It does seem odd that she just disappeared. "It's completely out of character from the person I thought I knew."

"Exactly. Now, I reckon a change of subject is what we need. Food. How about a few oysters to give the wine something to think about? What do you say?"

I smile awkwardly, amazed at how easily Erskine changes gear from character-assassinating my new lover to ordering raw shellfish. But that's a top lawyer in action, I guess. "Go for it. I've never had one before."

But Erskine doesn't need my encouragement. He's already calling the barman who smiles obsequiously at the request for half a dozen fresh oysters. When they're placed in front of us, the shells are already prized opened and ready to eat.

Picking one up, Erskine becomes my self-appointed mentor. "Two approaches. Either down in one, or give them a single chew before swallowing. I'm a down in one chap. Right. Tally ho!" And with that, he throws his head back and slurps the contents down. Humming with delight, he finishes off the performance with another slug of bubbles, before gesturing for me to take one. As he pushes the plate with the five remaining oysters in front of me, suddenly they look repulsive. Picking up a shell and studying the contents does nothing to warm me to the task, but I brave it out and follow Erskine's technique. Throwing my head back, the oyster slides from its severed moorings into the pit of my stomach, as in that moment, I know it will be the last fresh oyster I ever eat. Shoving the plate back in front of Erskine, I leave him to it, replenishing both our flutes with more sparkling wine in the hope that the spritz effect will jet-wash my mouth enough to obliterate the taste of Blackpool beach.

With less than an hour to go until we board our flight, any hopes I had of Fin making a dramatic last minute appearance evaporate. Deep down, I'd suspected they were irrational, but stranger things have happened. Now that I know she isn't coming, I need to try to focus on something else.

As I look at the departure boards, I notice that there are direct flights to Florence, something I hadn't considered before. "Why are we flying to Bologna when there are direct flights to Florence? Wouldn't it make more sense to fly straight there?" I ask him.

"Not in my experience. Plenty more flight options in and out of Bologna and its only half an hour to Florence by train. And it can be heaving with people at this time of year."

"Is Valentina joining us for dinner tonight?" I mentally fill Fin's void with a scenic alternative.

"That was the hope, but unfortunately she's busy. She has a long-standing client dinner she can't get out of. Bit of a bugger really, would have been useful to catch up. But never mind." Noticing our glasses are empty, the barman is straight on it. Wringing out the last drop of wine from our almost empty bottle, with around half an hour to go before we need to head for our departure gate, we decide another bottle would be perfectly acceptable. Remembering we're staying at the Grand Majestic Hotel, there really are worse places to sleep off a lunchtime session. As more sparkling wine courses through my body, the thought of being in Bologna's most prestigious hotel seems wonderful.

Before long, Erskine taps his watch and gathering my poise and belongings, we head for the departure gate. As we walk, Erskine seems unaffected by the bubbles, while I feel distinctly wobbly. Thanks to the travellators, we make it there in time. Once safely on the plane, I think back to my first flight with Erskine, a couple of months ago. Then we were off to see Valentina Russo, to sign all the paperwork and set things in motion. And here we are now, just a day away from the auction. The intervening weeks have felt like a personal rollercoaster, my emotions sinking to the point where I've doubted everyone involved, before being rocketed sky high. Then, in the last few days, Fin's entered the picture. And left it. But at last, I'm on a plane taking me to the final event, where I will watch my grandmother's jewels being sold for millions, a fortune that will change my life forever. With thoughts reeling freely around my mind, the plane begins to taxi, and my already heavy eyelids begin to close as I'm subconsciously transported forwards to my luxurious hotel bed.

What feels like a momentary lapse comes to an abrupt end as the plane makes a thumping first attempt to land. Its second landing, about three seconds later, is only marginally better, but as the engines scream into reverse thrust, at least we seem to be connected to the ground. Having slept for the entire flight, I come to terms with the fact that I'm not yet in the wonderful privacy of my hotel room.

Running my hands through my hair in an attempt to make myself look like I haven't been crumpled into a small seat for an hour and a half, I focus my thoughts on splashing water on my face, once we're inside the airport.

To his credit, as we disembark and walk through the terminal building, for once Erskine doesn't attempt to make small talk. Then after a freshen up and reclaiming our bags, we're in a taxi and being driven through Bologna's outskirts on the way to Via Indipendenza and the Grand Majestic Hotel. Feeling more human with each passing minute, I'm excited to be back in Bologna. Erskine had the right idea to be based here rather than Florence. To me, it feels like coming home.

Pulling up outside the hotel, it's the first time I've really felt that I want, even need, the trappings of wealth. The thought of staying in the small hotel I'd used a few weeks ago, no longer thrills me. Instead, I find myself wanting the comfort and, if I'm honest, the sense of privilege that comes with money. It isn't that I feel arrogant, but it seems like a shift has happened since my last visit. When I first walked up these steps with Erskine a couple of months ago, I felt out of place, embarrassed even, at what seemed like excessive extravagance. But now, the prospect of being treated like royalty whilst surrounded by luxury and comfort, feels almost justified.

As we get out of the taxi, I see the same old man who caught my eye, the first time I came here. Just as crippled and blind as I remember, he's sitting on a step, his upturned hat on the ground in front of him. My self-righteous mood instantly dissipates. Whatever I do when my money finally reaches me, I reaffirm my previous note to self to come back here and find him.

Going up to him, as Erskine disappears into the hotel, I press some ten euro notes into one of his hands, wishing I knew how to tell him that I won't forget him and I'll be back.

Hurrying up the steps to the hotel, inside Erskine's already at the reception desk. "Why don't we meet back down here in a couple of hours?" he suggests as he hands me my key card. "I've got a bit of catching up to do with the office and you could probably do with some decent rest after being scrunched into that plane seat."

After the flight, I can't think of anything nicer. "Well, if you've got work to do, I can certainly look after myself. I'll drop my bags up in my room and then go for a wander around the square." It's not quite what I have in mind but I don't want to be seen as lazy.

"Perfect. Let's meet back here say, six-thirty? Gives us just over two hours."

"Sounds like a plan. I'll grab the lift with you before I head out."

With my room on the fourth floor, and Erskine's on the sixth, I leave him to ascend the final two levels alone as I saunter loose limbed down the corridor, dreaming of the sumptuous bed that awaits me, with no intention of leaving the room until six-thirty, when I'll meet up with

Erskine again.

After the subtle click of the door when I touch it with the key card, I let myself in, the door closing automatically behind me. Dropping my bags, I kick off my shoes and shuffle across the room, where I remove the complimentary chocolates from the pillow. The time for a spread-eagle splat can no longer be delayed and standing at the end of the bed with outstretched arms, I fall like a tree.

As my head comes to rest, a deep rosy scent atomises from the bosomy softness of the pillows. A few moments of utter calm pass before I wrestle my clothes off, tossing and kicking them to the floor. Having just enough wherewithal to set my alarm for six, I sink into blissful semi-consciousness, then full blackout.

Falling through the air, as I hurtle towards the ground, I'm trying to release my parachute, while a few feet away, there's another parachutist falling at the same speed, waving his phone at me. Hearing my own phone ring, as I spiral out of control, I can't locate it. The other parachutist pulls his chord and jerks upwards out of view as I continue to plunge towards the ground. With the last few feet approach at blurring speed, I begin to scream. Then sudden silence before I'm hit by a familiar fragrance of rose petals as for a few seconds, I contemplate whether I'm floating in a beautiful afterlife.

My phone rings again, confirming I'm very much in this world, despite being partially incapacitated with a dead arm from sleeping heavily on it. Cocooned under the bedcovers, with what feels like a massively bloated hand on the end of an arm made of rubber, trying to locate the phone proves impossible, before it stops ringing. A minute later when the phone rings again, swiping away the bivouac of sheets, I'm sufficiently compos mentis to face answering it.

"Hello." In my haste to answer, I fail to notice who's calling.

"Peter, it's Erskine. It's nearly half past seven. Are you OK?"

"Jesus, really? Sorry. Same problem as last time. These beds are just too comfortable. Give me twenty minutes and I'll be down."

"I'm in Piazza Maggiore. Gave up on you! Just wandering in the evening sunshine. Why don't we meet at the bar opposite the church here? Shall we say eight o'clock?"

47

"Valentina, it's me again. I've just spoken to Peter. He was asleep in his room. I'll be meeting him soon for a drink here in the square. You have no need to worry about him."

"I'm allowed to worry, Erskine." Valentina retorted.

"That's why I'm calling you back." Erskine spoke curtly.

Valentina spoke slowly. "Obviously I was concerned when you said he seems to have disappeared this evening. He's the only reason I'm going along with any of this. With the auction tomorrow, and the blackmailing twins hiding somewhere, who knows what's going to happen?"

"Everything will be fine. But I just want to confirm a couple of things regarding timings. At some point after tomorrow's auction, the twins will order me to email Gallo-Moretti accounts department requesting confirmation of the bank details for the proceeds of the auction to go to. As soon as I receive confirmation back from Gallo-Moretti, I will forward it to the fraud twits as demanded, with the result that they will naturally believe the money is going to them. I will call you shortly after that, so you can switch the Bassinott's bank account details to mine. You will need to be at Gallo-Moretti all day tomorrow, because I don't know when they will ask me to send the email."

"I already know all this."

"One can never be too careful, Valentina. In any case, the fraud twits have done exactly what I thought they would, so maybe I could be given some credit. My predictions were spot on."

"Am I meant to be impressed?"

"Maybe you will be in the next couple of days when all this comes together, the money rightfully comes to us and you get your commission." The full force of Erskine's self-confidence was back.

"Commission I would have got anyway if you hadn't been blackmailed due to your dark history." Valentina sounded suitably scathing.

"Look we'd better leave it there. Peter will be out here in the square at any moment and I don't want him to think I'm talking behind his back."

"Even though you are?"

"Oh, for God's sake Valentina, let it go for a while. We need to work with clear minds to get this right. I'll see you at Gallo-Moretti in the morning."

"Enjoy your evening, Erskine. Maybe you

should avoid the spaghetti bolognaise tonight." Valentina said pointedly, abruptly ending the call.

With the line dead, Erskine addressed thin air. "I'll eat what I fucking well want."

48

Jogging lightly down the steps of the Grand Majestic, the September evening is surprisingly warm after the cool of the hotel. There's no sign of the old man who was sitting on the step opposite and I set off to find Erskine, who should only be five minutes away in the big square. Walking the short distance up Via Indipendenza, I imagine Fin by my side, thinking she would be here if Erskine hadn't stuck his oar in. With a few glasses of wine sloshing around my head, I'd begun to wonder if he might be right, but now I've sobered up I'm struggling to square his views with the girl I got to know.

I can picture her here - laughing and marvelling at the endless shoe shops and their colourful window displays stopping shoppers in their tracks. We'd be in and out of gelato stalls, little bars and atmospheric dusty shops that sell everything and look like they've been in families for generations. Before meeting Fin, I would have been happy enjoying all this alone, but now I'd give anything to be sharing it with her.

Once in the piazza, I spot him immediately outside the bar opposite the big church, looking like he's scrolling through something on his phone.

He looks up just before I have the opportunity to surprise him. "Arh, at last, sleeping beauty has woken!" Erskine manages not to attach any irritation to his welcome.

"Yes, sorry to be so late. That prosecco at the airport completely wiped me out. Anyway, I'm ready for some more! Calm the nerves before tomorrow and all that."

"Well, no-one can blame you - certainly not me. Incredibly exciting times. We should take it a bit easy tonight, I reckon. A good meal and an early night is my plan."

"Sounds perfect to me."

"Great. Well, I know a nice restaurant a few streets away. Camilleri's. Lovely old place." Taking his cue from my nod, Erskine stretches out an arm in the direction of the restaurant and we begin the short walk through the throng of late summer tourists.

The restaurant is full of charm and I'm particularly struck with the traditional décor and interesting touches, like kitchen equipment from a bygone era dangling from the ceiling. On Erskine's recommendation I order the steak, expecting him to have the same, so that I'm surprised when a plate of pasta is placed in front of him. "I didn't have you down as a spaghetti bolognaise man."

"Ooh... don't ever say that here!" Erskine scrunches up his face disapprovingly. "In fact, it's something of an insult to call it that. It's not a name that ever gets used in Italy. Ragu is what they call the sauce - usually with tagliatelle. But for some reason, I just fancied spaghetti."

As we start eating, I can't help feeling I've got the better choice of dishes. As we chat about the charm of Italian restaurants, I'm struck with Erskine's interest in spiralling the pasta onto his fork. It's both obsessive and clumsy, rather like a child's first encounter with spaghetti. A couple of times he holds the fork between us in an upright position while he emphasises a point he's discussing, as though he's trying to show me a thing or two. The only problem is every time he does it, the spaghetti rapidly unravels then falls off.

Whatever the reason, Erskine's put me off ever trying that technique, eventually resorting to cutting his spaghetti into shorter lengths and sucking them in. In fact, he seems quite lost in his food as he continues to tackle it, but then his phone rings. Again, it seems slightly out of character as he hurriedly taps various pockets, eventually locating it in the inside pocket of his jacket, hanging over the back of his chair.

"Hello? Hello?" Erskine looks at his phone. "Blast, they've gone. Sorry, Peter, but I need to call back. Please excuse me - I'll pop outside for a couple of minutes. Probably much easier. Back in a tick." With badly disguised urgency, Erskine leaves me alone at the table. A table that when we arrived earlier, he generously insisted I take the better seat with the window view. Now, without his carton head blocking most of that view, I'm able to gaze over an atmospheric slice of Bologna street life. On the other side of the street, pacing along the pavement, Erskine is obviously in a heated conversation with someone, emphasising his words with a raised hand. Is he in trouble with Mrs E again? Before I have too much time to dwell on his behaviour, he's quick-stepping his way over the road, then back at the table, blocking my view again.

"Sorry, Peter. Just some personal things I had to deal with. Actually, still have to deal with. Apologies, but can I suggest we finish up here as soon as, then head back to the hotel? I have some calls and things to do tonight. But you're obviously free to carry on doing whatever you wish. Unexpected events and all that, but I need to dip out early."

It's not an issue for me. Fancying a few drinks on my own in the piazza, in some ways I'm happy that Erskine is turning in. "Not a problem. I'll take a wander around the Quadrilatero and have a nightcap or two. Everything OK with you?" I try to sound unconcerned, but I can't help wondering. "The phone call... nothing's come up related to the auction, has it?"

Erskine suddenly looks horrified. "No, no, no. So sorry, Peter. This has nothing whatsoever to do with the auction! Totally remiss of me to let my personal issues cut across our evening. None of this should be about me. You should be looking forward to tomorrow without me putting a dampener on things. How about I settle up here and we'll have a grappa in the square, before I head back and deal with my workload?"

It's good to know there are no problems with the auction. It still doesn't take much to spook me. Still feels like I'm in a dream, sometimes. I'll be much more relaxed when it's all over. "A drink on the way back would be good!"

Leaving the restaurant, the evening is still warm as the last of the sunlight catches the tops of the taller buildings. Piazza Maggiore is alive with buskers and tourists and we take a seat outside the bar opposite the church.

Erskine orders two large glasses of grappa. "Cheers, Peter. Here's to tomorrow. It's a massive day for all of us. This is the culmination of a huge amount of work and I appreciate that since our first meeting, this must have felt like an eternity to you. But only a few hours to go now... so here's to it." Erskine clunks his glass against mine.

These are thick functional glasses, a million miles from the showy flutes we chinked at Gatwick's swanky bar only this morning. "Cheers to you, Erskine. And thank you for all you've done." My minimalist compliment clearing the way for us both to make short work of the grappa.

Our glasses have hardly made it back to the table when Erskine stands up purposefully. "Right, that was lovely, but that's me done. I'm back to the hotel. What are your plans, staying on here or heading back with me?"

"I think I'll stay a little longer. A bit more booze will probably help me to get to sleep!"

Patting me on the shoulder, Erskine laughs his professional laugh before heading back to the hotel. Even though the sun has fully set, sitting here in jeans and a t-shirt, the temperature is wonderfully comfortable. I think about walking to another bar just for the sake of variety, but every time I seriously consider moving, I find myself magnetised to the spot. It's the perfect place from which to watch life beautifully drifting by, while each time I think about tomorrow, pulses of excitement surge through me.

Nearly an hour and two large glasses of wine later, I catch the waiter's eye for the bill. Then just as he acknowledges me, I'm stunned to hear my name being called. "Peter? Peter... hello, how are you?"

As I look around, I can hardly believe my eyes. It's Valentina Russo. When I saw her here a few weeks ago, I avoided her, slightly embarrassed at having had a boozy lunch. But this feels different. It's a nice evening and she looks like she might have had a drink, too. In any case, she certainly seems friendlier than when I bumped into her on the stairs in Gallo-Moretti.

As she comes over to my table I get up. "Tina! First, we bump into each other in Florence, now here. Incredible!" I realise I must sound a bit pissed. "I was just about to get another drink. Are you just passing, or can I get you one too?"

"Not such an amazing coincidence." Valentina pauses as we double-cheek kiss. "I do live here! I've been out with a couple of girlfriends, but a nightcap would be lovely. Big day tomorrow!" Valentina takes the same seat that was home to Erskine's buttocks not an hour before.

"Yes. You've not long missed Erskine, actually. We had dinner, but he headed back to the hotel early. Something urgent popped up, I think." The waiter appears with my bill which I pretend I didn't ask for and after checking with Valentina, I order two glasses of chianti.

"Ah. Yes, Erskine. Shame I missed him. Busy man at the moment. Did you find a nice restaurant?"

"Camilleri's, down that way a couple of streets. One of Erskine's old haunts." I point somewhere behind me. "Shame you couldn't join us, Tina. He said you had something on tonight." Erskine had told me she was at a client dinner, rather than out with girlfriends, but not wanting to put her on the spot, I'm intentionally vague.

"Just a drink with friends. Nothing formal, I could have rearranged. Actually, I know that restaurant well. Interesting choice of his. Traditional Italian. Was the food good?"

"Mine was. Lovely steak. Oddly Erskine recommended it, but didn't have it himself!"

"Did he have spaghetti bolognaise, by any chance?" Valentina looks as if she knows the answer.

"Actually, he did! But he insisted it was called ragu. He kept trying to spiral the spaghetti onto his fork, but it kept falling off before it got to his mouth. Quite funny to watch. Not sure he saw the funny side, mind you. He seemed almost obsessive about it."

"I'll tell you a story about that one day." Again, Valentina is being mysterious. I think about asking her to elaborate, but she changes the subject before I get a chance. "So, apart from Erskine, you're on this trip alone?"

"Yes. I had planned to bring a friend... but sadly, it didn't work out."

"That's a shame." Valentina raises an arched eyebrow. "It's a pity you can't share this special time with someone close. Mind you, I suppose with an event like tomorrow's, you have to be careful who you'd bring. With great wealth comes great responsibility, as they say."

"I guess. But I don't mind spending time in my own company. It probably all goes back to being orphaned as a child." I stop myself. "Apologies. You don't want to know all this! I'm afraid the wine is talking. We should talk about something else!"

"No, it's fine. I'm sorry to hear about your loss at such a young age." Valentina says respectfully. "So as a result of losing your parents young, you're saying you don't have many close friends?

"Something like that."

"That's so sad. Really sad that there's no-one special."

I'm struck with how sympathetic Valentina seems towards my situation. I guess that's the magic of wine; in vino veritas. It's working for me too, and I can't stop myself from mentioning Fin.

"I met someone recently." As Valentina nods, I don't need any more encouragement to continue. "A girl. I really connected with her. It turns out she was orphaned too, and I totally related to everything she said. She was a little unconventional, but we got on like a house on fire. But I liked that about her - she was colourful."

"Is that the person who was going to come here with you?"

"Yes. But everything happened very quickly. Too quickly, probably. Meeting her, getting together, deciding to come here, then deciding not to. All within a few days. It was a whirlwind."

"I was going to ask..." She breaks off. "I'm sorry. It's none of my business."

I'm flattered by her interest. "No, not at all. Ask anything you want."

"Was it her decision not to come?" Valentina sips her wine.

It seems a strange question and I ponder for a few moments. "Hmm, interesting question. Yes, I suppose it was. But not directly because of anything I'd said. It was something that someone else said to me - about her. Her being Fin by the way - that's her name. Basically, this other person accused her of being a gold-digger."

"And she just decided to end things because you mentioned what someone else had said?" Valentina sounds surprised.

"Yes. It sounds bad, I know, as if she's been caught out and then ran away. But it wasn't just the words that upset her. It was more to do with the person who said them."

I watch Valentina raise her eyebrows with apparent bemusement.

"It was actually Erskine. He thought she was out to fleece me." This time Valentina's eyebrows now seem to have risen beyond the point of comfort. "It was after a meeting I had with him, on Monday. I took Fin with me to introduce her and ask him to organise flights, hotels etcetera. Everything seemed fine until after the meeting, when he asked if he could have a couple of minutes with me - privately. That's when he warned me. He had no doubt she was a con artist."

"And what do *you* think?" Valentina asks, her eyebrows now lowered to pretty much their normal location.

"I can see why Erskine jumped to his conclusion, but I'm not convinced he's right. I just can't believe she is a con artist. Sure, we only got to know each other over a few days, but firstly, I really can't see how she could have targeted me. And on top of that, there was something almost magical about the way we clicked. I did try to reassure her that it was Erskine's opinion, not mine, but the damage was done. I don't interpret her not being here as running away from the accusation. I'm sure she must be upset with me. After what he said, how could Fin possibly spend a few days with Erskine in the picture?"

"Will you try to get in touch with her again?"

I shrug. "I want to. She has my number, but hasn't called. Maybe, with luck our paths will cross again. It sounds crazy, but for the first time in my life, I feel there's a gap. I genuinely miss her. I thought I'd never say these words out loud, but I think, well... I think it may be love."

"That's tragic. And sweet. And everything else in between." Valentina looks at me sympathetically.

"Anyway, you haven't stopped by to hear about all my troubles. And how much trouble can

I really be in when Giovanna's jewels are being auctioned tomorrow?"

"Well, on that note, I assume Erskine told you there is a lot of new interest in your auction?"

"Really? That's fantastic! The more the merrier. But to answer your question, no he didn't mention it. Maybe he forgot. He seems busy with something else at the moment."

Valentina's eyebrows are given another workout, before she carries on. "Specifically, two Russian oligarchs have registered their interest in the jewels. That could be quite significant if it gets into a serious bidding war. Erskine really should have mentioned it. Never mind, not long until all will become crystal clear." Valentina finishes her wine. "And talking of tomorrow, it's time for me to get back home for a reasonably early night. I'll be heading to Gallo-Moretti before you and Erskine. I look forward to seeing you there, bright eyed and bushy tailed, as you English say. Thank you for the drink, it was good to catch up on your news. I'll keep my fingers crossed that things work out for you and Fin."

"Thank you. Good to see you too. I'm going to have one more for the road before I head back." I'm hoping it'll knock me out and I'll be able to stop thinking about tomorrow.

After another double kiss, Valentina glides away and I'm left alone at the bar to dwell on the auction. As I think about the additional, even more thrilling prospect of the jewels selling to the Russians in excess of the reserve, one nightcap isn't enough to switch off my excited, overactive brain. Signalling to the waiter, I order another.

49

As I pull open the heavy brocade curtains and another bright Bologna morning meets my eyes, any hangover remnants are completely obliterated from my constitution by the excitement and adrenalin coursing through my body as I realise the day of the auction has arrived.

Somehow, until now, I've kept a relatively tight lid on runaway thoughts of millions in the bank and being permanently free of financial strife. But as I get ready to meet Erskine for breakfast, that lid has very nearly worked its way loose.

Showered and spruced, I skip down the wide hotel stairs in preference to taking the lift. I have too much nervous energy, the stairs helping to disperse some of it, but not enough, and my springy restlessness carries me outside, down the hotel steps to the pavement, where I take a deep lungful of fresh air, before heading back up to reception.

Blood suitably oxygenated, I head through to the opulent breakfast room where I join Erskine.

"Peter, good morning. You're looking well!

You must be excited, you've actually woken up on time!" In a dark suit and open collar white shirt, he looks relaxed and in control.

"Indeed. Amazed I slept at all. The grappa helped. But now I need coffee."

After Erskine effortlessly catches the attention of a waiter, we order coffee and I follow his recommendation of *poached eggs with bacon, food of champions*, then watch him systematically unfold his serviette. "You'll never guess who I had a drink with last night."

Looking up, Erskine halts his unfolding. "Last night? When last night?"

"After you left me in the square. Valentina Russo walked past. She was on her way home, so we had a drink together."

As he listens, a look of surprise forms on Erskine's face. "Really?"

"Yep, she was heading back after a night out. Actually, thinking about it, didn't you tell me she was going to a client dinner last night?"

"If memory serves me well, I think that's what she said. But it was a couple of weeks ago I asked her."

"Odd. She said she could have rearranged and joined us. She was just out for a drink with a couple of girlfriends."

Looking perplexed, Erskine pulls another face to suggest he's scrutinising all his powers of recall. "I don't understand that. Must have got our wires crossed. Never mind. Did she stay long with you?"

I frown slightly. It seems a strange reaction, when surely *that must have been a nice surprise,* or *how was she* would be more normal. "She stayed a little while, long enough for a glass of wine, anyway."

"Did she have much to say?" Erskine asks what seems like another odd question.

"We chatted about everything and nothing. The restaurant, what we had for dinner. We even talked about Fin."

"Getting on like a house on fire, by the sound of it."

I can't decide if Erskine sounds disapproving. But then it hits me again. He's jealous! He obviously still fancies his chances and I represent a bit of a gooseberry. Poor old Erskine, suddenly I feel just a tad sorry for him, probably stuck in a boring marriage with Mrs E, as he calls her, his head full of Valentina Russo fantasies. If he thinks he's got any chance of schmoozing her, keeping me at arms-length would suit his agenda much better. After all, I'm younger than him and in a few hours, I could be considerably wealthier. Attributes that I imagine Erskine believes Valentina would find attractive. Then, as our breakfast trolley nears, he regains his focus.

"Well, you certainly are a man of coincidences, Peter Foster-Fewster. Shame we didn't all meet up last night, but hopefully Valentina will be able to join us for dinner this evening."

"That would be good. Incidentally, she mentioned that there was some Russian interest in the auction. She seemed surprised you hadn't mentioned it to me."

"Yes, that's right. I was in two minds whether to mention it or not. I'm always cautious about rumours. Can lead to tremendous disappointment. But now you know, just keep everything crossed they turn up! Anyway, busy day ahead. Time to crack on with this rather splendid looking breakfast!"

Agreeing wholeheartedly, I watch the waiter efficiently fill most of the empty gaps on the table with loaded toast racks, coffee, butter, jams, milk, biscotti, followed by two large plates of poached eggs on toast with bacon. Efficiently, we tuck in.

Returning to our rooms after breakfast, we collect overnight bags. Erskine had the foresight to book this hotel for the complete duration of our stay, even though we won't be here tonight, negating the need to check out. Leaving the hotel, it's a pleasant fifteen minute walk down Via Indipendenza to the station where we catch the 10:00 fast train to Florence. Less than thirty minutes later, our train has pummelled its way through the mountains and swings into Florence station. The bizarre reality of the day ahead feels so bewildering that Erskine has hardly said a word on the journey, until now as we walk past the Duomo. So magnificent is the cathedral that even just being near it inspires extended appreciation of its greatness. A few minutes later, we cross the Ponte Vecchio and turn into Via Crostini. Tapping on Erskine's arm, I stop momentarily to point to the jade green chesterfield in the antiques shop window. "That's the first thing I'm going to buy after the auction."

As he quietly nods his approval, we carry on walking. The sign for Gallo-Moretti is already clearly visible at the other end of Via Crostini, my legs feeling like jelly as we walk the last few metres and stand in front of the black glass doors.

"After you, sir." Standing back, Erskine gestures towards the entrance.

Even though I've been here before, as the doors open and I enter the circular reception area, it's as though I'm walking into a parallel universe. This is the day, the time and the place where my life will change, forever.

50

"So, it's finally here. Your big day!" Valentina looks wonderful in a red top and skirt, as she passes me a coffee in her office.

"Yes, I can hardly believe it. It's all very surreal!" I say, slightly embarrassed that I'm not feeling more commanding and that everything is happening around me, while I'm just a passive bystander.

Sitting on the same sofa, Erskine chips in. "It'll all be very real in just over an hour, when the bidding starts!"

Valentina agrees. "Yes, things will fall into place very quickly. And then when the hammer comes down, it will all be over. Well, nearly. It'll just be a matter of getting the money to you as soon as possible. Isn't that right, Erskine?"

"Oh, absolutely. Things will happen very quickly. Then you can get your green sofa!"

"Anyway, Peter, I'd like you to meet Marco Spinetti." Valentina says before taking a sip of her coffee. "He's been overseeing your auction lot, making sure the right people know about it. He'd like to say hello and put a face to a name.

"Sure, no problem." I don't have any burning desire to meet him, but with the minutes going so slowly, if it helps to kill some time, why not? I remember someone once telling me that the difference between genius and madness is almost non-existent and there's a strange version of the same counter-intuitive reasoning going on in my head. I ought to be cock-a-hoop, but instead, I feel completely terrified.

But my mood improves when Spinetti arrives, full of life and laughter. "Mr Foster-Fester! How lovely to meet you! I hope you are enjoying your time in Italy and here, in the beautiful city of Florence." He shakes my hand. "We are confident of a really fantastic auction today. All you have to do is sit back and enjoy everything here at Gallo-Moretti. Maybe after, I can give you a tour. And of course, if you ever need to release any valuables again, just get it touch with me."

As Spinetti juts a business card towards me with his chunky fingers, I realise this is all a sales pitch. But I take it happily, as like all good salesmen, he's naturally entertaining and relies on no input from his audience. After generous handshakes amid good humoured farewells, Valentina subtly engineers Spinetti out of her office, which returns to relative silence as she taps away at her computer and Erskine reads a magazine. I watch them both, noticing Erskine finding it difficult not to keep glancing at Valentina. He definitely fancies her, but there is nothing in her behaviour to suggest the feeling is mutual.

The peace is broken when a phone bleeps. Picking up her mobile, Valentina reads a message. "Right, this is it, Peter! We can go to the auction room. The doors will be closed to buyers for another twenty minutes, but I suggest we go down now and get good seats. Make sure you have your identity lanyards on." With Valentina sounding in control, Erskine winks at me as he stands, making sure his lanyard is properly suspended around his neck with the name card facing the right way around, at the same time patting his stomach, seemingly proud there's no obvious middle-aged spread.

"Right, here we go." Erskine sounds excited. "Let's see how deep those Russian pockets are."

With Valentina leading the way; Erskine and I follow. Leaving her office, we walk along a small corridor before reaching a regular set of stairs at the end. The auction room is on the next floor down and as we get closer, it's obvious from the looming hubbub that a lot of people are mustering. Unlocking a small door, Valentina pushes it open. Suddenly, we're in a corner of the registration area, among lots of nattily dressed people talking in groups, whilst more people emerge from the wide staircase leading up from the reception area. Indicating our direction of travel with a raised finger, Valentina guides Erskine and me towards the registration desks through air full of expectation and expensive cologne.

As Valentina breezes us through the registration and security process, it's a neat demonstration of 'it's not what you know, but who you know" before we push through the heavy doors and into the hushed auction room.

Today, it seems smaller than I remember, but no less impressive. A handful of officials whisper among themselves while technicians quietly run through their light and sound checks. Following Valentina's suggestion, we take a seat in the front row. I'm not sure it's how Erskine would have orchestrated the seating plan, but as Valentina invites him to sit first, then me to his left, before she takes a seat to my left, she seems quietly focussed. From my place between the two of them, I watch the big screen above the lectern come alive with a message welcoming everyone to Gallo-Moretti.

"You could hear a pin drop!" I say to Erskine, as quietly as a pin dropping.

"The quiet before the storm." Erskine jokes, addressing both of us.

"Interesting prediction." Valentina says pointedly.

When Erskine shrugs, for a moment, I'm left wondering if there's a deeper meaning to her words, but as the doors open noisily and the public start filing into the auction room, the moment passes. Watching the clock on the screen counting down to the start of the day's proceedings, with just under five minutes to go, I'm trying with all my might to be the model of calm, but already my butterflies are beginning to get out of control.

It's nothing like I imagined it would be. I'd imagined I'd be laughing and joking with Erskine, and I wouldn't have a care in the world. But even Erskine is unusually subdued, and to some extent, Valentina too. There's been so much build up to today, that now I'm so full of adrenalin, I'm feeling sick.

With one minute to go and at least a hundred people settled, the lights dim and a spotlight focuses on the lectern. My heart thumping, I glance at Erskine who's clearly tense, then at Valentina, who at least manages a reassuring smile.

Just as when I was here some weeks ago, the same smartly dressed auctioneer walks to the lectern and welcomes everyone. But not quickly. He seems to go on and on, in a process that feels like it's taking forever. Wishing he'd just get on with it, as if I've communicated telepathically, he stops.

"This is it," Erskine whispers in my right ear.

Then Valentina explains what's happening into my left ear. "The jewels are going to be sold in five lots." Her soft voice and perfume provide a surprisingly welcome distraction. "Starting with the items that have the lowest reserve, then going up in value. It's the set five of diamond broaches first. Reserve is €250,000."

"Can you keep whispering?" I whisper. "Otherwise I won't understand what's happening!"

As she nods once, the jewels are placed on the display area before being brought to life in high definition on the screen above. Moving his head away from the microphone, the auctioneer clears his throat in readiness to open the bidding.

Poised for the simultaneous translation which begins with the auctioneer's description of the item, Valentina's ready as it starts.

"OK. The opening bid is for the reserve price, on the internet. Next bid in the room at 275. Now 300. 350. 375. 375. I think that's it? No, 400 on the internet. No more bids. Sold. €400,000. Very good start."

Leaning forward, Erskine makes sure we can both see his emphatic thumbs up.

"Wow, that all happened quickly. Who bought them?" I ask Valentina, completely shell-shocked at the speed and price.

"We'll probably never know. It was an internet sale. Anyway, the next lot is just about to start. It's the diamond bracelets, reserve is €300,000."

This time as I sit there, my nervousness is

replaced by pure excitement as Valentina's muted commentary begins.

"Here we go. Starting bid is 300, hitting the reserve again. 325, 350, 375, 400, 425. Stuck on 425, it's with the internet. 450 back in the room. 475 internet, that's probably it. Sold. €475,000. Total so far, €875, 000. Three more lots to go."

While Erskine and Valentina take it in their stride, again I sit there, dumbfounded, by both the speed and the sums of money involved.

Erskine leans across and speaks softly "Looks like whoever's bidding online is going to go one more than the final bid in the room. It's good, but if we had two online bidders at it, prices could go sky high." He's looking considerably more animated than he did ten minutes ago. But then, we all are.

Valentina whispers. "OK, third lot. It's the first necklace. Amazing piece, gold with emeralds and diamonds. Reserve is €500,000."

"Looks absolutely stunning." I whisper back to Valentina. Rolling her eyes, she holds her hand against her chest as if to say, 'if I could, I'd buy it'.

"The first bid is in, again at the reserve. 525. 550. 575. 600. 625. Same as before, it's with the internet. Will the room go for one more? Yes, 650. Internet straight back with 675. And sold for €675,000. Running total €1,550,000."

"Now it gets interesting." Erskine whispers into my right ear. "The next two lots are sets of jewels, not individual items and worth much more. Watch this space."

Then Valentina whispers into my other ear. "This should now get much more interesting. It's sets of jewels, not just one." She points up at the screen. "Rings, brooches, bracelets, necklaces, all coordinated using gold, platinum, silver, diamonds, sapphire. The list goes on. Just stunning."

Genuinely speechless, I study them, thinking about their history and their incredible journey here today, as Valentina whispers. "It's about to start. Reserve is €2m. First bid hits the reserve. Going up in 50s. 100. 150. 200. 250. 300. 400, going up in 100s now. 500. 600. 700. 800. 900. €3m... €4m... €5m. €5.1m. It's stopped with the internet again. I think that will be it. Sold. €5.1 million. That's €6.650 million so far." For the first time, her eyes share my excitement. "And the biggest lot has yet to go under the hammer."

Leaning in front of me, Erskine looks at Valentina. "What's the reserve on the last lot?"

"Reserve is €3m. Based on the last lot, I imagine he will go up in 100s. This is the crown jewels of the afternoon. It has sets of rings, brooches, bracelets and necklaces, like the last lot, but the delicacy of work and quality of gems is out of this world. Also, it includes tiaras, so it really is fit for a royal family." As Valentina finishes speaking, the jewels appear on the screen and a hum of awe moves around the room. Respectfully tapping his gavel, the auctioneer starts his customary description.

"He's also saying that the first bid is over the reserve price. He's starting it at €5m. Here we go." As she talks, I'm holding my breath. Then the numbers start flying upwards. "100. 200. 300. 400. 500. 600. 700. 800. 900. €6m… €7m… €8m. The bidding has stopped. I think that's it. No, wait. Another internet bid is coming in, €8.5m. Sold!"

The room erupts into applause, probably a spontaneous reaction to relieve the collective tension as much as anything else. Valentina looks at me, delighted. "Incredible, €8.5m added to the other sales comes to… €15,150,000."

"Good day at the office." Erskine says, small beads of sweat formed on his brow, "I don't know about anyone else, but I need some fresh air."

Nodding my agreement, we get up and leave quietly before the next items are displayed. As we emerge from the black glass doors of Gallo-Moretti, sunlight is streaking along Via Crostini as the tension explodes out of me. The auction, the amount of money, the fact that it's happening to me, it's just too much to take in. Like an over-wound toy, I circle Erskine and Valentina, laughing and high-fiving them, whooping and adding fist pumps, my behaviour totally out of character, but the last half an hour has blown my brain to bits.

"I can't believe that just happened!" Uncut, class-A adrenalin of the purest quality is tripping me out and it feels incredible.

"Yes, yes, yes!! It did! Incredible result. Congratulations." Beaming, Valentina grabs my hand, rooting me to the spot while she plants kisses on both cheeks; cheeks I can feel are pulsing red after the drama of the last twenty minutes. Then Erskine clasps me in a comprehensive man hug which, either by design or accident, brings an end to my hoofing. Holding me firmly at arm's length, we stare at each other, both of us apparently gobsmacked. Wonderfully dishevelled, it looks as though it's all been too much, even for the unflappable Erskine. But before he can say anything, a look of relative normality returns to his face as his phone rings.

"Oh dear. Got to take this, excuse me." Erskine moves away to the privacy of a side street to take his call.

"No peace for the wicked, eh?" Valentina watches him as he walks away.

"Yeah, I'm not sure what Erskine's plans are for the rest of the day but I'm ecstatic - and exhausted! I just can't take in what happened in there. Not sure I'll ever come down! Reckon I could jump over the Duomo. Or drink fine Italian wine for the next few days. Anyway, what are your plans later? I know Erskine thought we might all catch up for dinner here tonight in Florence."

"Sadly, I can't. I would love to, but I have to get back to Bologna tonight. And I have to get back to work in there, before then." Valentina points towards Gallo-Moretti's front door.

"Not sure I could go back in there again today. Just too emotionally draining."

"It's very different for me. In theory, it's just another day in the office, though this has been incredibly exciting and I'm delighted for you. I feel I've been on part of this journey with you."

"Thanks for all your hard work. Hopefully today's amazing results will give your commission a boost."

"Commission? What's all this talk of commission?" Erskine returns and butts in with theatrical bluster. "A win is not a win until you collect, as they say in the racing world."

"Another one of your quaint English sayings, or should we be worried?" Valentina asks.

"Oh, you know, just trying to be funny. Failed, obviously. Probably the last half hour getting to me. We need a drink. I think we're all in a parallel universe at the moment. Can you believe what just happened in there!?"

"No, I can't." I say, looking at Erskine, "And I probably won't until I collect, as they say in the racing world."

Erskine deploys his best professional laugh. But there's an element of truth in my words. Even though I've witnessed the auction with my own eyes, I know I won't be able to fully relax until the money is in my bank account. Something I want to discuss with Erskine later, over dinner, hopefully when my head has returned to planet earth.

51

"Valentina, it's me. Erskine."

"Your name is listed on my phone, Erskine. I do know when it's you." Valentina sounded irritated. "Actually, you're not listed under *Erskine*. One day I might tell what name I use instead."

"Why not tell me now? It seems a good day to bury bad news." Erskine matched Valentina's tone, although with a few lunchtime drinks inside not quite so eloquently.

"If you really want to know. *Niccolo*. I have you listed as *Niccolo*."

"Oh, Nicholas? And why would that be?"

"Work it out for yourself. Search online for famous Italian Niccolos."

"Well Einstein's first name was Albert, so it can't be that. But I will check it later."

"Please do. Anyway, you sound like you've been drinking. I hope you've looked after Peter this afternoon. Where is he now?"

"He's sleeping it off here in the hotel. We had a very good lunch. He's rather got a taste for Chianti. And Valpolicella. And grappa. He's massively over-excited, but then who wouldn't be, thinking they've just become a millionaire?"

"Well, let's just hope he has."

"That's obviously why I'm calling. Can you talk at the moment?"

"Within reason. The auction is going on downstairs so it's quiet up here. I'm on my own in my office."

"Right. Good. Look, that phone call immediately after the auction this morning was Gerald Bassintwat. He was fully aware of the sale prices. He's on it, completely. And as expected, he wants me to send an email to Gallo-Moretti asking for confirmation of the bank account details of where the money is going. So if I send that now, can you locate the email and confirm them in an email back to me?"

"Just don't forget the sacrifices I am making here. If I get caught, I'll lose my job and... oh, forget it. What's the point of trying to get you to understand? I'll get the confirmation email back as soon as I can."

"It is appreciated, I can promise you. When I receive it, I'll forward it onto the Bassin-gits, as they've told me to do. When they see it, they'll be happily thinking the money is going to them. Then all that's left to do after that, is for you to change the account details back to mine on Gallo-Moretti's system. I'll confirm later when to do it, after I've emailed the twits."

"Sounds like you're sobering up as you speak. All this corruption, focussing the mind a little?" Valentina's words were loaded with sarcasm. "One other thing, have you completed the file against the Bassinotts, the one you'll hand to Scotland Yard if you need to?"

"Yes, totally. A bulging box file full of evidence to prove they've broken their parole agreement."

"And just so I'm clear, how will you use it?"

"When the twits realise the money isn't going to happen, they'll undoubtedly contact me. I'm 99.9% certain of that. They'll rightly assume I've got the money. Rather than carry out their blackmail threat to ruin me at that point, they'll have calculated it's worth trying to blackmail me again."

Valentina sounded confused. "Why would they try blackmailing you again? Surely, they would just carry out their original threat to drop you in it, wouldn't they? I don't get it."

"Because if they do that, they'll get nothing apart from the satisfaction of seeing me carted off to prison. So, when the twins contact me to have another go at getting the money, I'll tell them about the evidence file I have against them and the fact it will be on my contact's desk at Scotland Yard within ten minutes - unless they agree to sail off into the sunset with nothing. I'll have beaten them fair and square, honour amongst thieves.

I will make it abundantly clear that disappearing is by far their best option, otherwise the file will be sent and an arrest warrant will be issued immediately. It'll be game over for the Bassinott fraud twins once and for all. And if they decide to go down screaming and shouting about me, don't forget I have all their photographic evidence under lock and key in my office. Without those and just relying on anecdotal stuff they got from their time in prison, I'm confident I can demonstrate that they cooked up a reason to try and defraud me."

"Isn't Pikkow a potential problem in all this?" Valentina still sounded worried.

"Pyecoe? Not really. He's very ill and not likely to be around much longer. Anyway, he's got no interest in turning the spotlight on himself at this stage in his life. He'd be back in prison for perjury if he did. I'm sure I can put a few quid his way, make things a bit easier for him. I'll use Mike Reynolds to drop round a parcel of cash. That'll draw a line under that one."

"It all makes me incredibly nervous, Erskine. Makes me feel sick to be honest. I hope you know what you're doing."

"I do. Think about it. Every question you've asked, I've had an answer. Trust me, this will all work out."

"Trust you! Pleased to know you've kept that English sense of humour. Anyway, I can't talk anymore, there are people outside in the corridor. I'll reply to your email and confirm the bank details, as soon as I can."

52

Swimming underwater, cascades of tropical fish are darting around me, vivid rainbow colours shimmering and gleaming in the dazzling sunlight illuminating the blue waters. It's vibrant with life, yet silent and serene. And I can breathe, gulping in water like fresh air, tumbling with huge dolphins who high-five me before peeling away. Noticing an oyster shell on the seabed bubbling and making a strange noise, with just one flick of my webbed feet, I'm jettisoned downward to pick it up. When I do, it vibrates and gets louder. Then suddenly, I'm thrown into another world.

"Peter, it's Erskine. How are you doing?"

As I flail to the surface from my dream, I inadvertently press the speaker button on my phone.

"Um, yes. Sorry. I was fast asleep. What time is it?" I check there aren't any fish under the bed-covers.

"Ha! It's nine in the evening. I'm thinking maybe we should scrub dinner tonight. We had a splendid lunch and I think we're both going to be exhausted. A restful night, then we'll be in a good frame of mind to enjoy our last night in Bologna tomorrow. How does that sound?"

"I don't think I can move, so sounds perfect to me."

"Good. Well, shall we meet for breakfast downstairs at nine?"

"Yes, I'm sure I'll be firing on all cylinders by then. Actually, just before you go, any updates from anywhere after the auction? Jewels not been accidentally dropped down the drain by a clumsy auctioneer or anything?" I try to sound light, but I know I'm not going to properly relax until all those noughts appear in black and white on my bank statement.

"No, nothing to report since you last asked over lunch! Everything is ticking along as it should be. Absolutely nothing to worry about at all. Quite the opposite, you have everything to be happy about! I'll leave you to get some more rest and see you in the morning for the best coffee in the world."

"Sounds wonderful. See you then." Turning my phone off, I lay in bed, my brain engaged and far too wired to sleep, despite the lunchtime wine onslaught. Staring at the ceiling, my head is still buzzing with what happened at the auction today, as I try to contemplate the difference it will make to my life. Over the boozy lunch, Erskine said that even though it would have to be calculated officially, the higher hammer prices would at least double my expected pay-out. And assuming there were no hold ups at Gallo-Moretti, I could expect the money to land in my account any time after Tuesday next week. His words pound pleasantly around my head, but I want the money now. I want to know it's there. I want to call up my online bank statements whenever I feel like it and marvel at the ludicrous wealth at my fingertips. I want to view properties in Bologna knowing I could buy them there and then. Plan crazy holidays, maybe with Fin - if she ever comes back into my life. Tuesday feels like a million miles away. My excitement about the future merges with frustration at having to wait, until the after-effects of today's adrenalin make it impossible to keep my eyelids open.

I wake early, just as the sun is rising, a couple of hours before my scheduled breakfast with Erskine. All of last night's frustrations at having to wait for the money have dissolved and nothing but excitement fills my mind. From my hotel window, Florence looks spectacular - and quiet.

The thought of walking through empty streets draws me outside into the wakening city, where rising sunlight transforms the medieval buildings from dark edifices to golden temples. Caught in this magical atmosphere, I think about calling Fin for the first time since the auction - maybe after breakfast, giving me plenty of time to think about whether it's a good idea or not.

But I certainly won't be asking for Erskine's advice. Sauntering with no agenda, I think about other people, too, like the old man who was begging and particularly Bruce Browning, remembering my promise to treat the boys from the pub to a day out in the West End. Whatever else is happening in my life, Bruce's lot will keep me grounded for sure.

Studying ordinary life as it unravels around me, I watch shopkeepers getting ready for the day ahead, delivery drivers supplying them, wide-eyed young backpackers discovering the world on a shoestring, reluctant dog owners forced to walk their companions when they'd rather still be in bed. Having lived in a similarly functioning world for most of my life, it strikes me just how differently the outlook appears when money is not your first concern. Apart from the comfort blanket of knowing you're not going to starve, it gives you choices. Comfortable choices. I could go to Australia on a whim, if I wanted to. Or Disneyland. Or buy a Ferrari and screech around the streets of Florence. Or all of those things, one after the other. Knowing that options are available at the flick of a switch brings an electrifying sense of liberation. On top of that, if you take away the requirement to continually dance to someone else's tune, just to keep a roof over your head, the world becomes an entirely different place.

After an hour of blissful ambling, I'm back at the hotel. It's pleasant enough, though far less ornate than the Grand Majestic in Bologna. Imagining Erskine will already be in the breakfast room, when I walk in I see him straight away.

Getting up, Erskine shakes my hand. "Good morning Peter! You must be feeling on top of the world today!"

"Yes, indeed. I had no problem waking up this morning. Very ready for coffee!" I follow Erskine towards the self-service table, laden with various cheeses, cold meats, fruit, yogurts and drinks. After collecting fresh orange juice, coffee and random breakfast items, we set about tucking in.

"Everything still tickety-boo?" I ask Erskine, unintentionally crushing a croissant in an attempt to butter it.

"Yes, absolutely. As you know, I thought it was wise to hang on for a couple of nights after the auction, just in case of any unforeseen issues. But very pleased to report that everything is progressing without a hitch. I spoke briefly with Valentina, who will be working at Gallo-Moretti on Monday. Even though it's not her area of the business, hopefully she'll be close enough to things to know that the money is in from the buyers." Lifting his glass, he downs his orange juice in one.

"All sounds good, but thinking about it, why would you need Valentina to confirm that the money is in? Especially if it's not her area. Wouldn't it be much easier to just check with the accounts department?" Slightly toying with him, I suspect the old Romeo just likes an excuse to talk to her.

"Oh, no particular reason. It's just a quicker way to get the information. If I go through official channels, it'll take ages - confirming my identity and speaking to some office junior. It's just a more efficient route to knowing things are fully on track. Very efficient girl, Valentina."

He doesn't fool me for an instant. "So, when we get back to London, what's going to happen next? I don't want to be calling you every five minutes to ask when the money is being transferred. Also, about confirmation of the actual amount... when's that likely to be? If I know, it'll help my spinning brain!"

"OK, let's think about it. We fly back tomorrow, Sunday. I'll be back in the office on Monday and plan to get everything squared up including your statement showing your final payment. Everything will be detailed, the commissions, advances, expenses, bank fees, etcetera, etcetera. Being the rational human being you are whose life is about to change forever, I imagine the only figure you'll be interested in is the one at the bottom! As mentioned yesterday, I reckon that will be around 7.5 million euros, give or take." Erskine takes a large bite from an apple, then uncharacteristically carries on with his mouth full. "I can email you that statement, hopefully by close of play on Monday. All sound good?" It would sound better with his attention fully focused on me without the crunching sound effect, but I avoid the temptation to mention it.

"Yes, perfect. And you still think the money could be transferred on Tuesday?"

Erskine picks at an awkward bit of apple stuck in his teeth. "Slightly at the mercy of Gallo-Moretti on that one. Could easily be Tuesday, but then again, could just as easily be Wednesday. I'll obviously keep you posted with any updates I get."

"So, I just wait to hear from you?"

"Yes. Sit back and let the wheels churn away in the background and the money will be yours in no time." Closing his mouth, Erskine runs his tongue over his teeth. "Now, after breakfast I suggest we get ready at a leisurely pace for the midday train. Then once we're back in Bologna, probably makes sense to do our own thing this afternoon, then meet up for a last dinner tonight before we fly back tomorrow."

"Suits me perfectly." I imagine window shopping in Bologna, for everything from shoes to houses. "I'll have to watch myself or I'll have spent it all before it arrives!"

"Let's drink to that!" Erskine clinks his coffee cup against mine. "Cheers!"

Back up in my hotel room, I think about calling Fin. Picking up my phone and putting it down again several times, I eventually convince myself that it's not the right time and that I'll call her when I'm back in London, fully focussed, the money safely in my account. Not because I want to shout about it, but because this chapter needs closing, so that I can get on with my new life.

Even though I have no reason to doubt the money will happen, I feel in a surreal state of limbo, where the difference between a few quid in my pocket and a few million in the bank are worlds apart. And although it's lovely to live with that money on the horizon, I'm partially paralysed until it happens. I'd rather talk to Fin when all this is behind me.

Leaving the hotel and walking to the station with Erskine, I'm struck with how quiet we both are. Happily lost as I am thinking about all the things money can buy and watching the world go by, my own silence doesn't bother me. But Erskine's normally chatty. Thinking back, he seemed a bit blasé and not quite himself at breakfast. The one thing I've worked out about him is that when he's distracted, you never get close to what he's really thinking and on that basis, there's little point in asking him. I imagine it's Mrs. E, giving him the third degree for spending another weekend away from home.

But it's making me think. Do I really want to spend another evening with him? He's not going to have any more news about the money and frankly, this morning, he seemed more interested in his breakfast than talking to me. Now that the auction is done, I imagine he's probably consumed with his next assignment. Not wanting to waste my last evening in Bologna, I've a feeling it would be far more enjoyable spending it alone.

53

It's eight o'clock on Wednesday morning, five days after the auction. In the café in the Strand opposite Erskine's office, the coffee isn't a patch on the real thing I was enjoying a few days ago in Italy, but that's only an incidental thought as I watch his front door, waiting to see if he arrives for work. I know his usual routine gets him to work around eight-thirty, so sitting at a window table on the café's first floor, I have a clear view should he arrive early.

The last time we spoke was on Sunday afternoon at Gatwick, as we parted company after the flight back from Bologna. Before going our separate ways, Erskine had assured me that he'd be in touch on Tuesday morning at the latest, with an update on my final balance and confirmation of the transfer date. But Tuesday was yesterday, and I've heard nothing. And despite my calls to Erskine's office and to his mobile, he hasn't answered any of them. The best Jayne Renton could offer was to take a message and pass it on.

His failure to return any of my calls both

angers and worries me. All he's got to do is keep me in the loop, but ignoring me? What's that about? Pissed off and gimlet eyed, focused on the glass front doors of his office building, I wait.

At nearly eight-thirty, if he's going to the office today, he should be trotting up those steps opposite any minute. I'm not going to confront him. Well, not in the street, anyway. I just need to know that he's there. A couple more minutes pass before a few butterflies jump in my stomach as I see him, walking across the road, then purposefully jogging up the steps before slipping inside. As my butterflies tighten to a knot, I know something isn't right. I also know Erskine's skill for smooth talking. But any communication would be preferable to the current radio silence and one way or another, this morning, I have to make something happen.

Even if he has no news on the timing of the transfer, he should at least be confirming my final balance details. I decide I'll give him ten minutes to get settled before making my next move. Keeping close watch as I wait, in case Erskine leaves the building, after ten minutes I call his mobile. Then when it goes straight to answerphone, I call the office number.

"City Law Partners, good morning." I recognise Jayne Renton's voice.

"Jayne, good morning. It's Peter Foster-Fewster again. Could you put me through to Mr.

Erskine, please? Incidentally, he didn't return any calls yesterday. Did you pass on my messages?"

"Oh. I'm sorry about that. I did leave a message for him. For personal reasons, I don't think he's going to be in this week." Put on hold, I ponder Jayne's vague answer, for quite a long time, as it happens, before she's back. "I'm sorry, but Mr Erskine is out for a few days. He did just get a message to me to say he knows you are trying to call him. He apologises and says there is nothing to worry about, and he will get back to you as soon as he can."

"So, can you confirm that Mr. Erskine is definitely not in the office today? And just to be clear, I'm talking about the Strand office, the one you are in now." Feeling my hackles are rising, I'm sure it's noticeable in my voice.

"I'm not fully aware of all his movements at the moment, but he was very clear that he will be in touch as soon as he can."

It's a load of non-committal bullshit, but I decide not to shoot the messenger, instead thanking her as sincerely as I can manage in the circumstances.

Keeping my eyes on his office building, I consider my next move. Knowing I'm being lied to, my anger is raging. I have to confront Erskine, but I need to keep my cool. Taking deep breaths, I try to think things through. If I go and buzz on the door, Jayne will tell me Erskine is out. Maybe I'll go and wait outside the entrance. Either Jayne or Erskine will come out at some point.

A few more deep breaths later, I leave the café. Clanking up in the retro lift, I think about the first time I came here all those weeks ago, not knowing what to expect. Little did I know it would come to this, me pissed off with the lawyer I met that day, now pretending to be out of his office to avoid talking to me. Now, I want the truth and for whatever reason, I'm not getting it.

Once out of the lift, I hang about in the corridor near the door to City Law Partners. It's another of those moments where doubt alters my perception, my mood wavering from anger to horrible self-consciousness as I imagine Erskine's reaction to seeing me. It could be that he's snowed under and there's nothing remotely sinister or worrying about the lack of contact. Now that I'm here, despite all my earlier logic, could I be making a fuss over nothing? Before it all starts churning through my head again, I hear the lift ascend and stop at this floor. As a courier gets out with a parcel, he looks at me. "'Scuse me mate, is this where City Law is?"

I nod towards the door. "Yes, that door there, just ring the bell."

"Chiz mate." As the courier presses the bell, I hear Jayne's voice.

"City Law Partners, how can I help?"

"Package for... Erskint?" The courier says uncertainly, scrutinising the label.

Allowing myself a smirk, I wait for Jayne's reply. "Yes, that's fine, please wait there. I'll be through in a couple of minutes to collect."

The courier rolls his eyes at me. "Bloody hell, I'm going to get a ticket at this rate."

"Actually, I'm going in there. I know Mr Erskint. I'll take it if you want?"

"Really? That'd be great. Chiz, mate. Just a squiggle on there, if you don't mind signing for it. You're a gentleman."

Happy, the courier gets in the lift and descends out of view. A couple of minutes later I hear someone approaching the door, before Jayne opens it.

She looks warily at me. "Oh, hello. How confusing. Was there a courier here just now?" Holding the door open, she steps forward, craning left and right down the corridor even though there's evidently no one else present, presumably to cover her embarrassment that it's me standing in front of her.

Taking my moment, I step past her. "He asked me to take this personally to Mr Erskine. He couldn't wait." Speaking loudly over my shoulder, I leave Jayne standing in the corridor, already in the reception area by the time she catches up with me. Looking flushed, it's obvious that she's been lying about Erskine not being here today. Any self-consciousness I was feeling has evaporated.

"Is he alone in there?" I ask pointedly.

"Shall I call Mr Erskine and see what his movements are?" Attempting to ignore my obvious irritation, Jayne tries to be the model of reason.

"If you like. In the meantime, I'll leave this on his desk." Holding up the parcel, I don't wait for her reaction as I walk towards Erskine's office, knock on his door then push it open without invitation. Standing by his window looking down over the Strand, Erskine swivels around. When he sees me, he looks thunderstruck.

"Peter... you were next on my list to call. Take a seat. Bloody silly client mucking me around today. I was supposed to be out all day, but they scrubbed it without letting me know. I think it's still in the diary, in case Jayne gave you different information. Right. After all the fun and games in Florence, you'll be wanting to know what's going on!" Erskine fine tunes his delivery from shock to chummy bonhomie within a few sentences. But I'm not taken in.

"You could say." I instinctively hold my ground.

He clearly knows I'm pissed off. "Right. Well, very nearly worked out your slice of the pie. Should have that all squared off by close of play today, if not tomorrow. Then regarding the transfer of said funds, let me see." Erskine turns to his computer and starts tapping away. "No sign of anything yet, but it could happen any moment." Without raising his gaze for even a second, instead he's apparently intrigued by what he's looking at, all the while continuing to type incessantly.

I'm really not happy. "Jayne told me you wouldn't be in this week. Personal reasons." I pause, long enough to watch him grow uncomfortable. "And I'm sure you'll have perfectly good reasons for that." There's sarcasm in my voice. "But you said you would have my balance agreed by yesterday morning at the latest. So that's the first thing I'd like explaining. Why the delay, and why haven't I been kept informed? Secondly, the money is later than indicated by Gallo-Moretti. Can't you just ring them and ask them where the payment is or when it's happening?"

"Oh, I don't think we need to do that just yet." Erskine's chuckle and slight air of condescension are beginning to make my blood boil.

"Well, why not? You could do it now. While I'm here. It's hardly like asking North Korea for details of their nuclear programme. It's money they owe us and surely they'll have no problem confirming the status of the payment?"

"Ah, you might think so. Tricky lot the Italians, when it comes to money. No, far better leave it to me and I'll winkle it out of them. Maybe I'll see if Valentina can shed any light. But... I can see you're upset, and I can also see that I owe you an apology. I hadn't realised you were watching the clock so intensely through all of this. Leave it with me and you'll get a firm status report by lunchtime tomorrow, at the latest. Hopefully the money will be in your account by then, too. How does that sound?"

"I'll let you know how it sounds when you call me tomorrow lunchtime," I reply sarcastically. I'm still not happy and I want him to know. "I'll be honest, this delay has worried me. And pissed me off. Someone should have kept me informed." As I speak, Erskine holds up surrendering hands. Before turning to leave, I place the courier's package on his desk. "And this is for you. Don't worry it's not a bomb... as far as I know."

FIVE DAYS LATER

54

"So, to Lake Como, Signore? Have you visited before?"

"Actually no, I…" Cut short as we thump over a speed hump, I intensify the search for the other half of my fraying seat belt. "…haven't. How long is the taxi journey?"

"From the airport? Just over an hour, Signore. It's a beautiful drive. Even in this car! Business or holiday for you?"

"To be honest, I don't really know. I've been invited to an event there. Overnight stay. Grand house by the lake. All a bit of a mystery."

"Mystery? It means like a puzzle, no? Maybe a surprise?"

"Yes, exactly. A puzzle, a surprise."

"Maybe it's a good surprise for you, Signore."

"Well I'm hoping so. I could certainly do with one after everything I've just been through."

"Hey, listen Signore. If you want to talk, I'm tutto orecchi."

"Sorry, you're what?" I say, finally giving up on my seatbelt.

"All ears, Signore. I'm all ears!"

And so, with little encouragement from my affable driver, an unconventional therapy session begins, as I explain how I've ended up in the back of a taxi on my way to an unfamiliar address on the edge of Lake Como.

"It started in London a couple of months ago. I got a call from a company that finds lost inheritances. They told me I had one. Some jewels that belonged to my grandmother."

"Nice call to get, Signore, eh!?"

"Yes, except it was a bit complicated. The jewels had been stolen in the war by the Nazis." When my driver makes a spitting noise and slaps his forehead, I assume he's not a Nazi sympathiser. "Anyway, we had to get the jewels returned from Germany to Italy, then sold at an auction. They eventually sold for quite a lot of money, Russian money apparently."

"Hey, it's good for you, Signore?"

"Well, it would be, but I've yet to see a penny. The auction happened over a week ago, but after telling me there's a delay, my agent in England has virtually disappeared."

"Not so good, Signore. It would give me a stomach ulcer."

"Quite. But getting this invitation was nice timing. I thought if I were to get away for a couple of days, it would fill my head with something else, especially as it's in Italy. I love Italy! Hopefully by the time I get back, the paperwork will all be done and the money sorted."

"Paperwork. Officials! They're as fishy as the fish in Lake Como." The driver slaps his forehead again, as our eyes meet in his rear-view mirror. "I keep everything crossed you'll be a rich man soon, Signore!"

"Thanks! They tell me everything is fine. I just need to be patient. Anyway, this event at Lake Como could be useful. There is a connection. It's one of the main reasons I'm going."

"Sounds like you're 007. James Bond, Signore!"

"Who me? Hardly! The name is Foster-Fewster. Peter Foster-Fewster."

"Francesco. That's me, Signore. Same as my father and his father too. So, what's the connection at Lake Como, Signore Peter?"

"Well, a couple of days ago, I was considering what to do about my bloody useless agent in London when I received a surprise letter. I had to sign for it. An official invitation to an all-expenses paid event in Lake Como. The invitation came with a note apologising for the short notice, because my story had only just come to light. The event is to honour the repatriation of arts and artefacts from the Nazis to their rightful countries and owners. Lots of important people, speeches, an exhibition, even ordinary people like me who've been affected. Obviously, I accepted! I'm just a spectator, but there are bound to be people with similar experiences to mine, lost inheritances and auctions. Would be good to talk to them. They might have some advice on getting money out of flakey agents!"

"Sounds like the place to be. Who knows what you might find? Mystery, Signore, one big mistero!" Our eyes meet again in the driving mirror.

Eventually, as the surrounding beauty takes priority, our conversation gives way to silence. Descending towards Lake Como, late September sunshine shimmers across the wide expanse of water, stopping at the other side against verdant edges dotted with fantasy houses. Beyond, densely wooded hills rise to create a cosseted snug feel, despite the scale of everything.

On our side of the lake, the road hugs the water's edge passing dream houses for several miles before Francesco eventually slows to a crawl, trying to make sense of his satnav, while I watch in the mirror, seeing enough of his crumpled eye sockets to know that he needs to trouble an optician.

"We're close Signore. Very close." I'm grateful for the information as my friendly driver feverishly studies his satnav, while in theory keeping an eye on the road. After a couple of mildly terrifying minutes, we turn into a private drive and Francesco springs back upright. "This is it, Signore. Palazzo di Como. Magnifico!"

And magnificent it certainly is. As he stops the car, my eyes are locked on the house while I pay him and share a few distracted words. Wishing me good luck, he crunches away down the driveway with a couple of honks from his horn, leaving me standing there. I take in the vision in front of me; a palatial house of muted yellow and terracotta opulence, surrounded by an expanse of sweeping green. Columns and wide steps project from the huge front doors and there are more windows than I can comfortably count set across three floors.

But walking towards the house, I suddenly become aware that there are no signs of life anywhere. Checking the invitation again, it confirms everything; Palazzo di Como, the date is right, overnight stay and a reception party this evening. It's five o'clock now. I'd expect the place to be alive with activity. As I head for the main door, I convince myself that there must be more than one Palazzo di Como along the shores of Lake Como. Have I been delivered to the wrong place?

55

Almost certain that I'm at the wrong address, I decide to check it out anyway, in the hope of finding someone who can point me in the right direction. Arriving at the large double doors, I press the only button I can see. Within a few moments, efficient footsteps echo from within the house before the door opens.

"Buongiorno, Signore." A neatly dressed gentleman welcomes me.

"Buongiorno, do you speak English?"

"Yes, I do. How can I help?"

I pull the postcard sized invitation from my back pocket and pass it to him. "A taxi brought me here, but I think he's got the wrong house. Is there another Palazzo di Como around here?"

Scanning the card, the gentleman smiles. "No, this is the only one. Your driver brought you to the correct address. Please come in."

"Really!" I say, stepping inside. "I thought there'd be lots of people here by now. I guess I'm early?" But my surprise temporarily gives way to awe as I'm hit with the grandness of the hallway, leaving me wondering what sort of event is going on here.

"Please take a seat. Someone will be with you very soon."

Thanking him, I make my way to a jade green chesterfield among the choice of seats in the cavernous hall. Running a hand over the taut shiny leather, I lower myself respectfully and register how my weight has no impact on the dense buttoned cushion.

Reminded of the one I fell in love with in the furniture shop in Via Crostini, my mind inevitably wanders back to the auction in Florence and the bewildering circumstances surrounding it, both before and after. And talking about bewildering, what the hell is going on today in this sodding great empty house?

Back in England with Erskine frustrating the hell out of me, the surprise invitation here had seemed the perfect distraction while he sorted his shit out. I replay his last words to me, before I left his office, *"Don't worry, your money will appear at any moment. Try to put it to the back of your mind for a couple of days. Everything is absolutely fine."* Over and over, the words ringing in my ears until, as usual, I'm convinced that I've been overreacting and Erskine's right. But before the words can make another circuit of my brain, I hear, then see a casually dressed gentleman briskly descend the wide staircase. Not sure whether to ignore him or nod a smile, as he walks across the hall, I'm momentarily paralysed as I realise he's walking directly towards me – not unlike a mafia hit man. Instinctively standing as he approaches, the tension lifts wonderfully as he breaks into a smile.

"Good afternoon Mr Foster-Fewster. My name is Genaro. The event is already underway upstairs. Please follow me."

"So, are there lots of people here already?" As we ascend the stairs, we pass huge windows with stunning views over the gardens.

"Full house actually. We're just down the corridor here on the first floor."

I'm expecting to hear voices as we near our destination, but it's silent, so much so we could be walking through a trappist monastery.

"Third door along... Here we are. The Fortuna Selvaggia suite."

I'm taken by surprise when he knocks before entering, especially as it becomes clear that no-one else is in the room. The suite is bigger than seemed possible from the outside, each wall home to at least two leather settees, a large circular table in the middle of the room, surrounded by a dozen or so chairs. Three sets of French windows appear to open onto a huge connected balcony overlooking Lake Como and on the wall now behind me, a large electronic screen suggests the room is used for business meetings and seminars.

"Is there going to be a presentation or something?" I ask.

"Yes, a presentation, I think. Not from me. I only work here. Technical support. I just need to set up a couple of things. When I'm finished, someone comes to do the presentation." Sitting at the table, Genaro opens a laptop. After a few moments, as the electronic screen lights up on the wall opposite him, Genaro gets up. "I just need to close the curtains to help the screen definition, then I let the organiser know the presentation can start." After sweeping the large curtains into place, he leaves the room via a side door. After a few seconds the screen returns to blank, plunging the room into near darkness.

56

Freaked out and alone, suspecting this is about my money, I start to sweat, imagining a kidnap, or worse. I'm finding it impossible to think of a positive alternative. Panicking, I suddenly want to get out of the house, but as I head for the door, a tall man strides into the gloom from the same opening Genaro disappeared into.

"Whoa. It's pitch black in here. Hold on." The voice is authoritative and obviously English, coming from a tall figure making his way to the laptop. Pressing a couple of buttons, the screen comes back to life, filling the room with bright light. "Sorry about that. Don't know what happened there. So much for technical experts! Anyway, good afternoon Mr Foster-Fewster. Take a seat."

Still not sure whether to run or sit, as the apparent friendliness of the tall man washes over me, I decide on the latter.

"We've not met before." He turns to look me in the eye, "My name is Bassinott. Gerald Bassinott."

I shake the large hand on offer.

"I'll explain everything in due course, but I think you will be interested in today's presentation. To begin, I have arranged to video-call with a special contributor this afternoon. I'll be calling them very shortly. I'm going to move a couple of seats away from you, so they'll only be able to see *me* in the video. You might be tempted to speak during the call, but please don't unless I invite you to do so. I think you'll find it fascinating. Don't worry, all will become clear. OK?"

I'm far from OK but I've at least lost the sense I'm about to have a stiletto knife plunged into my gullet. "I have no idea what to expect, but please carry on." I try not to emphasise how worried I am.

"Right, here we go." Bassinott taps at his laptop before a ringing sound follows. After a short delay, the screen flickers and comes to life with a live video link. As if today couldn't get any more surreal, when I see the face on the screen, I begin to feel a lack of resistance at my rear end.

"What the hell… I know him… It's Erskine," I erupt, pointing at the screen.

Bassinott places a hand on my arm, "Please, try not to say anything just now. I had you on mute, because I anticipated your reaction. Just let me do the talking."

Lost for thought and rendered speechless, I have no problem obeying.

"All OK?" As he checks, I manage a nod, before Bassinott taps his keyboard and starts talking. "Mr Erskine. A very good afternoon to you. Can you see and hear me?"

Still stunned, I can see Erskine peering into his screen but instead of returning the same pleasantries, he shrugs reluctantly.

"I wasn't expecting congratulations, Erskine, but cheer up. No one likes a bad loser. You didn't play by the rules, did you? You played a risky game and you lost."

Oh my God. Suddenly I know Bassinott must be talking about the money. Has he somehow stolen it from Erskine? My mind is racing, as I try to work out what is going on. I'm desperate to say something, but frankly I'm crapping myself. I knew from day one this all sounded too good to be true and now I'm right in the middle of some horrendous pantomime. But why have I been brought in? And when I haven't got the money, what possible use am I to anyone?

Erskine's familiar tones come through the speakers. "You need to think carefully, Bassinott. I've got a file here that will sink you. Something that will ensure you're banged up for a very long time."

For reasons I can't explain, it's reassuring to hear Erskine getting angry with Bassinott, but what the hell is he talking about? What's anyone talking about?

"So, Bassinott. What are you prepared to give me to keep quiet?"

Keep quiet? What secret is Erskine sitting on?

"Well, the arrangement was to pay you off if you behaved yourself. But you most certainly haven't behaved yourself. Going behind my back? Trying to outwit me and get the money? Not clever. But tell me, Erskine. If I were to pay you something to shove off quietly, how much will you share with Mr Foster-Fewster? Give me a rough percentage."

I listen intently, my bafflement now off the scale.

Erskine waits before answering. "How much would I share? I don't know. Not enough to cause you a financial problem. A few quid to get him off my back?"

If I wasn't floundering and confused as fuck before, I certainly am now. Whatever else is going on between these two, it looks like my fortune is disappearing down the drain. Suddenly I'd be happy to walk away with nothing, just to get away from this madness.

My arm is getting sore from self-inflicted pinch marks, but there's no waking up from this as Bassinott carries on. "Enough to get him off your back? Sounds a little selfish to me. What do you think Mr. Foster-Fewster would say if he heard that?"

"We'll that's not very likely is it? I'm expecting him to come marching into my office any moment, demanding to know where his auction money is. I can't fob him off anymore. He turned up a here unannounced a few days ago despite my receptionist telling him I was away for the week. He'd been calling me incessantly. I think I've managed to shut him up for a few more days, but I can't do it anymore. You want me to believe you have successfully got the money? But I have no proof yet. Convince me. My lawyer's brain wants to know everything."

"I'll explain everything. But first, let me introduce you to someone. Someone who is totally confused by what's going on here." Bassinott taps at his keyboard again and I can see from the inset image on the big screen that Erskine can now see both of us.

As Erskine scrutinises the image in front of him, his face looms stupidly large on the big screen in front of us. The penny soon drops. "Holy fuck. Are you two in this together? You complete bastards." Standing up furiously, as Erskine's chair jettisons to the wall behind him, he paces out of camera view.

But I can no longer hold back. "I'm not in anything with anyone. I'm in meltdown here." Bassinott makes no attempt to stop me.

But as he sits down and examines his screen, Erskine ignores me. "Fuck. I didn't imagine it.

Bassinott and Foster-Fewster together, as if it couldn't get any worse." Erskine sounds utterly incredulous. "Somebody, please, tell me something."

I echo his words, my eyes flitting between Bassinott and Erskine. "Me too, please. Somebody, please tell me what's happening."

Holding up his hands, Bassinott smiles. Then as silence falls, his smile fades and his hands return to the table. "It all started several years ago. But I'll come back to that later. The first thing to explain is a rather wonderful coincidence. Three years ago, while I was in prison..." Before I have time to work out what level of criminal he is, the surreal scene gets an upgrade as Bassinott leans back on his chair. "Mr Bassinott, please join us."

As I watch, an identical man enters the room from the side door and joins us at the table.

Bassinott introduces us, "Peter Foster-Fewster, meet my identical twin, Thomas."

As we shake hands, I have no idea whether to smile, laugh or cry. When Erskine isn't included in the introductions, I'm guessing they already know each other and it's another relationship based on mutual hatred.

Gerald carries on. "Thomas and I were sentenced to two years in prison during which time I met a chap called Duke Pyecoe. Duke told me about a lawyer he knew. For the benefit of Mr Foster-Fewster, I should explain about your past activities, Erskine."

"Lovely." Erskine retorts with sarcasm. "Maybe you could elucidate a little on your own *activities*, while you're at it."

"With pleasure. Well Peter, Thomas and I were sent down for fraud. Taking money from those who could afford to lose it. But we were caught, and we served our time. Plain and simple. No complaints from us. Not quite the same for Erskine. Unlike us, the whole purpose of his position as a lawyer is to be a pillar of public trust. To uphold the law and expose the wrong-doers. So, it would be very bad indeed if he was found to be guilty of perjury and paying for false witnesses. When I say bad, I'm talking about losing his title, job, reputation, income, home and face a very long stretch in prison." Bassinott pauses for a few moments. "Now, here's the interesting thing. Erskine *is* guilty of professional misconduct. And he upset some people along the way. Notably, Duke Pyecoe, who was short changed by Erskine."

"Short changed? I don't get it." I'm trying to keep up, but need some help.

"Erskine was a prosecution lawyer in a high-profile court case. He was losing the battle against the defence and needed to pull something out of the hat. So, he found Pyecoe and *persuaded* him to be a false witness - in return for £25,000. Pyecoe carried out his duties to the letter and

Erskine won the case. But Erskine only paid Pyecoe £15,000 then ignored him when he requested the balance."

I look at the man on the screen who seems so far away from the man I know, as I try to work out if Erskine also has a twin brother.

But no, there's only one Erskine and he addresses me. "Don't be taken in by all this, Peter. When Pyecoe's shortfall was brought to my attention, I offered to pay the balance in full. Repeatedly I offered. Would anyone listen? Fat chance."

"But by saying that, you're admitting you hired this man to be a false witness?"

Erskine doesn't speak, just looks dumbfounded that I've even picked up on that point.

After a few seconds, Bassinott fills the silence. "So, you see Peter, all this begins with a very dishonest lawyer. Your Mr Erskine. Now back to the story. Pyecoe was in prison for burglary, nothing to do with the Erskine court case, but no doubt he was forced to turn to stealing after his inadequate payoff ran out. Anyway, he told me all about the way Erskine perverted the course of justice and short changed him, then ignored him. As my release date was before Pyecoe's, I told him that Thomas and I would track down Erskine and give him a fair opportunity to repay that particular debt. All clear so far?"

"Well, I'm beginning to get a new under-

standing of the phrase 'honour amongst thieves'."
I can't think of anything else to say, sanity forcing
me to suspend all normal reactions until all of
this is over.

As Bassinott smiles, I hear him whisper the
same words affectionately to his brother. *Honour amongst thieves*, as Thomas nods, his identical
face caught in the briefest flicker of sunlight as a
breeze ripples a curtain in front of an open balcony door.

Still mainly addressing me, Gerald carries
on. "After Thomas and I were released, we
thought long and hard about the best way to approach Erskine. Then as luck would have it, we
saw his name in the paper." Turning to the screen,
Gerald raised his voice, "You remember that
Erskine, the press story? It mentioned you and
your company and this amazing bit of heir hunting your parent company had done. Nazi theft,
lost fortunes, auctions - the story had everything.
It even mentioned Peter, here." He turned to me. "I
imagine you weren't very happy about that news
story, were you, Peter?"

"No, distinctly pissed off, actually. Never
found out where it came from."

"Well, maybe Erskine can tell us?" While
Erskine sits in stony silence, Gerald lets a few
torturous seconds pass. "It was you, wasn't it,
Erskine? You saw an opportunity to promote you
and your company. You used your contacts to get

the story into the press, but unfortunately for you it led us straight to your door."

I can't stop myself. "Is this true? You swore blind you didn't know how the story got in the press. Over and over again, you swore blind." I raise my voice towards a screen on a wall, furious.

After a brief silence, Erskine speaks. "Pure speculation."

"I think we both know I can prove otherwise, but we'll leave it at that for now." Gerald is firmly back in charge. "When we read about the jewels going for auction, we saw an opportunity to not only get Pyecoe's money back, but also divert the proceeds of the auction in our direction."

"You mean *steal* the money from Erskine... and me?" I have no idea which thief to back.

"Not exactly. I'll get to that. So, we tracked down Erskine and told him we'd seen the press reports about the jewels and the auction. I then told him about my time with Pyecoe in prison and how he'd told me everything about Erskine being a bent lawyer and the money he owed him. Naturally, when confronted, Erskine denied everything - very convincingly. Until we showed him the proof."

"You had proof? Why didn't you go to the police?" I'm aware of how naïve I sound, but I am so far out of my comfort zone, my speech is on autopilot.

"Well, because it was the perfect opportunity to blackmail Erskine!" As Gerald sounds triumphant, I feel sick. "Thanks to Pyecoe, we had photographs, taken by his brother. They clearly show Erskine covertly handing Pyecoe a bag. A bag of cash. It was the first instalment of £15,000. Had you honoured your full agreement and paid the £10,000 balance after the trial, none of us would be here today. How does that make you feel, Erskine?" Gerald turns to the screen.

"It's all very entertaining, but I think I'll keep my thoughts to myself." Erskine holds up a large envelope.

Ignoring him, Gerald carries on, "The thing was, even though we knew we could blackmail Erskine, we had to work out a way of doing it. Securing his silence was crucial. So, over several meetings, we made it crystal clear that he needed to keep his mouth shut about our intervention, unless he wanted us to expose his criminal past."

I look at Erskine, my anger growing as I realise, all along he's been double crossing me. "All this was going on in the background while we were making arrangements for the auction, visiting Italy and everything else?"

But when he doesn't answer, Gerald picks up. "To be fair to Erskine, he couldn't tell you. We made that impossible for him. In fact, we made it impossible for him to talk to anyone - unless he wanted us to contact Scotland Yard with our proof and watch him being carted off to prison.

He gave us every guarantee that he was playing ball. But despite those guarantees, he was playing a different ball game behind our backs. That's right, isn't it Erskine?"

I stare at the screen, waiting for Erskine to respond to Gerald's latest turn. But when Erskine remains silent, clearly unsettled, Gerald goes on.

"Maybe this will help jog your memory. Thomas, would you mind asking our next guest to come in?"

Silently, Thomas slips away from the table and through the side door. Moments later he returns with someone else and despite the subdued lighting in that part of the room, I can see it's of the female form. As she takes a place at the table, in the light cast from the screen it's suddenly obvious who it is, but before I can say anything, Erskine's head balloons into the screen again as he scrutinises the view in front of him, slowly taking in his audience.

I expect him to explode, but he sits down and talks quietly. "Gerald Bassinott. Thomas Bassinott. Peter Foster-Fewster and now Valentina Russo. Hardly my idea of the dream team."

Gerald ignores Erskine and addresses me, "Peter, I'm aware that you and Valentina have met and know each other reasonably well." Sitting either side of Gerald, Valentina and I nod to each other. "But obviously you'll be at a loss as to why she's here today. As will Erskine. Let me explain."

I watch as Erskine swivels his chair sideways and leans an arm on his desk, propping his head in a hand, before Gerald goes on.

"When I told Erskine about our plan, it wasn't without potential benefit to him. We agreed to pay him a cash sum, to keep quiet before and after the auction. But what did he do immediately after he agreed? He went to visit Valentina in Bologna and asked her to be an accomplice in helping him thwart our plans."

Although I'm confused, it seems like Erskine was doing the right thing and despite being disturbed by earlier revelations, I feel compelled to defend him. "I don't know exactly what's going on here, but this is *my* money you're all talking about. You have no authority to offer Erskine cash sums. He was speaking to Valentina to protect my money. You were simply trying to blackmail him out of the money. My money. He was doing the right thing... by me at least."

Erskine swings back round to look at his audience, seemingly pleased he has an unexpected ally in me. I wait for Gerald to shut me up.

But on the contrary, he is calm. "I think Valentina is best qualified to deal with your quandary."

"Thank you, Gerald and nice to see you again, Peter." The omission of Erskine's name from Valentina's introduction is notable. "After Città Legale Italia were first involved in the

Foster-Fewster case, everything was progressing normally, including a meeting at our Bologna office where I first met you, Peter."

I nod, at last agreeing with something.

"As you know, the meeting was to sign various forms and to confirm your identity, passport etcetera. Then a few days later, Erskine contacted me and asked to meet me urgently in Bologna. I was surprised and had no idea what he wanted to discuss. We met at the Grand Majestic Hotel in Via Indipendenza."

Remembering my chance sighting of Valentina walking up the hotel steps, my eyes stray from Valentina to Erskine. But he's still slumped sideways to the screen.

Valentina's soft voice draws me back. "Erskine told me that the Bassinott twins had visited him a day or two before. They said they had proof he was a bent lawyer and unless he agreed to do what they said, they would go to the police with their evidence. It was blackmail, no other word for it. The twins ordered him to obey their ongoing orders, meaning the auction money would ultimately go to them, not him."

Gerald intervenes. "And for Peter's benefit, please explain why Erskine asked you to meet him at the hotel in Bologna?"

"Because he wanted my help. He told me the only hope of him getting the money was if I helped him."

"And what did you say?" Gerald asks, wanting me to get the full picture.

"I said no. Absolutely no way. I told him whatever was going on, it was nothing to do with me."

"What did Erskine say to that?" Gerald probes further.

"He explained about what he'd done, the Pyecoe false witness story. He said he was in hole and there was only one way out. He needed my help and if I didn't agree... he would blackmail me."

"Blackmail you? Can you say that again Valentina, so that we can all hear it loud and clear?" Gerald sounds more like a lawyer than Erskine.

"Yes. Blackmail." Valentina sounds upset.

"How could he blackmail you?" Gerald sounds sympathetic, but he wants me to know everything.

"I am not proud of this. In fact, it disgusts me really. But five years ago, at our office party in Bologna, Erskine hit on me. My only explanation is that I was drunk on wine and grappa, which he was very happy to keep topping up."

Erupting into life, Erskine starts shouting at the screen. "You're a grown-up woman, for fucks sake. You can't blame me for how much wine you drink. Take some bloody responsibility for once. Jesus Christ, what sort of kangaroo court is this?"

A brief silence fills the room, but any intended impact is short lived as Valentina continues without acknowledging a single word. "The end result of that evening is that I slept with Erskine. In truth, I remember almost nothing about it, except waking up full of regret. A short while after, I was devastated to discover that I was pregnant."

I break my silence. "Pregnant by Erskine? Bloody hell, can this get any more surreal?" When no one answers, I throw my hands in the air and slump back in my chair.

Glancing apologetically towards me, Valentina continues. "Sorry Peter, this must all be overwhelming. But this is what happened. That's why I couldn't really talk to you when we bumped into each other on the stairs at Gallo-Moretti. Erskine was blackmailing me. He threatened to tell my husband about the pregnancy. He also threatened to tell him about the subsequent termination, which Erskine paid for. The problem for me was that when I got pregnant, I was engaged to be married. If Erskine told my husband, it would end my marriage and cause untold damage within my husband's family. A mix of devout catholic and mafia sympathies is a dangerous combination. My husband would never forgive me. Or probably worse than that."

My eyes leaving Valentina, I focus on Erskine as I try to replay our conversations that would have taken place at the time. Even though there was no clue about him blackmailing Valentina or that the twins were blackmailing him, I'd been plagued with a sense of uneasiness. And now I know why.

Gerald takes over again. "Thank you, Valentina. So, Peter, I think you'll be forming a very different opinion of the Mr Erskine you thought you knew?"

Shrugging my shoulders, I raise my hands in a *I don't know what the fuck to think* gesture as Gerald goes on.

"Well, let me pick up from where Valentina got to. For the record, I didn't know her when all this was going on. I was busy trying to finesse my plans to divert the upcoming auction money away from Erskine's bank account and into mine. Part of my groundwork involved visiting Gallo-Moretti in Florence to get a better understanding of how they operated, specifically how they paid clients after an auction. I visited a chap called Marco Spinetti, under the name of Peter Hobday, I certainly didn't want any record of Gerald Bassinott visiting them. Having wrapped Spinetti round my little finger and got the necessary information, Thomas and I headed back to the hotel." Gerald turns to Valentina, "Would you like to take it from here?"

As Valentina nods, Erskine listens restlessly. "So, the day that Gerald, or Peter Hobday, visited Gallo-Moretti, I was working there. As you know,

Peter, I'm based there a couple of days a week. When Spinetti was giving Gerald a tour of the auction house, I recognised his face immediately. I'd previously researched the internet after Erskine told me the Bassinott twins were blackmailing him, so Gerald's face was fresh in my mind. After Gerald left my office, I waited and watched from my office window. A few minutes later, he got in a cab and drove away along Via Crostini. I immediately went down to talk to our staff on reception…"

I cut in, feeling the need to say something, "The young man with the blue glasses who prods them back up his nose all the time?"

"Yes, Gino. He used to be a model." She's momentarily distracted. "So, I asked Gino if he booked a cab for the guest who just left. He told me he did and gave me the hotel he was going to. Because I'd been dropped in all this shit by Erskine, I wanted to track him and find out how the twins were planning to take the money. When I left work a short while later, I went straight to their hotel and waited in the bar. I saw the twins drinking wine at a table and I managed to sit near them. Near enough to hear their conversation."

Erskine comes to life again, "You didn't tell me any of this." He sounds almost hurt. "I guess you didn't discover anything remarkable. Nothing worth reporting back to me, anyway."

"On the contrary, Erskine. I discovered

something *very* remarkable. So remarkable in fact, that I had to go and introduce myself." Valentina sounds pleased.

Gerald moves into the driving seat. "You don't need to know what was said that day, Erskine, except to say Valentina was no longer working in your best interests. Instead, she started working for us."

"And what about my best interests?" I pipe up, still at a loss to work out if anyone here is on my side.

"You do have a role in all this. All will become clear." Gerald is short and to the point.

Erskine leans forward, "Let me get this right, Valentina. After Mike Reynolds told me the Bassinotts were going to Bologna, I rang you. But this means you knew already. And I'm now guessing they were going to see you."

"Correct." Valentina sounds more confident every time she speaks. "When I met them in the hotel bar after their visit to Gallo-Moretti, there wasn't much time to discuss anything. We made introductions and agreed in principal to work together. So, we arranged a meeting for a few days later - in Bologna - to talk through everything more carefully."

"So, Erskine, the long and short of it is, we knew all about your plan to switch bank accounts after the auction. Valentina was keeping us informed at every stage." Gerald was now veering towards smugness. "If Valentina hadn't tracked us down and offered to work with us, our job would have been much harder. A lovely bit of luck - or maybe it was poetic justice?"

"Well, I'm really delighted for you." Erskine falls back into full sarcastic mode. "All of you. Look at you, sitting there thinking you've screwed me over. Well, I'm afraid it's not that simple. You seem to have forgotten, Mr Bassinott, that you and your fraudulent brother are on parole. I don't know where you're all hiding right now, somewhere in London I guess, but I have a file here which will get you flushed out within hours. And OK, bully for you, you've pulled this off, but unless you want to talk to me about coming to an amicable agreement, I have a file of evidence against you in my safe that within the next ten minutes, is going to Scotland Yard."

Gerald lets Erskine dwell on his own words before speaking. "Fighting talk. But you need to think carefully, because we have evidence too, Erskine. Proof of you paying off Pyecoe. Evidence he's guarded with his life, for years, and keeps safe under lock and key."

"Evidence like this?" Erskine taunts, wafting an envelope into the screen. Without waiting for an answer, he unseals it then slowly produces one photograph after another, holding each one for several seconds as it fills the display.

While he's doing this, Thomas Bassinott

slips away, moments later returning with another man who looks lean and purposeful, sporting a beard and baseball cap. Sitting at the table next to Thomas, after Erskine finishes his pantomime with the photographs, I watch his eyes grow wider as he stares at the newly enlarged group of five in front of him.

57

"Good afternoon, Mr Erskine." The new addition at our table speaks with a slight Irish accent. Then as he removes his cap, his shape becomes more familiar.

Once again Erskine's head fills the screen. "For fuck's sake. You're kidding me." Erskine is apoplectic. "Mike Reynolds? You're in with this rabble? You double-dealing bastard. I'm certainly not paying you any outstanding bills. Jesus Christ. What the hell are you doing there?"

Reynolds takes in Gerald's nod of approval. "I told you not to underestimate these guys, Erskine. That was my opinion and feedback after tracking the twins to the pub that night. I had no idea, but they were onto me the moment I followed them into the pub. They contacted me a few days later and made me a counter offer. And when they told me what you'd been up to in your professional life, I had no problem agreeing to work with them. And, how shall I put it, their pay and job prospects looked much brighter."

"And Mike helped us with these." Gerald held

up an identical set of photographs to the ones Erskine had just shown. "Once Mike told us about your plan to switch the photos in Pyecoe's flat, we made sure we kept the originals and you got a set of duplicates. Which means we still have the evidence against you. Incidentally, while you sat in Mike's car that night you hired him to swap the photographs, we were in Pyecoe's flat enjoying a cup of tea with him and his mum. Pyecoe and his mum had walked around the block and in through the back door. They let Mike in and gave him a duplicate set of photographs. Breaking in was just a performance for your benefit, to keep you believing you were one step ahead of us. I think Mike deserves an Oscar nomination. What do you think, Erskine?"

Erskine's reply is curt. "I knew he wasn't nervous enough about breaking in that night. Should have twigged it then."

Gerald laughs, "Never mind, Erskine. We're very grateful to you for putting Mike our way. He is now on our payroll, so to speak. You do at least get ten out of ten for working out the Baileys connection, it gave us an opportunity to get a few more grand out of you through Mike's work. He's going to be a very useful person, going forward."

"You're welcome to the little shit." Erskine falls back into his chair.

Gerald ignores him. "So let's move onto the auction. The only thing we all needed to do now, was to string you along so that you believed Valentina was on your side. You needed to believe she would switch bank accounts back to yours. With Valentina fully on our side, we just needed to register a bank account at Gallo-Moretti that got the money straight to us. Normally, this would represent a problem - bank accounts are easily traceable. You might remember Erskine, when Thomas and I were sent down for fraud a few years ago, it was an international scam that went wrong." As Erskine grunts a form of recognition, Gerald carries on. "At the trial, we protected the identity of one of the insider's we worked with. He was a high-ranking financier who subsequently gravitated to banking within the principality Lichtenstein. Protecting him cost us extra time behind bars, but we knew it would pay us back handsomely one day. And when that day came, he repaid his dues without question, agreeing to set up a new bank account within the wonderfully secretive tax haven. Behind the scenes, he organised things so that when the money arrived in Lichtenstein, it would immediately transfer out to several new accounts that only we had access to. The first account would then be closed, gone and forgotten. Nothing for anyone to trace. It's not the sort of thing they do every day there, they're specialists in clandestine tax avoidance. Much more lucrative I'm told. But our man came good, and all in return for not grassing on him. Honour amongst thieves, you might say." After repeating those words again, Gerald stops speaking, doffing an invisible hat in gratitude to his absent accomplice, as I realise this is the first mention of where the money is. But I'm still no closer to understanding why I'm here. Drawing breath to demand some answers, I stop short as Gerald turns to face me.

"OK, let's move this on. To Peter. You've been sitting very patiently throughout our explanation to Erskine, but both you and he will be at a loss as to why you're here."

Erskine jumps in. "Yes, what role have you been playing with this lot of back-stabbing shits?"

Ignoring him, Gerald carries on, "As I said at the start, a lot of this story goes back a long way. In fact, in the case of Thomas and me, it goes back to the day of our births. We were adopted just a few days after we were born and never knew our real mother and father. Our adoptive parents broke the revelation about our adoption on our eighteenth birthday. Before that, we had no clue. Not a scooby. It was obviously weird, but they had brought us up strong and we didn't dwell on it. A couple of years later, we got a letter from an agency saying our natural mother wanted to know if we were prepared to meet her. We chose not to. Roll forward about twenty years and Thomas had second thoughts about tracing her. This was shortly before we were convicted of fraud. We were sent to different prisons, but once there, Thomas went into overdrive, tracing our history, writing to lots of people, scouring the internet. He had endless time and dedicated every waking moment to it. Unfortunately, he discovered that our mother had died some years before, so we never got to meet her. When we came out of prison two years later, he had bags of research. Nothing particularly significant and he nearly threw it all away as we walked away from prison. But fortunately, he held onto it all."

"Fascinating. Forgive me if I start snoring." Erskine's flat tones punctuate Gerald's monologue.

"OK, I'll get to the point. A few weeks after our release from prison, the press article came out about Erskine and the auction. It went into a lot of detail about the Nazi thieves and people who lost the jewels in the war. When Thomas read it, he turned as white as a sheet. He's a man of few words. In fact, no words. Thomas is a mute. But I knew something was burning inside him. He was trying to tell me something, but he became so animated, it took several minutes to interpret his sign language."

Gerald breaks off to look around the room slowly, his eyes falling on his brother, then Mike Reynolds, before moving slowly to Valentina, Erskine, then finally stopping at me. "It was then he told me."

I'm frozen. What's he going to say? How much weirder can all this get? Then suddenly, unable to contain myself any longer, I demand to know. "He told you what? What the hell did he tell you?"

Gerald's eyes still locked on me. "This is the moment. After all this time and Thomas's research, there is no doubt. No doubt whatsoever. Peter Foster-Fewster... you are my brother. And Thomas's. You, me and Thomas. We are all brothers. We share the same mother." I stare at Gerald, speechless.

Valentina beams at me. "Isn't it amazing, Peter?"

"You knew?" I manage to squeak to Valentina.

She nods excitedly, "That's what I discovered when I tracked down the twins in Florence. You're their lost brother. I overheard them talking about you. That's when I started working with them. But I couldn't tell you!"

Around me, I feel the room start to spin as having lived with this secret for weeks, everyone at the table comes to life. Sitting there, I feel faint. As far as the money goes, I still don't know what this means. I manage a glance at Erskine whose head is face down and motionless on his desk, only vaguely aware of another man entering the room from the side door.

Erskine raises his head just in time to see the

new addition join the table. "Pyecoe?" he whispers, incredulous, before his head thuds back onto his desk.

With everyone talking in what seems like a blur, I turn to Gerald. "Are you absolutely certain we're brothers? Why didn't Erskine's company find that out?"

Gerald quietens the room with a raised hand. "Erskine's clumsy mistake was the press article. It joined the dots in Thomas's research into our ancestry. The name Foster-Fewster is very unusual, but it provided the key to unlocking ancestral threads. Threads that linked back to Aunt Daphne in London and our shared Italian grandmother, Giovanna. Links that unless you were an OCD mute banged up in a cell for two years, you'd have no hope of tracing and connecting. That's why Erskine's research agents missed it. So, not only did we luck out on being able to extort Erskine, but through his greed and the press story, we unwittingly got drawn into discovering our own inheritance. Now, if you're Erskine, that's incredibly bad luck. But for us, it was a lottery win with a bonus – it came with a new brother!" Another grunt emanates from Erskine. "Armed with this information and entitlement, we knew we could take Erskine for the whole lot. It was worth putting a major plan together for several million quid."

Although my mind is all over the place,

somewhere in there are Aunt Daphne's occasional stories and questions, about my two brothers. Maybe it was her dementia preventing any of this coming to the surface when I was living with her. But something else is confusing me. I turn to Gerald. "As direct descendants, the estate was rightfully yours... or I should say, ours. So, I don't understand, why you didn't just come forward at that point and claim your rightful share?"

"Because, with our plan, we could leave Erskine with the workload of getting the auction done, then take him for a lot more. His commission, for starters. Then with the help of our colleagues in Lichtenstein, we'd avoid any nasty tax bills. And maybe the biggest reason of all... the satisfaction. We'd be paying him back for ripping off Pyecoe. And we'd be doing it in the most gratifying way possible. Ever since we were kids, Thomas and I have always enjoyed the thrill of the chase. It's especially sweet if we believe we have the moral high ground. Erskine's been hiding behind his professional exterior for too long. We decided this was the perfect way to increase our fortune, at the same time as bringing down a truly bent lawyer. It's the perfect crime!"

I'm still not entirely sure whether to be terrified or excited. "What happens now, to the money?"

Gerald smiles. "This is the lovely bit. We divvy it up! And because the jewels sold for more than the reserve, there's far more to share out than originally expected. Mind you, that's not entirely accidental either. Once we heard there was a Russian oligarch interested, our banking colleague helped increase the price by bidding online just below the point he thought the Russians would go. Even if he'd got it wrong and had to buy them at the inflated price, he knew he'd be able to sell them onto the Russians at a much higher price than the auction reserve."

I allow myself a word of genuine admiration. "Brilliant."

Gerald doffs his invisible hat again. "So, here's the proposal. The final figure of approximately fifteen million euros splits three ways, me, Thomas and Peter. Except as Thomas and I are twins and have always considered ourselves one entity, we will take one third to cover us both, leaving two thirds, or around ten million euros, to you, Peter. We all end up with far more than we would have done if we'd let Erskine handle things in the normal way. It also leaves us plenty of money to keep Mike Reynolds and Valentina on a very healthy retainer until the next project comes along. And of course, Duke, who is as fit as a fiddle." Gerald turns to the screen. "We needed him to seem a bit doddery to help make our story work out, Mr Erskine. And we'll be looking after him properly, not like you did." Leaving Erskine to contemplate the repercussions of his life decisions, Gerald addresses me again. "We're all delighted with the arrangement, and Peter, you walk away with a genuine fortune, our good wishes and two new brothers."

Suddenly I'm back at the top of the emotional rollercoaster again, my adrenalin pumping, my thoughts whizzing all over the place. But then something hits me. "This is all incredible, but why did you keep it a secret from me? If you all knew we were brothers, why not tell me all about Erskine's dark past so I could have gone along with it too? Surely it would have saved so much trouble?"

Gerald smiles again. "Because you're far too decent. You'd never have been able to cope with the deception. You performed your role perfectly. If Erskine had smelled a rat and put you on the spot, it could have scuppered the plan. This way, Erskine believed he had you under his spell and no matter what other problems he was dealing with, he knew you were just an innocent. It was hard to watch sometimes, but this way you lived in blissful ignorance to the very end. Now you're one of us, we'll make sure you get your money without causing anyone to raise an eyebrow."

Erskine raises his voice. "Well, you might think it's all neatly in the bag, done and dusted, but don't forget all this is in my head. I can cause you serious problems out there in the real world, wherever you are now. As for you Valentina, my threat to let your husband know about our little relationship is still real and I have a file of evidence I can get to him at the drop of a hat. In fact, the whole lot of you, I could stitch you all up in less than five minutes. Unless of course, you want to get your chequebook out and start talking money. After all the bloody work I put in, it wouldn't hurt for a little bit of the pie to go my way. Just enough to guarantee my silence."

As Erskine rants, I notice Mike Reynolds pick up his mobile. When Erskine stops, Reynolds speaks. "OK, Jayne sweetheart, you can show them in now." We all follow Mike's eyes to the screen as Erskine's face is distracted by the sound of his office door opening.

"What the…" As two uniformed policemen stand behind him, Erskine falls silent.

"Mr Hilary John Erskine, you are being arrested on the charge of perverting the course of justice, perjury, paying for a false witness…"

When the arrest statement finishes, Gerald raises his voice to be heard. "And sirs, don't forget to take the large brown envelope of photographs on Erskine's desk. That's all the evidence you'll need. Oh, and he's syphoned off all the auction money. He'll scream and shout that he hasn't, but lock him up long enough and one day he'll probably tell you where he's hidden it." With that, Gerald abruptly ends the video call.

"Fucking Hilary! No wonder he kept that

under wraps!" Pyecoe shouts, as we all erupt into laughter.

Gerald turns to Mike Reynolds. "That was great, Mike. So pleased you and Jayne Renton became romantically entwined recently. You were both instrumental in leading the police to Erskine's door anonymously and super-efficient at getting into his safe and destroying the files of evidence against Thomas, me and Valentina. It's wonderful news that Jayne is flying out here tomorrow to join you." Smiling broadly, as Mike replaces his baseball cap, his cheeks gently flush.

Valentina raises her hand to speak. "Oh, just one other thing, Peter." I look at her quizzically. "When we met that last time in Bologna, you told me about someone you'd met recently. It was someone that Erskine didn't trust. He sent me passport details to see if I could find out if this person was an international con artist. But I checked it out and Erskine was wrong, as you knew all along. Not a con artist but after a long conversation, someone I now know to be a genuine artist and sincere person."

As Valentina finishes speaking, a curtain slides open from one of the balcony windows and Fin walks into the room, an aura of early evening sunlight accompanying her. She looks absolutely wonderful, especially with her new platinum hair which catches more light as Gerald sweeps open the remaining curtains. Staring at each other, we burst into laughter before wrapping ourselves in a spinning hug.

As we move towards the French doors, I notice the balcony has been set with a dining table ready for dinner.

"Come on. Everyone, outside, it's time to celebrate!" As Gerald shouts, waiters appear from nowhere with trays of champagne flutes and canapés. Fin and I untangle ourselves, then hand in hand, step outside to take in the view of Lake Como, stretching out in all directions under the warm sun.

I stop a waiter and take two glasses of bubbles. "So, we're eating out here? What's on the menu?"

"Well Signore, special request of Mr Bassinott."

"And what would that be?"

"Spaghetti bolognaise, Signore. Spaghetti bolognaise!"

THE END

Acknowledgements

Having succeeded in writing my first book, I would like to say a few heartfelt thanks for some wonderful support.

Firstly, Debbie without whom this book would have kept the déchetterie in Périgueux busy for weeks. Nik and Judy Scopes for providing the most inspirational backdrop to write against, and for Nik's patient and thoughtful edits. Nick Gilbrook for being my best friend since being forced to sit together at school (for alphabetical reasons) and his reliably focused editorial help. To my sons to whom this book is dedicated: Jamie, for his studious critique and attention to detail and Tommie, for his endless support. Richard, my brother for being so encouraging from the other side of the world and for creating the inspirational cover. And Betsy, my sister because she's just always there for me. Bean the little black kitten we adopted in the Dordogne and who improved our lives in a way that is impossible to believe. My Subaru, which blamelessly criss-crossed Europe for three years requiring nothing more than a new dust cap and headlight bulb. And to everyone else I've ever met, you've either inspired me to be more like you, or less like you. Whatever, whichever, thank you! x

Printed in Great Britain
by Amazon